Praise for *US*[illegible]
Maisey Yates

"The clever dialogue and steamy encounters make *Unbroken* a real page-turner."

—*RT Book Reviews*

"Get ready for some sizzling romance, twisted intrigue and scandalous revelations."

—*Goodreads* on *Avenge Me*

"Maisey Yates puts just enough sizzle in this prequel to get you hooked. *Take Me* will definitely have you wanting more!"

—*Fresh Fiction*

Praise for *New York Times* bestselling author
Erin McCarthy

"Erin McCarthy serves up an incredibly sexy yet wonderfully sweet story that takes the friends-to-lovers angle and adds in a fun little twist, making it extremely enjoyable."

—*Goodreads* on *Perfect 10*

"McCarthy kicks off a fun trilogy, From Every Angle. Readers will look forward to the next installments in the series."

—*RT Book Reviews* on *Double Exposure*

"*Perfect 10* is funny, sexy and thoroughly entertaining."

—*Bibliojunkies*

Praise for HelenKay Dimon

"Dimon brings back characters from her delightful series, but she delves deeper into the psyche of Corcoran and its members in this first-rate story rife with action and passion."

—*RT Book Reviews* on *Traceless* (4½ stars)

"Nonstop action, suspense and romance."

—*Goodreads* on *Traceless*

"As is usually the case with a HelenKay Dimon book, the sex scenes were hot and the dialogue sparkled."

—*Dear Author* on *Lean on Me*

Maisey Yates knew she wanted to be a writer even before she knew what it was she wanted to write.

At her very first job she was fortunate enough to meet her very own tall, dark and handsome hero, who happened to be her boss, and promptly married him and started a family. It wasn't until she was pregnant with her second child that she found her very first Harlequin Presents® book in a local thrift store—by the time she'd reached the happily-ever-after, she had fallen in love. She devoured as many as she could get her hands on after that, and she knew that these were the books she wanted to write!

She started submitting, and nearly two years later, while pregnant with her third child, she received The Call from her editor. At the age of twenty-three, she sold her first manuscript to the Harlequin Presents line, and she was very glad that the good news didn't send her into labor! She still can't quite believe she's blessed enough to see her name on not just any book, but on her favorite books.

Maisey lives with her supportive, handsome, wonderful, diaper-changing husband and three small children across the street from her parents and the home she grew up in, in the wilds of southern Oregon. She enjoys the contrast of living in a place where you might wake up to find a bear on your back porch, then walk into the home office to write stories that take place in exotic urban locales.

USA TODAY Bestselling Author

Maisey Yates,

New York Times Bestselling Author

Erin McCarthy

and

HelenKay Dimon

#SEXYMISTAKES

HARLEQUIN® COSMOPOLITAN RED-HOT READS

ISBN-13: 978-0-373-60969-7

#SexyMistakes

Recycling programs for this product may not exist in your area.

This edition published by arrangement with Harlequin Books S.A.

For questions and comments about the quality of this book, please contact us at CustomerService@Harlequin.com.

Printed in U.S.A.

CONTENTS

CRAZY, STUPID SEX

Maisey Yates

To Jessica Lemmon.

Remember that time we brainstormed this book in a hotel lobby in Kansas City?

I do. Thank you.

CHAPTER ONE

ACQUIRE SOCIAL LUBRICANT. Check. Step three of this theoretical man-landing mission was complete. She'd already put on panties that would make her feel confident and sexy, then found a bar in the right part of town that was sure to contain the right sort of people.

Now she just needed to relax so she could engage a potential mate.

Evie James looked down into her pink drink and frowned. She didn't feel particularly socially lubricated. Or lubricated in any fashion, really.

She was nervous. Shaky and neurotic and nervous. This was what years of hiding in her office had gotten her. What years of dating the same boring man who hogged the covers and treated the female orgasm like an elusive, nonexistent unicorn that didn't bear hunting for had gotten her.

She didn't know how to pick up men. She knew how to program apps. How to manage a team of creatives. How to sell and market what she created, to a whole roomful of people if necessary, and she had a few million dollars in her bank account that stood as a testament to that. On a personal note, she also knew how to find a moving service to get your rat-bastard ex's shit out of your apartment and have it delivered to his mother's house in boxes marked "things to clutter up your basement when your man-child returns."

Yeah, she knew how to do that.

But picking up men? New men she had never talked to before? Men she wanted to do sexual things, not business things, with? Not so much.

Not that she was actually going to do any sexual things with a guy tonight. She just needed to see if she could get one to take her bait. So to speak.

She sucked up more pink drink through her straw and waited for some magic to happen. None.

She tugged her iPad out of her purse and opened up the basic mock-up of the app she'd been using as a guide. *Flirt* magazine had commissioned her to create this app that would be a field guide for fashion, flirting and hooking up.

Right now, the app needed some beta testing. And she was the one testing it. Because hell, if it could work for her it could work for anyone.

She clicked on the "10 Dating Tips" article and skimmed to number four.

Put yourself out there! You don't have to wait for a man to approach you. That went out with corsets and stays. The rules of the dating game are in your hands.

Her shaky, sweaty hands.

Sweet.

She looked around the bar. It was so dim. She wasn't sure how anyone was supposed to tell how attractive the people around them were. Though, maybe that would work in her favor. Whilst she'd followed the "How to Get a Smokey Eye in Three Easy Steps" guide religiously while getting ready, she was privately afraid she looked like she'd been punched in the face.

So maybe the dim lighting would work in her favor.

The guy across the bar was actually pretty nice looking. He was wearing that standard blue business shirt, collar open, his tie probably ditched in whatever fleet car he drove. A company car, she was willing to bet. He had an eight-dollar haircut. That she was sure of. She could see the razor tracks from twenty feet away, but that wasn't so bad.

He probably sold something. Insurance maybe.

So maybe she could get a little ego salve and a good rate on a policy for her motorcycle all in one night. That would kind of rock.

She stood up and started walking toward him before she could overthink it. Before she could think at all.

A wall of cheap body-spray scent greeted her when she got within five feet of him. She nearly gagged. They needed serving-sizes on that crap. She'd banned it in her offices. The young male interns completely believed the commercials that promised random ménages with strangers and seemed to bathe in the stuff before work. It gave her a headache.

It was giving her a headache now.

That didn't bode well for the flirting.

She really would like it if she could manage to stun a guy with her witty repartee and stunning beauty. If she could get a guy to ask her to come back to his place. Partly because she was trying to figure out how successful her app was, and partly because she really needed the boost to her self-esteem.

The loss of Jason the Ass, and the fact that he'd been

sleeping with another woman, had dented her confidence. A little male interest would go a long way in fixing that. Not all the way to the bedroom, mind you.

She couldn't even imagine that being worth it. In her memory, sex had never been so hot, in spite of rumors to the contrary.

It had been a long time for her. Even longer since sex had thrilled her in any capacity.

Jason had been boring in bed. There. She'd admitted it. And yes, she was probably a little bit boring in bed, too, but that man hadn't made her toes curl in years, and even then, he hadn't made them curl with any consistency.

Someday, she would investigate if the toe curling was real. If the panting and sweating and things that her friends always talked about, that the magazines said were possible, were in fact possible.

Her entire sexual career boiled down to one man who seemed to think foreplay was a golf term.

It was partly her fault. Because she'd been seventeen and a virgin the first time she'd been with him, and she'd basically just kept being with him because she hadn't known what else to do. They'd followed each other through life. Through college and their first apartment. Their first jobs. And then her quitting her job to develop apps. And her ensuing success.

Success, which had, apparently, made him feel neutered and had forced him to seek greener pastures. And by greener pastures, she meant another woman's vagina.

Bastard.

The thing that sucked, really sucked, was that when

she'd come home from her office to find him with his head between another woman's legs she'd been pissed about two things.

The first being that he'd said he didn't like that. Always. He'd tried it on her once, and said he hated it. And he'd never done it again. So, there he was after ten years with her, doing it for another woman with an enthusiasm she'd never seen from him before.

Yeah, that had pissed her off.

The second thing was that she wasn't brokenhearted.

The realization that she didn't love him anymore either was a hard one to swallow. Because in some ways, even though she was angry, she just felt free.

Free to move his things out. Free to tell him to leave. To tell him to enjoy life without his meal ticket. Free to put on music he hated and dance in her panties and go to bars to pick up men who got her much more excited than Freaking Jason.

It had made her angry because it was ten years of her life, poured out on a guy she couldn't even cry over.

Her most righteous and frightening anger was at herself. Six months she'd had it stewing on the back burner. She hadn't wanted to date. She'd barely wanted to look a guy in the eye because it just made her a little stabby.

Her poor interns.

Then she'd gotten the offer to do this app for *Flirt.* And that had plunged her into research on dating, hookups and sex. Which was why she had sex, and toe curling, on the brain when she'd successfully ignored the concept for quite a few months.

She'd already compiled a profile for herself in the app. The things she would need, with her personality and experience level, to pick up a guy.

Now, it was time to see how it worked. In theory, at least. All she needed was for him to indicate he wanted to hook up, and then she'd know that her app was a success. And that she actually had a snowball's chance in hell of having another relationship someday.

"Hello," she said, moving to where the guy was sitting. "Evie, Evie James." She stuck out her hand and stood, waiting for him to reciprocate.

He did eventually, but he had that look in his eyes that her sisters usually got whenever Evie was trying to explain something techie to them.

"Brent."

"Nice to meet you, Brent," she said, smiling broadly. She mentally went through the list again. "A drink," she said. "I'd like to buy you one."

"Okay," he said.

Damn this was awkward.

But she was pressing on. She had her *Flirt* profile all set. She had "10 Tips to Land a Guy," and she was going to do just that.

CALEB ANDERSON HAD watched the thin, awkward redhead approach three different men and bomb out in the last ten minutes.

It was like watching an overeager puppy try to make friends with cat people. Sad. It was sad.

Of course, he was a thirty-five-year-old man in a

bar on a Friday night hoping to pick up a stranger for sex, so he imagined he was a little sad, too.

But his chances for success were much higher than hers. So there was that.

He could hear her voice carrying over the music. She was loud. Everything about her. From her steps in her stilettos to her laugh, was damned loud.

"These heels are making me blister."

Oh man. She was so awkward.

"Really, I never wear shoes like this." She was still talking about her feet. And now bending down to pull a shoe off. She was wobbling, but caught herself on the bar before she face-planted onto the glossy marble floor.

The guy she was talking to seemed willing to overlook the awkward. At least for now. Probably because the girl had a fine rack on her, at least it seemed that way from his vantage point.

Might be one of those lying gel bras. False advertising at its most insidious.

And now her shoe was off. And her weirdness officially trumped her rack. The guy she was talking to was zoned out now, his gaze on the blonde across the room.

Caleb had assessed the blonde already. She was boring. She wasn't awkward, but there was nothing special about her. Her legs were nice, but he'd had a lot of blondes with nice legs. He could see exactly how the night would go. He could take her back to his place, take her to his room. She'd wrap those legs around him and they'd both work their way to orgasm, while the blonde did her best not to sweat her makeup off.

He liked the ending, but the journey just didn't excite him much.

Damn. Sex was starting to get boring. He really did need a hobby. One beyond picking up women in bars, apparently.

The redhead wasn't boring. She was weird. But she wasn't boring. Sex with her? He couldn't predict that. And that interested him.

Caleb got up from his table and walked across the bar, his eyes on her. She was trying to get her shoe back on now, and she was oblivious to the fact that she'd lost her audience.

She looked up, her hair spilling over her shoulders, all glossy and sexy, her lips drawn into a pout.

For the first time since he'd seen her, hot surpassed weird as his primary descriptor. Her eyes were still on the guy who was now very much trying not to look at her. He'd never seen a woman as pretty as her strike out so hard so many times in a row.

"Can I buy you a drink?" he asked.

She looked up and her eyes went wide. "Me?"

"Yes, you."

"I had one."

"Only one?" he asked. He'd sort of imagined she was a little tipsy. If she was sober then she was extra weird.

"Yeah, just the one. I didn't want to get drunk."

"No, I can see why you wouldn't," he said.

"I was talking to Jeff here," she said, looking back at the man who was no longer looking at her.

"You were done talking to Jeff," Caleb said. "Or rather, I think he was done talking to you."

"I think he's playing hard to get," she said, arching a brow.

"I think he can hear you," Caleb said.

The woman stepped away from the bar and lowered her voice. "Well, he was."

"Men don't play hard to get," Caleb said. "Men want to have sex. Every guy in here by himself wants to have sex tonight. Hell, every guy in here with a woman wants to have sex tonight, their odds just aren't as good as the guys who are alone."

"You think so?"

"I know so, Evie."

She frowned. "How do you know my name?"

"Evie, Evie James, you've introduced yourself very loudly to several men in here since I walked in. I observed."

"Well…I…I…that's just annoying," she said. "Eavesdropping, I mean. Eavesdropping is annoying."

"This is where you ask my name," he said.

"I'm not sure it is."

"Yes, it's polite. Caleb Anderson. And your pickup techniques aren't working."

"I'm doing research," she said, her tone sharp. "For an app."

"An app?" he asked, interested now.

"I'm an app developer, that's what I do."

"See? That's interesting. Your heel blisters aren't."

Freckled cheeks turned deep red. "But they hurt."

"Sorry. Want me to rub ointment on it?"

"Having a man rub ointment on your feet is nowhere in the guidelines."

"Guidelines?"

"I have these guidelines. I'm using them to make the app. For *Flirt* magazine. Yeah. That one. Maybe you've heard of it. It's like…a big deal."

Now, that was a twist he couldn't have predicted. But then, this was the hangout for people who worked in that arena. Which he knew, not because he did, but because it was a good place to pick up businesswomen who wanted to blow off steam.

He knew the magazine well. One of the many glossy-paged ponies in his father's media stable. It had been enlightening to him as a teenage boy discovering women.

It had been like being behind enemy lines.

Part of the empire that would have been Jill's. Now it would be his someday as the sole surviving heir. He didn't like to think about it much anymore. And the connection almost sent him walking back the other way.

He didn't need any emotional baggage; he just needed a little fun.

But Evie James was interesting. And the desire to be interested was stronger than the desire to turn away.

"The women's magazine with all the sex tips?"

"Yeah," she said. "That's the one." She leaned in, one eyebrow arching. "And I've been reading up."

Evie was starting to wonder if she really was drunk. A feeling of desperation was making her behave like an ass, and she knew it, and now this guy was talking to her. This guy who didn't even look like he could possibly be real.

He looked like he'd stepped off the pages of some

business magazine. Perfectly cut suit, expensive watch and shoes. And his haircut had not cost eight dollars.

No, his dark hair was perfection. She wanted to run her fingers through it. Or pull it. That was one of the sex tips she'd read. Some guys were into that.

And now he was talking to her. She wished she were in a business meeting. Then it wouldn't matter how hot the guy was, she would know what to say. She would know what to do with her hands.

She wouldn't be so sweaty.

She was beyond competent in every other area of her life and she just didn't know how to do this.

The damn app needed to be able to flirt for her. Give a command, and it would do her bidding. But that was asking a bit much of artificial intelligence.

Siri, I'd like to get laid…

There are ten horny, sexy men in your area.

Not likely.

"So, what's in your app?" he asked, leaning on the bar.

"Nothing finalized yet. I mean, I'm not writing all the content, I'm programming it. Though I am taking some things straight from articles. You can create a profile that helps customize your fashion and flirt type. It has…hot spots, to help you find the right kind of guy for you. You know, athletes, businessmen. You can send messages. There's quick dating tips and… sex tips."

"Sex tips?"

"Yeah," she said, putting her hands on her hips. "Sex tips. Fifty of them."

"Fifty? I'm going to have to hear about those."

Evie took a deep breath and leaned in a little, ignoring the fact that she wobbled on her heels a bit. Ignoring the fact that she was so nervous she could hardly breathe. She had nothing to lose. Three unsuccessful attempts already and she was starting to feel like a failure.

It was time to lay it all on the line.

"What if I showed you instead?"

CHAPTER TWO

STEPS FIVE THROUGH eight had effectively been skipped. She'd moved straight to step nine: The Proposition. The only thing after this was Closing the Deal. And that was a thinly-veiled euphemism for "letting him put his penis inside you." Which was not her desired end result, but, really, this should provoke him to suggest a deal-closing. Which would technically mean she was a rousing success and could go home and put on her flannel pajamas.

In theory.

Her dating history wasn't super illustrious. One man. She'd been with one man, and they'd hooked up in high school, and back then, her standard for a datable male had been A) breathing and B) not oblivious to her existence. Jason had been both of those things, and so one night they'd sort of ended up sitting at the same table at a popular burger hangout and the rest had been history.

She'd given him her V card as a matter of course. He'd asked her to prom, he'd brought her a corsage. And he'd gotten a hotel room you could rent by the hour. He'd done the expected things, so she'd done the expected things.

And thus it had gone on.

Well, that wasn't her anymore.

She didn't need a relationship. She didn't want one. Hell, she was a woman at the top. A blinking multimillionaire by age twenty-seven, and no one had helped her get there. It was all her.

She was in charge. And she was going to have Caleb the annoying bar hottie to demand she show him her sex tips!

"You want to show me your sex tips?" he asked. His lips were curved into a half-smile, and rather than looking uncontrollably aroused he looked…amused. That wasn't what she was going for.

She tucked her hair behind her ear. "Yeah. That's what I said. You. Me. Sex. Tips."

"Tell me something, Evie."

"Okay."

"Why is it you're out to pick up a man tonight?"

"The app."

He shrugged. "Okay, you win the prize. You've picked me up. Now you don't have to follow through. Your methods worked. The app is a stunning success."

She frowned. This was supposed to be sweet victory, and yet, in the moment it rang hollow. "You seem so into it, far be it for me to doubt whether or not I've scored," she said dryly, "but I sort of doubt it."

"But say you had. And that it all worked. Do you want to follow through?"

She blinked. She looked around the bar, at the guys she'd struck out with. If they'd asked her to go back to their place she'd be back at her place alone drinking a Moscato. She for damn sure would not have said *yes*.

But Caleb asking if she wanted to follow through?

The idea was tempting in a way she hadn't anticipated.

"I…the data is skewed because you know about the app," she said. "I can't ever be sure."

"Sure you can. I would like to take you back to my place and have sex with you, Evie. What's your answer?"

She opened her mouth and nothing came out. And that's when she realized, she was seriously considering naked touching with a stranger. And she'd been warned about strangers. No matter how much candy a guy claimed to have in his van, she knew better than to go with him. She knew that.

Yeah, she was nervous as hell. And if any of the other guys were standing where he was? She would be saying game over. Flirt level: Awesome, achieved. No sex required. Just as planned.

But now? Now she was looking at this guy, the hottest guy she'd ever seen, and thinking *why not?*

Because this wasn't about an app, or a flirting experiment. This was about demanding something other than mediocrity. Something better than a guy she got naked for just because he was there and it was expected.

She wanted a guy who would tear her clothes off like she was a present on Christmas morning. And she'd never had it. She'd never been able to ask for what she really wanted. And any time she'd tried, Jason had just acted like she'd asked him to hide a body, not go down on her. That list of sex tips? She would have been too embarrassed to leave it on Jason's pillow, much less verbally ask for any of them.

And what was that? She was a professional woman who had total control over her life, and yet she'd never asked for what she wanted in bed. She'd never pushed for excellence there, even when she demanded it in all other areas of her life.

"Okay, you want the truth?" she asked.

"Depends."

"On?"

His smile widened. "If I'll like a lie better."

"I don't lie well. I'm honest. Painfully so. It's part of the awkwardness, which, I am aware of, by the way. It works for me in some settings."

"If you say so."

"*Forbes* says so, actually, but that's beside the point."

"*Forbes* has never said anything about me," he said.

"Don't feel bad. You're young yet. Make something of yourself and maybe someday you'll be as important as I am. That point aside, though," she said, taking a deep breath, "here's the truth. I just got out of a really long-term relationship. Like, if socks were as old as that relationship, throwing them out would have been the obvious thing to do."

"Socks?"

"Metaphorically, it actually holds up well. It stunk and it was full of holes. Again, much like old socks. And then I lost the asshole in the wash, so to speak."

"Okay."

"Anyway, long-term relationship. So done with it. So done with him. And I don't know what the hell I'm doing. I know how to turn a few lines of code into a fortune, but I don't know how to get a date. And I am…

desperate for sex that's more exciting than lukewarm oatmeal. Desperate. So…I'm sure I broke a cardinal rule by confessing my desperation, but—and this is a big *but*—I probably won't be pursuing that non-bland sex with a stranger from a bar. Sorry."

"Confessing desperation is probably a serious rule-breaker, you're right."

"No doubt."

"I'm sure you're supposed to be playing aloof. Hard to get. Like Jeff over there," he said, gesturing to the man she'd made a pass at only a few minutes earlier.

That thought made her feel a little dizzy. She'd only been in the bar for an hour. She'd talked to four men. And she was going to go home with the fourth one if he was into it.

All in all, it was one of the more eventful hours in her life. And she'd had a few eventful hours in her lifetime.

"Well, I thought any more aloof and the bar would reach maximum aloofness capacity so I figured I'd tone it down."

"I like honesty."

"You just said you wanted the lie if it was better."

He smiled. "Either I'm very honest or a good liar."

"That shouldn't be charming. How did you do that?"

"I'm good at flirting."

"You have to show me. Because I think I need to understand the flirting since I'm making the app that's supposed to help with the flirting. That is why I'm here, after all."

"I'll make a deal with you. I'll help you with the flirting after you show me your sex tips."

"Is that an offer?" she asked.

"I thought you were the one offering. I'm accepting."

"I already told you it was more of an experimental offer. But for the sake of argument, is this a happy acceptance or a pity acceptance?"

He moved toward her, his eyes locked on hers. The glitter of humor in his eyes taking on a dark light that seemed to pull her in. He didn't smell like sweat coated in cheap body spray. He smelled like soap, a hint of cologne and an undertone of musky man that she hadn't realized she'd been missing from her life.

"Care to guess?" he asked, his voice soft, barely rising above the music and conversation in the bar.

She shot a quick look over to Jeff the Aloof. He was looking more interested now. Well, screw him. Or rather, not.

But maybe, just maybe, she would screw Caleb.

"Eyes on me," he said, his tone suddenly not so teasing at all. And she obeyed.

Heat shot through her, the commanding tone of his voice pushing off the edge of aroused and straight into a pool of lust. She wanted him. Research had nothing to do with it.

And if she wanted him…well, why shouldn't she have him? She didn't have a deadweight boyfriend keeping her from pursuing him.

Yes. Oh yes, she was going to have him. Decision made. There and now. But she wasn't going to tell him that yet. The app suggested she not make herself a "sure thing." She had to make him seduce her.

Though, she felt pretty well seduced.

"Do I what?" she asked, suddenly unable to remember anything except the color of his eyes. Warm and golden like whiskey held up against the light.

"Do you think I feel sorry for you? Or do you genuinely think I want you?"

"I'm not sure. Was it all my talk of being hard up or my foot blisters that got you?"

He bent down, his lips hovering just above hers. "I think it was the combination."

"I can see how that would get you," she said, sounding a little bit breathless now. "After all…there could be…ointment involved which is…not sexy."

He winked and pressed his lips against hers. Light. The pressure so faint she almost thought she'd imagined it. "Not really," he whispered. "Luckily, you are quite sexy."

"Even with the awkward?"

"It's charming."

"Is it?"

"I don't know. I've been staring at your breasts this whole time. I can tell you without a doubt that they're charming."

Her heart jumped, a little shiver of pleasure skating over her skin. "How do you do that?"

"What?"

"Say the most douchey things and make them sound hot?"

"It's a gift. I wasn't good in school. I've been fired from almost every job I've ever had. But I can pick up a woman in a bar without even trying. In fact, I can actively attempt to push a woman away and still wind up in bed with her."

"That's douchey, too, and it's still making me feel fluttery. Which was probably also detrimentally honest of me."

He cupped her cheek and kissed her again, deeper this time, his tongue sliding along the seam of her lips. It was so strange, to kiss another man for the first time in a decade. For the first time ever. His lips felt so different. His technique made it like another activity entirely. She opened for him and the hot slide of his tongue against hers nearly buckled her knees.

He cupped her cheeks, his hands hot, rough on her skin, his mouth insistent on hers. If she hadn't been certain about going home with him before, she was now.

She was making out with a stranger in a bar. And it was amazing.

When they parted, they were both breathing hard.

"Ready to go?" he asked.

"Did I agree to go with you?"

"I'm sure you did. Anyway, doesn't your list say you need to go with me?"

It did, in fact, say that leaving the bar and securing a hotel room or returning to a residence was the next step. "Yes, it does."

"Do you have a car?"

"No, I got a cab so I could drink. Which…not drunk but a little bit dizzy, so probably a good thing I'm not driving."

"I'll have my driver bring the car around." He pulled out his phone and pushed a couple of buttons. "Ready." He hung up again.

"A driver?"

"Yes."

"I thought you said you got fired from all your jobs." Granted, his clothes spoke of money, and she'd noticed that from the first moment she'd seen him.

"I'm surprised you didn't notice the silver spoon in my mouth," he said.

"You'd think I would have noticed when we kissed."

"You would think."

A sleek black town car pulled up to the curb and Caleb opened the door for her, waiting. "So I just get into the car with you?"

"Yes."

"Are you going to hurt me?"

He arched a brow. "Only if you're into that sort of thing."

Heat flooded her cheeks. "I'm not."

For some reason, just then, she pictured him wrapping her hair around his hand and giving it a hard tug. That was tip number twelve. She remembered it well because reading it had made her feel warm all over.

Made her think that it was something she might really, really like.

"Then no. I won't."

"Good to know."

"Getting in the car with me, going home with me…I don't take it for granted that means you'll sleep with me. But you want me. So I don't think you should say *no*."

"You're so sure of yourself?"

"Sure of this," he said, tracing her lips with the tip of his finger. "Don't tell me you don't feel it."

"Okay," she said, feeling a little fuzzy.

"Are you going to make me beg?" he asked. "Because I just might. I could get down on my knees if you want. Though, I'd rather have you on yours."

Heat coursed through her veins. Yet another line that shouldn't have turned her on, but did. But who the hell even cared what should turn her on? The fact was that he did.

"I won't do anything you don't want," he continued. "But if you ask…there isn't a lot I won't do."

She looked around and took a deep breath. "That might actually be nice for a change of pace," she said, getting into the car and leaning back against the seat.

"Will it?" he asked, his tone cautious, his movements slow as he got into the car. Like he was taking special care not to frighten her off.

"Well, you know, battery-operated devices can only do so much."

"And they can't talk dirty to you."

"No. But then, neither did my ex. The buzzing sound is actually an improvement over listening to him mouth breathe during the main event."

"Ouch," Caleb said, chuckling. "My place, right?"

Evie pictured her apartment. It was clean, and it was nice. Redecorated since Jason had moved out. But she still had the same mattress. Which she'd never really thought of. But now it bothered her and she wasn't quite sure why.

"Your place," she said.

She'd rather contend with the ghosts of Caleb's hookups past than her own.

"Take us home," he said to his driver. "So, do you think you'll be able to use this for your app?"

She almost said *what app?* but stopped the words from spilling out just in time. "Oh…yeah. The app. This will be very helpful. The ten man-catching tips are verified…"

"Sort of."

"Yeah, sort of."

"And now you can see how those sex tips work," he said. "If you really want to."

"Some of them are pretty wild," she said.

He laughed. "I'm sure they aren't going to shock me."

Well, that made one of them. She had a feeling she would be shocked a few times. She was shocked now. Or maybe in shock. She was numb everywhere except for her lips, which were burning from that kiss, and between her thighs.

There, she was wet and aching. She wanted him so much it hurt. Wanted in a way she hadn't since before she'd discovered how sex really was. Since before her body had become conditioned to expect the buildup to be better than the finale.

"I might like it if you shocked me a little," she said. She wasn't sure if she'd said the words loud enough. It was hard to hear over the traffic. Even harder over the pounding of her heart.

"How shocked do you want to be?" he asked, his voice husky, low.

"Well, this would be one of those one-night things, right?" she asked.

"That's all I do."

"Okay then. So if it's one night—" she looked up, met his eyes in the darkened car, and playing hard to get was completely forgotten "—then you'd better make sure I never forget it."

He nodded slowly, his eyes darkening, a muscle ticking in his jaw. "I think I can handle that."

CHAPTER THREE

OF COURSE HE had a mansion on the beach. He was that kind of guy. A sleek, modern mansion that looked like a cubist work of art.

Windows faced the ocean, the moon glinting off the waves. Palm trees and oleander surrounded the property, making it feel secluded. An oasis on the crowded strip of Malibu coast.

"Wow. How laid do you get?" she asked, standing on the front step, waiting for him to key in the code that would unlock the door.

"What?"

"I mean, if your ridiculous lines at the bar hadn't worked…this place…"

"It's not bad."

"I've been thinking of buying a house, but for now I'm in a loft downtown because…well, I don't need a yard or anything. But you're making me rethink."

"I think a loft downtown is an excellent seduction location," he said.

"You do?"

"I do. If you'd taken me there I would have given it up in five seconds flat. Any man would be powerless to resist your city views."

"And now that we're here, how long will it take for you to give it up?" she asked.

"Five seconds flat," he said. "I'm impatient." He pushed the door open and she walked inside, her hands shaking big time now. She was turned on, and nervous as hell, and for some reason the nerves element was only making her more turned on, which…which was making her teeth chatter.

It was a whole lot of adrenaline running through her just then. She needed to run a marathon real quick or something.

"Could you kiss me again?" she asked, as soon as he closed the door behind them.

"I was about to get to that. But I thought you might want a drink. I'm not taking anything for granted with you."

"That's…flattering. But I don't want to drink. I want a kiss. Because when you kiss me, I can't think."

"And that's a good thing?"

She nodded. "If I start thinking I might run out the door. I've only just wrapped my mind around this one-night stand thing. I'm a little shaky."

"You flatter me."

"Well, I don't do this kind of thing."

"I do. A lot."

She laughed. "That makes me feel better. I don't think it should."

"Why not?"

"I should be offended that I'm just one in a long line of women you take back to your place for sex and good views."

"You're the only one tonight."

"Screw you. That should not be hot."

"It is, though," he said, putting his thumb on her cheek and tracing a line from there to her temple. "You like it. And as it happens, I like your response. Because I would very much like you to fuck me."

Her chest tightened, her heart rate speeding up. No man had ever, ever said anything like that to her. Ever. And she'd never thought she would like it. But she did. She really did.

"I'd like that, too."

"So polite."

"Too polite?"

"For a discussion about getting screwed? Maybe."

"This is why we should just kiss," she said, moving toward him.

"I won't argue."

Caleb wrapped his arms around her and pulled her in close, brushing her hair back from her face before he leaned in and captured her mouth with his. It was deep, intense, not like any kiss she'd ever experienced before. Hotter than any sex she'd ever had and he wasn't even touching her body.

It was just his lips, his tongue, his teeth.

The little zip of pain that shot from her lip straight down to her core when he bit her gently rocked her. Shocked her.

And it made her think of him pulling her hair again. Bending her over the back of the couch. It made her think of hard, rough sex. The kind she'd never experienced.

The kind she'd always secretly craved but never asked for. Because Jason didn't even want to go down on her, so what the hell would he have thought if she'd started begging him to bite her?

But it didn't matter what Caleb thought. This was just one night. It was all for her. And she could have whatever she wanted.

And dammit, she would.

"What do you like?" he asked. "Tell me your fifty tips," he said while he kissed her neck, down to her collarbone.

"I like…I want…"

"Tell me."

"I want you to decide," she said.

"I thought you were in charge?"

"No." She shook her head. "I want you to do be in charge." The minute she said it, she knew it was true. Knew that what she wanted was a man who would direct things. Push her. Show her what she'd been missing.

She'd been the leader in her past relationship. And while in some ways that suited her, always taking the lead in the bedroom, while simultaneously having to ensure she didn't ask him for anything he "didn't like" was taxing and vanilla and boring.

And she didn't want that. Not tonight.

"And I retract the pain statement from earlier," she added.

He froze, one eyebrow raised. "You're going to give a stranger that kind of power?"

It was wrong that it got her hot. But it did. "Yes. I don't think you want to hurt me, not really. And I don't want you to hurt me, hurt me. But…sex tip number twelve."

"Care to let me in on that?"

She extricated herself from his arms and pulled her phone out of her purse and pulled up the document, scrolling down to the aforementioned tip. He read it. "Hair pulling, eh?"

"Yes."

He reached behind her head, wrapping his fingers around her hair, pulling it all into his grasp before winding it around the back of his hand and forcing her to tilt her head back. The position left her vulnerable, her throat exposed to him, a little tingle of pain prickling over her scalp.

"Like this?" he asked.

"Yes," she said, her voice a whisper.

"I wouldn't have thought you were that kind of girl," he said, leaning in, pressing his lips to the tender skin of her neck.

"Me neither. We surprise ourselves. Oh!" He bit her again, tugging a little harder on her hair as he did.

"Good?"

"Yes. But I think I need you to touch me. I'm… I'm…" She was about to come and he'd never even touched her breasts.

He kissed her again, this time tender. Soft. A line of sweet kisses that stood at odds with the firm grip he had on her hair. The contrast was intense. Intoxicating.

She thought she might melt into a puddle. Just before her knees gave out, he pushed her back against the wall. It was hard behind her, his body hot in front of her, his chest pressed against hers.

He released her hair, slid his hands down her arms

and lifted them over her head, his grip strong on her, holding her in place. Captive.

"You want me to touch you?" he asked.

He kept her prisoner with one large hand, lowering the other and drawing his finger over her lips, tracing the outline of them.

"Yes," she said, desperate now. There was nothing teasing or humorous on his face now. All the light and fun was gone, burned away by a deep intensity that echoed inside her.

"Not yet," he said. "I'm going to make you wait."

She arched her back, bringing her aching breasts more firmly against his chest, looking for some relief from the pounding need that was roaring through her blood. She didn't know if she could survive this. And all he'd done was kiss her.

All he was doing was holding her now, his hand tight on her like an iron cuff, his eyes intent on hers.

That was all. And yet she felt like she was on the edge of orgasm. Desperate. Shaking. The nerves were gone now. Replaced by desire and curiosity.

"You put me in charge," he said, "and that might be a decision you regret."

The rough edge of his voice whispered over her skin, leaving goosebumps behind. "Somehow I doubt that."

"So trusting, baby," he said, cupping her chin, holding her.

"Are you trying to scare me?"

"No. Am I?"

"No. You're turning me on."

"Good," he said. "That's what I was going for."

"What else you got?"

Then his hand was back in her hair, her arms freed, his thumb and forefinger still on her chin. He pulled her head back, and kissed her lips, her mouth open to him as he delved deep.

He pulled away. "What do you have under your dress?"

"What?"

"Panties? No panties?"

She thought about the red lace thong she'd put on earlier. She'd dressed for success, as one of the tips to land a man had suggested. Feel sexy all over and you'll look sexy all over. Or something.

She lifted the hem of her dress. "These."

He looked down at the lace, framing the V at the apex of her thighs more than they concealed it. "I like them. A lot. But I think right now they have to go."

He hooked his fingers in the waistband of the underwear and drew them slowly down her legs, his body following the motion until he was on his knees in front of her.

"Got any sex tips for me while I'm down here?" he asked, leaning in, his breath hot on her.

Oh...jeez. A total stranger was eye level with the most intimate part of her. And she was more excited than embarrassed, which was epic in its amazingness.

"I'll get back to you. I can't reach my cell phone right now. And I can't think, either."

"I think I can improvise." He leaned in, parting her gently with his fingers and flicking his tongue over her clit.

She put her hands flat on the wall behind her, curling her nails against the smooth plaster as he slid his tongue over her slick flesh.

"Spread your legs," he said, his tone demanding. And she had no reason to disobey.

He cupped her butt, blunt fingertips pressing into her skin as he licked her, sucked her, his tongue sliding deep inside her.

She laced her fingers through his hair, holding him to her. Using him to keep her from melting into a puddle.

He tugged her hard against his mouth as he continued to assault her with pleasure. She was so close… so close.

Then he moved his hand, slid his fingers between her thighs and slipped one finger deep inside her. The penetration combined with his tongue's expert movements pushed her over the edge.

She was dizzy. Her blood pounding through her, her head fuzzy.

Then he was kissing her. She could taste herself on him. Her desire, her loss of control, coating his lips, turning her on all over again. A reminder of what he had done for her.

As if she needed a reminder when her body was still on fire.

"We'll make it to the bed later," he said, tugging his shirt over his head, revealing toned, defined muscles she'd rarely seen outside of a magazine. She lived in Southern California and still, bodies as fine as his were hard to come by.

"Okay," she said, sure she sounded a little bit dim but not really caring.

"I need you," he growled, kissing her hard while he worked to free himself from his pants. "Now."

He shoved her dress up to her stomach and hooked her thigh up over his hip. "Shit."

"What?"

He abandoned her for a moment, taking his wallet out of his back pocket before shoving his pants all the way down to the floor and kicking them aside. It took her a moment to realize what he was doing because her eyes were glued to his erection.

He was a very, very big man.

Just one more way he bested her ex. By inches. Which in this case counted for a lot.

He took a condom out of his wallet, then looked at her, smiling when he saw just where she was looking. He rolled on the protection, the smug smile not fading.

She had the belated thought that she should maybe try to look bored or something, but that ship had clearly sailed. She wasn't bored. She was hotter than hell. She couldn't wait to have him inside her.

"Now," she said.

He resumed the position they'd been in just before he'd gotten the condom, testing her entrance with the head of his cock, pushing inside her slowly, the tendons in his neck standing out. He looked as though it was taking every ounce of his control to keep from coming.

And nothing had ever looked hotter.

He braced his hand on the wall as he filled her to the hilt, stretching her, a small grunt escaping his lips, a matching one on hers.

"Are you okay?" he asked.

"Yes," she said, panting. "I've just never…not with anyone this…"

"You're okay?" he asked, genuinely concerned now.

"If you stop, I'll kill you."

"I'm not going to stop." He moved against her, his pelvis coming into contact with her clit, sending a spike of pleasure through her.

"Good," she said, rocking against him.

He pulled back, then thrust back into her, hard, the motion hitting all the right places. She'd never had sex like this. Against a wall, unable to wait to get to a bedroom. Unable to wait for her partner's next thrust, for him to be deep inside her again.

Every time he moved away from her she wanted to pull him straight back, and every time he plunged back into her she wanted to cry out from the pleasure. She did cry out. A lot.

He put his hand on the back of her head, closed his fingers into fists, tugging hard, the pain mingling with her pleasure, so much sensation she felt like it was too much to contain inside of her.

Then he bent down and kissed her neck, his lips warm and soft, followed by a slow scrape of his teeth and the soothing heat from his tongue, just as he thrust back into her. And then the world shattered, her orgasm bursting through her. She dug her nails into his back, his hard muscles tensing beneath her fingertips as he lost himself in his own pleasure.

Afterward they stood there, panting, bodies slick, her hands shaking.

"Well," he said, his breathing fractured, "it's a damn good thing we have all night."

CHAPTER FOUR

CALEB ANDERSON WASN'T bored anymore. Evie, Evie James, had blown his fricking mind.

He'd been right about one thing—he couldn't have predicted this. He couldn't have predicted her. This wasn't that smooth-practiced seduction. With a strip tease from him, one from her, knowing smiles and smooth movements.

This had been something raw, something elemental that he hadn't expected. Or particularly wanted. This went past "pleasant diversion" and into something else entirely.

But it was only for a night, and they had all night.

He wondered if he would survive. More to the point, he wondered if his dick would survive.

He opened his mouth to say something along the lines of *let's take this to the bedroom* which was The Line for moments like this, but for some reason, it didn't come out.

Because she was there, flushed pink, rumpled and half-naked looking like she'd just walked through a hurricane. And it grabbed his words and pushed them back down like a gale force.

"Get into the bedroom." That was what came out instead.

Her eyes widened, her lips a perfect little O.

"Did you still want me to call the shots or not?"

She nodded slowly. "Yes."

"Then get your pretty ass into the bedroom. Now." She took one step forward and he realized she didn't know where she was going. "Walk in front of me," he said. "I'll tell you where to go."

She nodded slowly and pushed her dress back down over her hips, taking slow, unsteady steps down the hall, her high heels clicking on the marble floor. Her hair was completely destroyed in the back, from her head being against the wall. He liked the reminder. As if the buzz in his blood wasn't enough.

"End of the hall," he said.

She walked on, his own private show. And he didn't feel the least bit guilty about checking her out. But there was one thing he needed to know.

She was asking for a very specific game. And he was fine with that. He'd been honest when he'd told her there wasn't much he wouldn't do. He was a rich guy with good looks and no particular ambition beyond having fun. That meant he'd had a lot of alcohol, and other things, and he'd had a lot of sex.

But this was pushing into territory he hadn't been into. The newness, the novelty, was intoxicating as hell, but it also meant they had to get some shit straight real quick. Simply because there was a trust element involved. And he didn't stay with one woman long enough to develop that.

He didn't know her; she didn't know him. And this was the kind of game that needed minimal guessing in order to be okay.

"You want to take orders?" he asked.

"Yes."

"You're sure?"

"I am."

"Be damn sure, Evie James. You're playing a pretty heavy game with a stranger."

She lifted a bare shoulder, the slim strap of her dress shifting with the motion. "Will you make me regret it?"

"No," he said. "I'm going to make you scream."

"Then I'm not worried."

"That's good. Worried isn't how I want you."

"How do you want me?" she asked, pausing at the bedroom door, turning partially, her fiery hair sliding over her shoulder and shimmering like a flame.

"I haven't decided yet. I might want you on top. Or, I might bend you over the bed so I can look at that pretty ass of yours. Watch my cock thrusting inside you. That's an option."

Her eyes went wide again and he felt, in that moment, a little guilty. Because she seemed innocent in a strange way, and he almost felt like he was corrupting her.

Still, better him than some idiot from a bar who would take advantage of what she offered without giving anything in return. Or worse, some animal who would hurt her the moment they were alone.

That thought didn't erase the guilt. But it was okay. He sort of liked the guilt. A novelty in many ways since shame was something he'd become numb to a long time ago. Deep emotion in general had been ripped from him on a sunny day ten years ago.

That it had been sunny made it particularly shocking. Because it was always sunny in Southern California. Because it was a day that looked like every other day, but it had changed everything.

He shook off those thoughts. Those memories didn't belong here. They didn't belong anywhere.

This was a fantasy. And in his fantasies, that day didn't exist.

She opened his bedroom door and went inside and he followed her, closing the door behind them. He didn't have to close it. He didn't have a family member who might show up. No roommate. There wasn't even a cat. But he liked the idea of closing them in. Of drawing a hard line between themselves and the world.

He looked at the bed, the black headboard the perfect height for a lot of different purposes. A reason he'd chosen it. No self-respecting playboy bought a bed that didn't serve multiple purposes.

But there was one thing he'd never used it for before.

"I could always tie you to the bed," he said, gripping the knot on his tie and loosening it until it came free. "Then I could do whatever I wanted with you."

He slid his tie through his hands, the silk heavy and cool against his skin. It would be soft on her wrists. And it would hold her tight.

There was something intoxicating about the thought of total control, and dammit, he'd never considered himself that kind of guy before.

But life was a big mess. A giant, uncontrollable beast that moved forward with the force of a freight train, whether you wanted it to or not. Which was why all you could really do was your best to have as much fun as possible until it ate you.

Except right in this moment, time seemed to be slower. And here in his room, he felt like he might be able to master it.

Or at least master something.

"I think that's what I want," he said. "You. Tied up for me. Naked. Take off your dress."

"All the way?"

"Yes. All the way. Your bra. I'm on the fence about the heels. We'll decide about those after the rest is gone."

Her fingers shook as she reached around and undid the zipper on her dress, letting it fall down past her hips. She had one of those strapless bras on. Not much support or padding to speak of if the jut of her nipples through the fabric was anything to go by.

And that meant she had every asset she'd promised to have.

At this point, though, he didn't care. Regardless of how she looked naked, she'd proven she was hot.

And he was hard for her again already.

She unhooked her bra and he almost lost it right then. She was totally naked for him, and she was perfect. Full, pale breasts, pink nipples. The sweet spot at the apex of her thighs. He'd already tasted her there, and now he craved more. She was better than ice cream. And he wanted to lick her all over.

"Now, get on the bed. Put your hands up over your head."

She obeyed, sitting on the edge of the bed, raising

her arms up over her head, her wrists crossed. "Yeah, like that," he said. "Hold still."

He approached the bed and wound the tie around one wrist, then the other, then around both before knotting it. She could escape if she wanted to. But she wouldn't. He was certain of that. Of her commitment to him. Her commitment to giving him the control.

And he had no idea what she was getting out of it, but he knew what it did for him. That was all he needed to know. This was just one night, not a relationship. And it was a bed, not a freaking psychiatrist's couch.

"Put your arms down. Hands in your lap," he said.

She obeyed, and she was watching him far too closely for his liking. Her eyes were arousal-glazed enough. They were too clear. Too smart. Too watchful. Like she was seeing through his suit. His chest. Down to the things beneath that. His heart. His soul, if you believed in shit like that.

He needed her a lot more mindless.

He started to unbutton his shirt and he kept his focus on her. Now she was starting to look glazed, her breasts rising and falling sharply with each quick little breath she took.

He pushed his shirt off his shoulders and shoved his pants and underwear down, gratified by the hitch in her breath when he was naked in front of her.

"Do you know what I want you to do?" he asked.

She looked up at him and shook her head.

"I want you to suck my cock."

The color in her cheeks deepened, the speed of her breathing increasing. He could see her pulse fluttering at the base of her neck. *Oh*, *Evie*. That was what he liked about her. Every emotion, every want, every thought, spoken out loud by her body.

He moved closer to the bed and reached behind her head, sinking his fingers deep into her hair and tugging back, tilting her face up. "You have such pretty lips," he said. "I want them wrapped around me."

She fidgeted, her cheeks brilliant pink, her eyes bright. "Whatever you say."

He guided her to him and she pressed her mouth against his length, testing him delicately with the tip of her tongue. Her hesitance only got him harder, hotter. And the guilt stabbed at him again. The combination of her tongue, her innocence and his own physical response to it was enough to send him over the edge.

He wrapped one hand around the base of his erection and squeezed tight, trying to keep control. She looked up at him, her tongue sliding along his length, from the head down to where he held himself tight, before following the same path back up.

Then she adjusted her position, her hands tied, his grip still solid on her hair, and took him in deep. His knees almost gave out. He tugged hard on her hair, to brace himself, to prove he was still rooted to the earth.

She moaned, the sound vibrating through him. He pulled up hard as she maneuvered her lips down over his length and he was rewarded with another deep sound of pleasure that shot straight through his body.

He tugged her head upward, pulling away from her at the same time. "Enough. I can't…I can't possibly take any more of that."

"You liked it?" she asked, a small smile curving her glistening lips.

"Hell. Yes."

She laughed, and it hit him like a lightning bolt. Shocking considering the situation. Arousing, which he found strange.

"What?" he asked.

"No one has ever said things like that to me before. But then, no one's ever given me an orgasm against a wall, tied my hands and given me orders, either."

"You have to start sleeping with better men."

"Consider this the beginning of that."

He chuckled. "Okay. Now we have to get serious again."

"Okay."

"Lie down."

She scooted back on the bed and lay across it, her hands still resting just over pertinent body parts. Like a renaissance painting in bondage, with her flowing red hair, milk-pale skin and the slate-gray tie on her wrists.

"Hands over your head," he said. "And spread your legs for me."

She hesitated. It was a small moment. A pause in her breathing, a tensing in her muscles. And then she obeyed. He put his hand between her thighs, stroking her slick head, pushing one finger deep inside as he moved his thumb over her clit.

"Ohhh…cheese and rice," she said throwing her hand over her forehead.

"Did you just call out food names in bed?"

"I…no…it's a…" she panted. "Kind of a swear word replacement. A little curtailed blasphemy. Just…habit. Didn't you ever say anything like that in front of your parents?"

"No. And if I did, it wouldn't be what I was thinking about now."

"I wasn't thinking at all," she said. "Clearly that's not a great thing for me since…since I just said that."

He moved up her body and planted his hands on either side of her head, then bent and kissed her lips. "I like it when you don't think. You don't have to think. And you don't have to be embarrassed. Not with me."

"That's good. Because you've done things to me no man ever has. So I'd hate to have to make our interactions more formal now."

"Sort of hard to have formal interactions when I'm doing this." He put his hand back down between her thighs and pushed his middle finger between her slick folds, deep down inside her and back across her clit. "Though, we could try," he said, teasing her as he leaned in, his lips a whisper from hers. "The weather was very nice today, wouldn't you say?"

"Perfect," she gasped, "like always."

"Good. Now stop talking," he said, kissing her cheek, then moving away from her. He went over to his nightstand and opened the drawer, taking out a condom and sheathing himself quickly. "I'm not in the mood to wait."

She started to lower her hands and he pushed them up, settling between her thighs. "I didn't tell you that you could lower your hands."

She blinked. "I'm sorry."

"You have to obey if you want to come. And you do want to come, don't you?"

She nodded.

"Tell me," he said.

"I do."

"You what?" he asked, pressing his length against her clit, moving slightly. She arched against him, her nipples brushing his chest. "Tell me, or I won't let you."

"I want to come," she said.

"Do you? What's going to make you come?"

"You," she said, "inside me."

"Do you want me to screw you?"

"Yes."

"Say it."

She met his eyes, her lips set in a determined pout. "I want you to screw me."

"And now I'm the one who's going to take orders," he said, pressing himself against the tight entrance to her body and testing her, watching her face as he pushed deep inside.

"I want to touch you," she said, her eyes locked with his, desperation visible there.

"No, baby, that's not the game," he said. "You're mine. And that's better than touching me, isn't it?"

"Yes," she said, her eyes fluttering closed as he withdrew from her and thrust back inside. "Yes," she said again.

And then he was lost, completely. There was nothing but the feel of her, the smell of her. Of being surrounded by her. She threw her head back, arched against him, her arms stretched up behind her head, her internal muscles tightening around his cock as she came.

And then he let go. And for the second time that night, Evie James had blown his mind.

CHAPTER FIVE

EVIE HADN'T MEANT to fall asleep. When she woke up, she was in a gigantic, unfamiliar bed alone, the sun just staring to rise up over the ocean.

"Crap," she muttered, looking around the room and spotting her discarded dress, shoes, bra and…her panties were elsewhere. "Crap, crap, crap…"

She stumbled out of bed, the sheets balled up against her chest in a protective, silken wad. She tiptoed through the room and collected her things, then scurried into the bathroom, locking the door behind her.

She put her clothes on quickly, then made the mistake of looking in the mirror. "Oh…oh dear." She was the epitome of the walk of shame. Bedraggled was the word. Her hair was sticking out at weird angles and her makeup had slid down her face, leaving tracks of black beneath her eyes.

She turned on the faucet and put her hands beneath the cold water, before splashing herself in the face. "Ah, darnit!"

This was not a moisturizer commercial, and she was not a model. She did not feel refreshed. She felt soggy and half-drowned.

She looked at herself again. Well, at least the

makeup was gone. But she looked like she'd had a fight with a hose.

She smoothed her now-damp hair and walked out of the bathroom, back into the empty bedroom. She wondered where Caleb was. And why he hadn't fallen asleep.

She tiptoed down the hall and to the kitchen, and that was where she saw him, sitting in a chair at the table, upright, asleep.

He obviously hadn't wanted to sleep with her. Shame prickled her scalp. Obviously she'd violated the rules of the one-night stand. But she didn't know the rules of the one-night stand because she'd never had one before. Because she was woeful and pathetic and not at all sophisticated.

And she felt even less sophisticated, and a bit more woeful, now that she'd had one. Because she just felt… strange. A little bit hollow, a little hungover and a lot embarrassed.

She walked through the room, past Caleb, and out into the living area, where she retrieved her panties and stuffed them in her purse before slipping out the front door and into the cool morning air.

She pulled her phone out of her bag and started searching for a car service. She was not calling anyone she knew. No one ever had to know about this, ever.

It was clear to her that Caleb already wished he could forget it, and she was starting to feel the same way.

But even while she felt slightly hot and shamefaced, calling a car out to an address she had to do some investigation to find, standing there in last night's dress, just advertising what she'd been doing, she knew she wouldn't forget all of it.

She would never forget the way he'd made her feel. Would never forget that for one night, she'd had the kind of sex she'd never even imagined was real. That she'd had the kind of sex she didn't think a woman like her could have.

Her ex could suck it. Or rather not, because she didn't want him anywhere near her. Not after a transcendent experience like Caleb.

She would focus on that. Not the morning after. Morning afters were supposed to suck, but if the night before was awesome enough, who cared?

Yes, Monday she had to go back to business as usual. No one would ever know about this. But she would know. She would know, and she was determined to hold onto only the good stuff.

And the good stuff was legendary. His hands between her thighs, his fist wrapped around her hair... oh yes, there was a lot of good to take away.

So she would leave the bad stuff, the regret, the embarrassment, here. She'd had enough of that to last a lifetime. She was moving on, a new, properly ravished person.

The car she'd ordered finally wound up the drive and to the front of the house. She looked back and saw that the windows were still dark, no sign of Caleb rousing evident.

"Goodbye, Caleb Anderson," she whispered before she got into the car, "thanks for the good times. And thanks for proving my app a success."

"EVIE, YOU BETTER get out here."

"What?" Evie looked up from the instant noodles she was eating at her desk, and at Raj, one of her interns.

"There's someone here who says that he's from *Flirt.* Or higher up, actually. And that he's here to start…overseeing the app development."

"What?" she slammed the foam cup down on her desk and stood up quickly, feeling a slight head rush. She blinked rapidly and tried to make the room stop swimming. "Why would they send someone? Everything is going fine."

"Something to do with coordinating content, and… making sure appropriate testing is done?"

"What does that even mean?"

"Just come out here," he said. "But…wipe the broth off your chin."

She wiped her arm over her face and ran her fingers through her hair. She wasn't exactly dressed for a meeting. She was just supposed to be working in her little office, with her little interns and employees. She was not supposed to be dealing with corporate suits.

She straightened her T-shirt and stared down at the words "Trust me, I'm the Doctor" with no small amount of regret. Not the best outfit to go to a meeting with bigwigs, but whatever. She'd been ambushed. It wasn't her fault.

Then she took a fortifying breath and walked out the office door behind Raj.

And stopped cold in the wide-open expanse of the office. Standing right in front of reception was not the corporate bigwig she'd envisioned. It was Caleb Anderson. And he was in a suit, his hair perfectly coiffed, his tie straight, his appearance immaculate.

But that didn't matter because she'd seen him naked, and frankly, that was all she could imagine now. That and those big, masculine hands wrapping his black tie around her wrists and…

"Mr. Anderson," she said. "What a surprise."

"Is it?" he asked.

"You don't seem surprised."

He put his hands in his pockets. "I'm not."

"My office," she said.

He lifted a shoulder. "Sure."

She turned, her face burning, unbearably aware that every eye in the open-plan office space was on her, and Caleb in the suit.

Of course, they would all assume she knew him from previous interactions with the *Flirt* corporate office. She was sure of that. They wouldn't know she knew him from letting him tie her up and have his wicked way with her.

Unless it was stamped on her forehead. She felt a little like it might suddenly be stamped on her forehead.

"Now," she said, turning and walking quickly back into her office, holding the door for him until he sauntered inside.

She slammed it shut behind him.

"What the hell are you doing here?"

"Nice shirt? Are you supposed to be Doctor Who?"

"It's just The Doctor," she said, annoyance coursing through her. "And that's beside the point."

"Is it?"

"Well, no. I mean…it's a point that needs to be

made." She closed her eyes. Oh, Evie, focus. "Yes. Why are you here? How are you here?"

"Did I not mention?"

"You said you didn't have a job!"

"I didn't. But I called my dad over the weekend and mentioned that I might like to try and get back into the family business."

"Your dad owns *Flirt* magazine?"

He laughed. "Don't be silly. My dad owns Holden-Anderson Media. *Flirt* magazine is just one piece of the empire."

"What?"

"Where do you think my money comes from? Did you think I followed the rainbow to its end and stole a pot of gold from a leprechaun?"

"Obviously I assumed you had family money. But I did not assume that you were somehow connected to the project I was working on."

"You know what they say about assuming."

"Seriously, what are you doing here?"

"I'm overseeing your project."

"Thanks in no small part to nepotism and manipulation. I got it. But why?" she asked.

"You're different in the office," he said. "It's interesting."

"This is my natural habitat, and you just walked into it. You might be king of the bars and…and bedrooms, but I am a business badass. So don't try to BS me or I will hand you your balls. Metaphorically. Not literally. Because literally your balls have nothing to do with this and I will not be touching them. Again."

He nodded slowly, walking over to her desk and rapping his knuckles lightly on the surface. "Sure. Point taken. But that's sort of counter to my plan."

"Which was what?"

"To help you work through your list."

"What?"

"Well, and I was thinking it was time I had a job again. There's only so much sedentary luxury a guy can take before the luxury starts to go to his head. I honestly found myself concerned by my lack of a female servant to feed me grapes and fan me the other day. That's not normal."

"No, it's not. But I don't think this is normal, either."

"Granted, it's probably not, but truth be told normal isn't my primary concern."

"What is your primary concern?" she asked, hands on her hips.

He frowned. "I want you still."

She sputtered. "I don't…I can't…what?"

"I want you still, and you left."

"You slept at the kitchen table rather than sleeping with me. I didn't exactly feel like you were hanging out to spend quality time with me."

"I don't want to spend quality time with you, I want to spend naked time with you. And I don't sleep with people."

"I don't even know what to say to this."

"You can't say much about it, because this is now my job."

"Sleeping with me?" she asked, blinking rapidly, her heart slamming hard against her breastbone.

"No. Weirdly, they won't cut a check for me for that particular activity. But overseeing this app is now my official job."

"What the hell title did they give you for that?"

"Third Party Technology Development Manager."

"Are you serious?"

"That's what it says on the little plaque on my desk."

"They did not…emboss you a plaque that quickly. That is not how that works. There's bureaucracy and, and…"

"Did you not hear the part about my dad owning almost every media outlet in the country?" he asked.

"This is unbelievable. I am not sleeping with you again."

"Technically, we've never slept together."

"I am not banging you again," she hissed.

"That's more accurate. Also, I don't think it's true."

"Oh, it is true."

"Why?" he asked.

"Because. Because I was supposed to just…do it with you and forget about you. You were not supposed to follow me into work like a lost puppy."

"Fine. Forget about the sex."

Her cheeks felt like they were on fire. "I can't, because my one-night stand has followed me to work."

"Try," he said. "And so will I. Just focus on helping me do my job. I'll be like a real boy, employed and everything."

"So you suddenly want to what…try at life?"

"Sure, if you want to put it that way. Yes, I partly wanted to see you again for…the thing we're now forgetting about, but honestly, I find you inspiring. You're young and you've done a lot with…hell, I don't know what you started with, but I'm sure it was with less than me, if only because ninety-nine percent of Americans have less than my family."

"So now you want to…reform?"

"Don't go that far, but maybe I want more. You seem like you have it together and you have to be… how old are you?"

"Twenty-seven."

"Okay, you're a good eight years younger than me, and clearly you have your shit much more together in the professional arena."

"You're full of crap," she said.

"Maybe. But this is the situation. I'm not going to harass you into sleeping with me, that would get HR involved, plus, it's a dickbag move. Also? I don't need to coerce women into my bed. They come willingly. As I'm sure you recall. Therefore, my efforts will now be focused elsewhere."

"Did you expect me to just…take my panties off when you walked in?"

The look on his handsome face clearly said: *Yes, yes I did.*

"I expected you to take them off and beg," he said, a completely unashamed smile crossing his features.

She cleared her throat and shuffled a stack of papers on her desk noisily. "I see. Well, sadly for you my panties are staying firmly…on my ass. So…there will be no dropping…of them." She cleared her throat again, and shuffled the papers even more loudly. Maybe if she did it enough times it would distract him. "Also, I think your confident brand of pickup swag works a lot better in a bar than in an office."

"You have a point. We're both very sober and the lighting isn't anywhere near as dim."

"Interesting, because you commented on how I seem different in this environment. So do you."

"Do I?" he asked.

"I think I have the upper hand."

He frowned. "I don't think so. Because, in addition to being your superior on this project, if I told you to take your panties off right now, you would."

Heat bloomed in her face, her heart thundering hard. "I would…not."

"Oh baby, if I told you to slide them down your thighs and show me what you have under those…leggings, you would."

"No. I absolutely would not. Nope. No. No. And you're inappropriate."

He lifted a shoulder. "Am I supposed to be apologetic?"

"I wouldn't expect anything so…decent."

"Oh good. I lack decency in most areas. But I find that makes me a much better lover. Which you've benefitted from."

Her face was so hot she felt like she'd just stuck it in an oven. "Sure. Once. But no more. This is…the workplace. Not the…not the bedroom," she said, calling on all the business class ballsiness she possessed. "And you just have to remember, that in this office, I'm the boss."

"You're The Doctor."

She put the papers down on the desk. "No…I'm not. I don't…time travel. I manage things. That's… stop distracting me." She regathered the papers and shuffled them again.

"Sorry." He didn't sound sorry at all. He looked… pleased.

"Either go back and clean out your newly minted desk, or stay and actually do a job," she said, looking at the wall behind him then trying to gather herself up, taking a breath and staring him down. "I'm not playing games. You're right—I didn't come from extravagant money. What I have, I earned on my own. So you may want to come in here and play at a job, but this is my life. And you are not playing around in it. Asshole."

CALEB HAD EXPECTED to be having sex by now. Actually, he'd expected to be basking in a post-orgasmic afterglow on Evie's desk by now. He had truly expected to show up at her office and have her sweep everything off her desk and demand ravishment. Because he hadn't been able to stop thinking about her.

And that never happened. Ever. So it had logically meant, in his mind, that since he hadn't been able to stop thinking about her, she must have been hanging out thinking about him.

So yes, he'd assumed that when he showed up, panties would be dropped.

Rather, he'd been met with Evie in leggings and a T-shirt, brandishing an evil eye that was enough to make pertinent bits of him wilt. Gone was the rambling, awkward woman he'd picked up in the bar.

Well, no, she wasn't gone, she was still there. But she was a hell of a lot more confident in her rambling in this environment.

So now he was working an office job. Without office sex. *Fan-freaking-tastic.*

But why? There were women here. Cute women. There was no reason he couldn't get himself some office sex. It didn't have to be with Evie.

His body responded to that with minimal enthusiasm.

That was a new one to add to the list. Along with: *screwed a woman, can't get her out of my mind.*

So now he was in a cubicle—a damn cubicle—waiting until Evie was ready to have him look at her "progress." She'd managed him. Like a child. It would have been more amusing if that wasn't how his father always handled him. Not that he hadn't earned the treatment. He damn well had.

But he was not used to women treating him this way. Which, were it not for his thwarted libido, would make it funny.

More importantly, she'd turned him down. It was unbelievable.

"Why did she put you in a cubicle?"

He looked over and saw a group of guys in skinny jeans and hoodies looking at him. "Because she wasn't willing to share her desk space. Don't you people have coffee to brew?"

The guy who'd already spoken, with dark scruffy hair and a beard, shrugged. "No, we're making a new game app. With unicorns."

"Sounds cool," Caleb said, his tone dry.

"We weaponized the horn," said the shortest guy, shifting in his bright red sneakers.

"I want to play," Caleb said.

The first guy shrugged. "Sure."

CHAPTER SIX

EVIE WAS SITTING at her desk getting increasingly antsy. She was trying to figure out some fun, interactive things to add to the different lists in the app so it wasn't just sedentary text. But she'd gotten to the sex tips portion and her brain was starting to short-circuit. As was her body.

She blamed stupid Caleb Anderson. Stupid Caleb Anderson and his lack of Whovian knowledge. Stupid Caleb Anderson who had invaded her space, her office, her domain. Stupid Caleb Anderson who was supposed to stay a one-night stand, and who had not.

One night of reckless abandon didn't work when it followed you back into real life. Then it became a consequence. Dammit, she didn't want a consequence. She just wanted a brilliant sexual experience, exquisite oral sex and absolutely no reckoning for her pleasure. Was that so freaking much to ask?

She skimmed down the list. Her entire body heating with every item read. Because she was picturing doing it all with Caleb.

Number five: when you're going down on your man, make sure to use your hands. Cup his testicles—

Oh, cheese and rice.

She skipped ahead. She had the idea.

Number six: surprise him at work. Nothing breaks up a mundane day at the desk job like having sex on the desk!

She choked.

Next.

Number seven: don't be afraid to get a little kinky. She shifted in her chair. A little pain can be fun. Hair pulling—yeah, she knew that—and spanking add a little spice to the bedroom. A light swat from your man's hand, or some more intense action with a belt, can really get things going.

She grabbed her iced coffee from the desk and popped off the lid, tilting the cup back and crunching ice cubes between her teeth, even though she knew it was bad for them—nine out of ten dentists could, like her ex, suck it. She needed to cool down.

And stop imagining office sex. Caleb bending her over her desk and—

No!

She stood up and rounded her desk; this had to stop. She glared at her desk, as if it were responsible for her filthy fantasies, and pushed open her office door.

And saw that all of her employees and interns were huddled in the corner, with Caleb at the center. *Huh.* Him and that damn, indefinable charisma.

"What's going on?"

Cassie, one of the employees she'd had longest, lifted her head and pushed her giant hipster glasses up her nose. Beneath said glasses she looked positively twitterpated. And it made Evie irrationally angry. "Caleb is on level twelve of 'Unicorn Strike.' Dude!

No! Get the horn of justice! The horn of justice!" She shrieked, turning her attention back to Caleb.

"Ah, no! Died." Caleb put the iPad back down on the desk in front of him and everyone around him sagged a little. "What's the horn of justice anyway?"

"When you impale your enemies it resurrects all the gnomes and fairies they've killed, then you get a swarm to come and give you aid."

"Well, I should have known," Caleb said, standing up, his eyes meeting hers.

Her stomach crushed in on itself, like it was a soda can Caleb had wrapped his fist around. "Can I see you in my office, Mr. Anderson?" she asked.

"Am I in trouble?"

"Of course not," she said, ignoring the sensual shiver his words sent over her skin. "Why would you be in trouble?"

"I'm slacking on the job."

"You're my boss, aren't you?" she asked, regretting the words when they came out.

"On select projects," he said, his words heavily laden with double meaning. Dear Lord, how did everyone in the room not hear the subtext? It was enough to make her overheat. She wished she'd brought her cup of ice with her.

"Yeah, fine, in my office." She waved her hand and headed back into the room, waiting for him again, before closing the door behind them.

"I'm having déjà vu from this morning," he said.

"You're a nuisance, Mr. Anderson." Her lips twitched. "I'm sorry, I can't say that without laughing."

"What?"

"Mr. Anderson. *The Matrix*."

"Okay."

"You know what, that makes you even worse. How do you not know *The Matrix?*"

"When did it come out?" he asked.

"Ninety-nine."

"Oh yeah, I was getting laid."

"You're a nuisance, Anderson," she said again, irritation spiking through her bloodstream.

"Am I?"

"Yes. You're out there being all…friendly with my staff and they have work to do. Much like for me, a job isn't a little game they try to amuse themselves with for a couple weeks at a time before they go back to a slothful existence of sleeping till noon and taking Jell-O shots off the stomachs of coeds."

"You must have been at last year's spring break event down in Puerto Vallarta."

"I don't want to know if what I just said was true!" she wrinkled her nose. "The point is, this is serious business to us."

"Yes. Weaponized unicorn horns and some ridiculous space-themed TV show on repeat on all the monitors on the walls. Serious business, I get it."

"It's our passion, Anderson," she said. "You get off on picking up random chicks at bars. We get off on this. More than that, we need it. It's our livelihood and our future. So don't come in here and screw with it. With your suits and your…your shoes and your expensive hair."

"I didn't come here to mess anything up."

"No, you were here for the nooky. Sorry I ruined

your plans." She was just annoyed now. Which was kind of nice because it made her feel less stumbly and awkward.

"Oh, I'm still here for nooky," he said.

"What?" The stumbly and awkward was back.

"That's why I'm anywhere, Evie."

She coughed. "You have a problem."

"Is it really a problem if you're totally happy with it? Though, I did tell you I'd help with the flirting stuff. And I will."

"Fine." She opened and closed her hands. "Have a seat. I have app crap to show you so pay attention."

"I think 'Unicorn Strike' is probably more to my taste level."

"Too bad, bitch," she said, "you signed yourself up for this project, now you're going to help. You're a manwhore, you ought to be able to help me figure out just how to lay out all this pertinent info. And you can tell me if any of the tips are BS. In that regard, your role as consultant makes perfect sense."

"I think I'm flattered. Let me see what you've got."

She handed him her phone. "Okay, what I'm working on right now is some kind of interactive features for the lists so they don't seem stagnant. But the problem with the sex tips is that everything I think of is pornographic."

He laughed. "Really?"

"Yes, really. Okay." She sat at her computer. "Scroll through. I've got the most up-to-date beta version on my phone."

"Yeah..." he said, "I think including pictures of

women licking popsicles on your blow job tutorial section is a touch overboard."

"Well, I couldn't put them licking actual penises. I have standards."

He actually laughed at her. "I like it when you talk dirty."

"This is an issue, Caleb. And it is now your job. Oversee."

"It's a no on the popsicles. I mean, if you're concerned about people being offended, which is sort of funny considering the content of the article. But strange things offend, trust me."

She leaned back in her chair. "I imagine you're an expert at offending."

He shrugged. "I'm okay at it."

"Any other ideas?"

"I think we should call the geek squad in for a consultation."

"No. There's a reason I've been doing most of this project on my own."

"Are you embarrassed?" he asked, swiping his finger over the screen.

"Are you…are you perving on the animation?"

"Yeah." He looked up at her. "Did you…did you do the art for this?"

She blinked. "Yes."

His focus went back down to the phone. "It's really good. You could transfer this skill."

"To what?"

"Drawing me dirty cartoons."

"It's tempting. Especially considering that your general affluence likely means you could set me up for early retirement if I did something dirty enough."

He continued messing around with the phone screen. "But you were in *Forbes*. I heard, somewhere, that you were kind of a big deal."

"From me. You heard it from me, and the sadness of that is completely noted, just saying."

"Okay, I'll be honest with you. It's going to be hard to do classed-up graphics for this."

"So what do I do?"

"You're overthinking. It's not a game, right? It's imparting information."

"Sure. But I just think some Easter eggs would be fun."

"I think the content is the star."

"Well, you're a guy."

"What's that supposed to mean? That for women this stuff isn't interesting? I call bullshit, Evie. I know it's interesting to you."

Evie shifted in her seat and looked very determinedly at the computer screen. "Sure. I mean, obviously I'm a sexual being."

"I like that. It sounds very elevated. And above common, sweaty, base desires like the rest of us have. Though, I know you aren't opposed to getting a little sweaty."

"Inappropriate workplace conversation."

"Sorry. The lines are blurring since we've already discussed the merits of animated penis licking."

Evie arched a brow and bit her lip, trying to keep from giggling like an adolescent. "That's business."

"I never planned on keeping things strictly business

with you. Remember? I'm utterly without shame. My sole purpose of coming here was to try and lure you back into my bed. That, in a sense, is my business."

The statement, like so many that Caleb made, should have pissed her off, and yet it just made her feel warm. And languorous. Like melted honey was spreading from her stomach out to all of her limbs.

"Yes, well, you should have consulted me on your plans."

"The thing is, Evie, my plans sort of went ahead without even consulting me."

"What does that mean?"

"I want you," he said, so simple, like it was obvious. Easy to admit.

She swallowed hard. "So you said. But I don't get..."

"I'm not the kind of guy who thinks about a woman after we have sex. I don't really mean it that way, I do think about women after. I have nice memories of hot times. But I don't...ache for them. I don't feel like I need them again. And you...I couldn't sleep Saturday night. I kept thinking about how you felt. About how good it was. I burned for you and that...doesn't happen. And so I figured I would put myself in your path again and you would say yes because...because..."

"Women say yes to you."

"Yeah," he said, his lip curling up slightly. "I am a bag of dicks."

"I don't know if I'd go that far. You're...entitled. But that, I guess, is what comes from having an easy life."

He laughed, and there was something bitter in it.

Something not entirely authentic. "Yeah. That's my problem. Life's been too easy."

"Back to the issue of my sex graphics."

"Yes, let us not forget your sex graphics."

"Typography?"

"What?"

"Maybe it's just about playing with the typography for these particular sections. Maybe I was going too elaborate. Or rather, too literal."

"Though, nothing says you can't go a little naughty," he said. "People like that."

"Okay, sure. So what if there's a naughty and nice version? Oh! And then like…the kinkier stuff can be in the naughty part. And you can pick if you're feeling nice or naughty and then…well, in the naughty version you can watch girls suck popsicles and read about getting bent over your desk and taking it from behind while your coworkers are only a thin, shoddily built wall away."

Caleb froze and dropped the phone on the desk. "I see. And…which section would you pick? I'm asking for beta-testing reasons."

She could see, from every taut line in his body, that this was not a hypothetical question. And she knew that the way she answered it would have a lot to do with what happened next.

Her breathing quickened, her heart pounding hard. The thing was, she wanted Caleb. Of course she did. She'd practically been aerial silk dancing in her sheets every night trying to get to sleep. And mainly she'd ended up sweaty, and horny and dragging out her vibrator.

And it had not been Benedict Cumberbatch on her mind during those late night sessions. Which made her feel a little guilty for cheating on her fantasy boyfriend—since he'd basically been the man assigned to said device back when she bought it—with fantasies of a man she'd actually slept with. And that was stupid.

But that was the state of things. Caleb was all she could think about. Caleb was all her body wanted. And why shouldn't she have him again?

He wanted her. Hell, he'd stormed into her building to…take her. Like a marauding pirate, which…no guy had ever done for her.

Jason was more the reluctant wench who would lie there and think of merry old England while he consented to her advances. Which did not do a hell of a lot for her ego.

What was holding her back, anyway?

Probably the fact that she'd decided it would only happen once. And that Caleb was around looking to make it more than one night was…not something she'd bargained for.

And, probably, because she was a little afraid that he'd somehow tricked himself into thinking she'd been awesome in bed, and a repeat performance, in the cold light of day and sober, would prove she was more what Jason thought, than what Caleb seemed to think.

That any illusion she had of being some sort of sexual tigress would be put to rest when she and Caleb touched again—it would be like trying to start a fire in a pile of damp driftwood.

And her moment of empowerment, her sexual triumph, would be destroyed.

So that was bullshit, because who cared? This had nothing to do with Caleb and what he thought of her. He wasn't her boyfriend. And what did some mythical triumph have to do with anything? It was only triumph if she was happy.

That was her whole problem. It was why she'd stayed with Jason. She got married to ideas, and she put them above her actual wants.

Her actual needs.

And here she was, bent on making her experience with Caleb a magic one-night deal, when she wanted more magic. When she wanted…and just wanted, because she was afraid of making a fool of herself. Afraid of wanting too much.

Well, no more.

She had nothing to lose here. She didn't love this guy. She could demand whatever she wanted, and if he didn't want to give it, he could march back to his cubicle and play "Unicorn Strike."

"Me?" she asked. "I'm naughty." Her voice cracked on the word, which sort of undermined her point. But oh well.

"How naughty? Popsicle-licking naughty or…"

She tried to swallow past her dry throat and she just felt like it ended up kind of…stuck together. "Bent-over-the-desk naughty," she said, feeling a little dizzy.

She'd never been that kind of naughty before. She'd never been any kind of naughty before Caleb. And now she wanted to try. To have him, here and now. During work hours. With people nearby. It was the perfect time. She had a guy who'd said he'd do anything she wanted, and a list that had given her all kinds of good ideas.

She was done resisting.

"You want me to bend you over your desk?" he asked, standing, planting his hands on the hard wooden surface, his palms sliding gently over it, like he was priming himself. And her.

"I didn't…say that…" She was backtracking. She was being a coward. "Yes," she said. "I do."

"Are you sure about that?"

"Who gives the orders around here?"

"You," he said, loosening his tie, "you're the boss, last time I checked."

"But someone has to keep me in line."

"I see. Are you interested in transferring power?"

"You're from the corporate offices, after all. A minion of the evil overlord of the company that paid me a lot of money to create this app."

He tapped on his chin with his forefinger. "I suppose that does put me in charge."

She saw the moment that it all flipped around. The moment he took her request and made it his command.

He walked over to her door and turned the lock, making his way back over to her desk. "Come here."

She obeyed, rounding the desk and standing in front of him, her hands crossed and clasped in front of her, as she'd done their first night together.

She didn't know why she was doing this. She didn't know why she wanted it. She only knew that she did. There was a strange kind of freedom in it. In letting go and giving Caleb the power, even if it was only the power she'd given him.

But then, that was what made it a safe game. The rules. Rules she'd laid down. And she knew he'd respect them. He had the night they were in his house, completely separate from anyone else, and he would certainly do it here, in her office where she could easily scream for help.

*Oh my...*in her office.

That added more fire to her arousal. Only made her hotter.

"Take those leggings off," he said.

"I should have chosen something better than leggings to wear today," she said, pushing the elastic-banded pants down her legs and pausing when they encountered her Toms. She flicked off her shoes and pushed the stretchy black fabric the rest of the way over her feet and onto the floor.

"Put your hands on the desk, face away from me."

She obeyed, the action thrusting her butt in the air. Her butt, which was now covered only by her stripy boyshorts. Horizontal stripes even. So hot. Not. Her ass probably looked like a giant rainbow zebra.

She felt his palm on her butt, warm, firm. He slid it down, beneath the waistband of her panties, gripping her bare skin hard. "You like that?" he asked, his breath hot on her neck, her ear.

"Yes," she said.

He gripped the back of her neck with his other hand, holding her steady, holding her still. "You want this?" he asked, sliding his palm from beneath the waistband of her underwear and bringing it down lightly over her fabric-covered skin.

There was no pain, only a sharp pang of need that crackled out from where his hand met her ass, to her core.

She bit her lip to keep from making moany-sex noises because…there were people outside her office. Why did that make it hotter? Why did that make it so much more…wicked?

She looked over her shoulder at him and nearly lost it then and there. His tie was draped over his shoulders, his shirt collar undone, revealing a wedge of perfect man-chest. And her eyes drifted lower, to his belt, to the bulge just beneath it.

She wanted it. All of it. She wanted it now, even though it was wrong. Even though she shouldn't want him. Not here, not now, not at all. But she was going to have him anyway. Because she didn't care about should, shouldn't or what anyone else might think. This was about what she wanted. What she needed.

After years of settling, she was so due.

He pushed her panties down her hips and she kicked them to the side. He moved his hand up beneath her T-shirt, cupped her bra-covered breast. "I might leave this on."

He released his hold on her breast and moved his attention back down to her butt, his warm palm sliding over her skin.

"Yesss. Oh…" She took a deep shaking breath. "Yes, Caleb. Touch me."

"You are a naughty girl," he said, his voice rough, his touch firm.

So cheesy. It should have put her off, but it turned her on. Because she'd never thought of herself as a naughty girl. A hardworking girl. A nerdy girl. But not terribly naughty, not terribly appealing. Not the kind of woman who abandoned all good sense, reason and deference to moral codes. To societal norms.

But today she was. And damn she liked it.

"You want me, don't you?" he asked.

"Yes," she said.

"You want me to take you with everyone just outside. If I make you scream, they'll all hear. They'll all know. Is that what you want, baby?"

"Are you asking? I thought you were in charge."

"Damn right I'm in charge," he said.

At least he was asking what she wanted, not making her fumble around to figure out what he liked. At least his response to her request wasn't, "you know I don't like that freaky shit." Which had, honest to goodness, been her ex's response to her request for sex from behind. Which, she seemed to be in prime position for now.

But not yet. Not until after he'd teased her more. Not until he'd made her want it more.

She heard him working on the belt buckle, one hand still firm on the back of her neck, holding her to her spot at the desk. As if anything beyond an earthquake could move her now.

She closed her eyes and listened, the soft sound of his belt being tugged through the loops of his pants sending a shiver of anticipation down from where he still held her with his hand, to the base of her spine. Gathering there, a knot of need, of longing that only he could relieve.

She heard his zipper being tugged down. Who

would have ever thought she'd be listening for a zipper sound? And that it would bring her close to the brink of orgasm.

It was in his control. His control to relieve the unbearable tension, or to hold her on edge like this forever. The waiting was delicious, almost as good as satisfaction.

She was trembling, shaking from her lips on down. And he was waiting.

"Tell me how wet you are for me," he said.

"I…I…" She was going to die. He was going to kill her with the waiting and his words.

"Tell me, baby, or I'm not going to give you what you want."

"I'm…you make me…you make me so wet," she said, shifting, trying to alleviate the ache that was burning between her thighs. "I want you so much it hurts."

"Where do you want me?" he asked.

"I want you…I need you…inside me."

"Like this?" He moved, his fingers delving between her thighs, spreading her open. She felt exposed, powerless. In the very best way. She was at his mercy, and she had no idea what he would do next. Only that she would like it. Because there was nothing Caleb had done to her so far that she hadn't liked.

"More," she said, the tease excruciating now. She was ready to beg. She had no pride at all where he was concerned. Where this was concerned.

His fingers grazed her clit before he dipped one inside her. She gasped, her entire body tensing, poised right on the edge. "Or did you want it like this?"

She nodded, biting her bottom lip. There were no words, at least none she could find.

He moved his finger in and out of her body. She bucked against him. Needing more now. Needing all of him.

"Caleb," she said, his name a long, low moan. And she didn't even care if anyone heard.

"You want me," he said. There was nothing obnoxious or cocky in his tone. It was a sort of intense growl that reverberated through her. It was a reflection of how she felt.

It wasn't light, easy wanting. Not now. It was something hard. Intense and demanding. Something that was taking her places she'd never been. Making her crave things she'd never known she wanted.

He moved his hands and gripped her hips, his tongue sliding over her slick folds, the sudden change, the warm, slick friction making her jump. She bit her lip and put her head down, curling her fingers in, her nails biting into her fists.

"Oh...Caleb," she gasped, wishing there was something for her to grab onto. Something she could do to help hold herself together.

Instead, she just leaned on the desk, hoping that would be enough to keep her from melting into the floor. Hoping it would be enough to keep her from falling apart.

He pushed his tongue deep inside her, the shock driving a hard spike of pleasure through her stomach and all the way down.

He continued to work magic on her with his mouth,

taking her to the edge before pulling back, teasing her with satisfaction and taking it away.

Anticipation had never been so sweet. Pleasure had never hurt so much.

It was pain, needing him so badly and not being filled by him.

"Take me," she said, without even realizing she was speaking out loud. "Please, Caleb. Please. I need you."

She was begging. She didn't care. Who had room for pride when they needed this badly?

"Caleb," she said, his name a prayer on her lips. "Please, Caleb. Please."

He stood up and she heard him tearing open a condom packet. She looked back over her shoulder and watched him roll the condom over his thick length, his pants shoved partway down his lean hips, their partial state of dress only making it all feel hotter. Feel that much more urgent.

And it was urgent. Damn urgent.

He pressed his chest against her back, one hand on her stomach, the other on her hip as he thrust slowly inside her. He made a hoarse, tortured sound as he sank in her to the hilt, his hand sliding up, over her breasts, stopping at the base of her neck.

He flexed his hips against her butt and she let her head fall back. He angled his head and kissed her mouth as he moved inside her, his hand keeping that possessive hold on her throat. Not hard, not painful. Just steady and firm, a sign of ownership. One she was happy to give him.

Because in this moment, she felt completely owned by him. Completely lost in him.

Amazing how a stranger could know so much more about her body, about her needs, than the man who'd shared her bed and her life for ten years. Amazing how he could make her feel so much more than the man she'd thought she'd loved.

Amazing how free she could feel when she was held captive.

He pulled her hard against him with each thrust, every movement inside her drawing a feral sound from his lips. This wasn't the smooth man in the suit. The playboy with easy one-liners. This was a man on the edge of control. And that seemed fair to her since she'd left her control on the floor with her panties quite a while ago.

"I can't hold back," he said, his voice rough.

"Good. Don't."

He growled, freezing as his orgasm washed through him, the pulse of his cock inside her pushing her that final way, over into oblivion. Her mind went blank, her entire body feeling like it was in a free-fall, weightless, tossed around in wave after wave of pleasure and release that crashed over her, hard and fast so she couldn't catch her breath. Until she was afraid she would drown. Until she almost hoped she did.

He held her tight against his body, transferring them to the other side of the desk, sinking down into the chair and bringing her with him, seated firmly on his lap. He was breathing hard, his chest rising and falling rapidly, his shirt stuck to his skin.

She leaned in and pressed a kiss to his exposed neck.

"Damn," he said.

"Yeah. I think we just violated the workplace code of conduct," she said, still gasping for air.

"No one would be surprised to know I violated a code of conduct," he said.

"No?"

"It's sort of what I do." He tightened his hold on her waist.

"Why?" she asked.

"Why what?"

"Why do you violate codes of conduct?"

"I don't know. Why not?"

"It's just…a funny thing to make Your Thing. But whatever, man. I'm in no place to judge. I just begged for it in my place of business. And got it, I might add." She lifted her shoulder and wiggled out of his hold, standing up and wobbling a bit. "Whoa."

"You don't have to get off me."

"I'm on the clock. I kinda do."

"I think the boss would understand."

"The boss is showing questionable judgment today," she said, picking her clothing off the floor and wiggling back into it.

"Do you regret it?"

She frowned. "No."

She should regret it. She should feel utterly weirded out, but she didn't. She felt…fine. With all of it. And that made her feel a little giddy. And like maybe the app she was making was magic. Because somehow, all of the things in it had helped make her brave enough to do things she'd barely let herself fantasize about.

"But I do have work to do," she said. "That's what you do when you have a job."

"Ah," he said, standing up and tucking himself back into his pants.

She almost couldn't handle watching him redo his belt. Just looking at it made her a little shaky, in the best way.

"You'll get the hang of this work business."

"I guess I'll have to."

"Yeah, you have to oversee me."

His expression turned to granite. Very sexy granite. "I guess I do."

"I assume I'll be going to your house tonight after work," she said.

"Do you?"

"Well, yes. I can't only bang you during business hours. And I do intend to bang you again."

"That's charming."

"Well, I thought so."

"Sure. How long do you want to go on with the… banging?" he asked.

"Until I've fulfilled my contract," she said. "How does that strike you?"

He smiled and walked toward her, extending his hand. She put hers out, and he shook it. "You have yourself a deal."

CHAPTER SEVEN

EVIE HADN'T ARRIVED YET, and Caleb found himself feeling...*nervous?* Surely not that. He didn't get nervous about whether or not a woman would show up for a date. For sex. It wasn't even a date. He didn't do dates.

Hookups. He did hookups. And he didn't feel even a little bit bad about it. Life was short—you had to live it while you could.

Usually, he chose to live it with a different woman every night. But Evie was...available. Because he'd... gotten himself hired on at his father's company so he could get a position in her office building.

Whatever. She was around. And she was coming over.

And if she wasn't it didn't matter, because he could get a woman whenever he needed one. Though, he'd never had an encounter with a woman quite like the one he'd had with Evie earlier today.

Or on Friday night.

He'd never been into tying women up, or screwing them in public. Hell, beds worked just fine for him, thanks. But she'd been so hot. So into it. It was like she was exploring her sexuality for the first time, and using him to help. And what guy wouldn't get off on that?

There was something about the way she wanted

him, about her mixture of boldness, innocence and total sense of adventure that got to him. Made him crave more.

But in order for him to get more, she had to show up. And he wanted her to. Okay, he needed her to. He could admit that much, even though it galled him.

He didn't do need. Or attachment. He wasn't up to it. He had nothing to offer back. Woe to the person he needed because there was nothing he could do to adequately compensate them for fulfilling his needs.

Yeah, he was good in bed, he knew that. But there was more to life than that. Or there was more to most people's lives, anyway. In his life, that was basically the beginning and end of it. Which was fine.

The doorbell rang and he strode toward the entry. "Thank God," he muttered, jerking the door open. "You're late," he said, looking at the woman standing out there on the step.

She was bar hookup Evie again. Not work Evie, in stretch pants and dorky T-shirt. She was wearing killer heels and a tight red dress that showed off just how flawless her curves were. She also looked big-eyed and nervous, slightly awkward.

"Sorry, I couldn't decide what to wear."

"What do I care what you're wearing? It's only going to end up on the floor."

She frowned. "I spent time on this selection."

"And you look amazing. But you looked amazing to me earlier, too."

She blinked rapidly. "I did?"

"You're beautiful. What you're wearing doesn't have anything to do with it. Now come in."

She did, walking in slowly, her hands clasped in front of her. He shut the door behind her. Evie was back out of her element again.

"It's not any different than earlier," he said, gripping her chin with his thumb and forefinger and tilting her face up to look at him. "You remember what you did to me earlier."

"I remember what you did to me."

"Come on, baby," he said, sliding his hand down her arm and guiding her palm to his cloth-covered cock. "Feel what you do to me?"

He was hard already. Had been hard from thinking about her. From fantasizing about what might happen tonight. His Evie was full of surprises. He was the first to admit to being jaded. To finding very little about life exciting or interesting.

But she was exciting. She was interesting.

And in a world where nothing was, it was something like finding water in the desert.

"I thought maybe we should have dinner…or talk or…okay." He pulled her in and kissed the words right from her lips. He had to, because he wasn't sure what he'd say if she wanted to talk. He felt weird. He *felt*, period, and that was weird.

He kissed her deep and long, his tongue sliding against hers. She made little kittenish sounds of pleasure, her fingernails kneading his shoulders. He couldn't remember the last time just kissing a woman had been so rewarding. Couldn't remember the last time he'd wanted to linger on a kiss.

This wasn't about rushing through to the main

event, but with her, it never had been. With Evie, it had always been the lure of the unknown.

Not because she was slick and mysterious, but because her honesty was so unpredictable. She was sort of scary to watch, too. She was someone who didn't seem to know how to protect the most vulnerable pieces of herself.

It scared him for her. Made him want to demand she cover up, put on a helmet to keep from the missiles that would fly her direction when other people saw just how unprotected she was.

But at the same time, he wanted her to stay the same. Because he liked what she gave to him. Which was a hell of a douchey thing. To want to use that sweetness, that guilelessness for his own satisfaction.

But then, he'd established early on in his life that he was in fact a dickbag, so it seemed in keeping with his character. If you could call what he had character. And he couldn't say he cared much either way.

He was all about satisfaction. The here and now. And Evie catered to all of that.

"You got more on your list?"

"Yes, yes I do."

A LONG TIME LATER, they lay in his bed, their limbs tangled together. He didn't like to linger in bed with women, normally. That was why he'd left her sleeping on Friday. But he didn't want to leave her tonight, and he honestly couldn't figure out why.

Maybe because the weight of her body felt good. Or because her hair was really soft. Or because he was just too destroyed to move.

"So tell me something about you," he said, and he didn't know why he wanted to know that either. Anonymity was safe for everyone involved.

But then, they weren't anonymous. He'd seen where she worked. She knew who his father was.

They'd exchanged firsts.

"What…anything?"

"Yeah, sure, anything."

"I…was not very popular in school."

He laughed. "No kidding. I was."

"No kidding," she said, kissing him on the chest. He felt the small gesture with all the impact of a bullet.

"Something else," he said, "make it good."

"I lost my virginity on prom night."

"Me too," he said. "Not my prom night. I was too young to go to prom. But I think a prom may have been taking place somewhere."

She smacked his shoulder. "I'm baring my soul, asshole, come on."

"It was formative for me."

"Unfortunately, my first time was also formative."

"How was it?"

"Boring as hell. I remember lying there thinking 'that's all the way?' He'd given me orgasms when we were making out, heavy petting and all that, and then we finally 'did it' and it was…meh."

"I think first times are usually like that."

"Was yours?"

"No. But it was fast. Thankfully, it wasn't her first time, so I don't think she held it against me."

"Want to know the worst part?"

He shifted and looked down at her. "What?"

"I stayed with him. For ten years. And it never got better."

He'd known that she was inexperienced, she'd said as much, and obviously since they were playing out all these fantasies she'd never tried, her sex life hadn't been particularly varied, but that she'd stayed with one guy, a guy who sucked in bed, just made him mad.

Not at her, but at the man. He should have given more. If you had a woman like Evie in your life for ten years, why wouldn't you give more? Why wouldn't you do what you could to keep her?

He shoved the thought aside as soon as it entered his mind. Nice of him to judge, since he had no intention of keeping Evie. But that was about him, not her.

"He made me feel like there was something wrong with me, and honestly, I mainly stayed with him out of habit. I didn't love him. But the way he treated me still changed me, and I hate that. I hate it. I never even got to know what I liked in bed, or what I liked in men because I tied myself to Jason when I was seventeen and stayed."

"You don't seem like the kind of person to accept blah, Evie, I have to say. Look at how accomplished you are in your job."

"I know. But I think that's partly why. My work was what I really loved. I wanted to be successful and I sort of thought, great, personal life sorted, and onto the main event. But he…he hated it all. Not right at first, because he sure loved the money. But he said it marginalized him. To have a girlfriend who was so much more successful."

"What did he want from you?"

"Honestly? I think he wanted out, but like me wasn't willing to make the move. Or maybe I'm giving him too much credit. Maybe he wanted me to quit working, be his stay-at-home housewife while he spent the money I already made. Either way, he ended up cheating on me…and blaming me. But it was the best thing that ever happened to me really."

"When was that?"

"Six months ago. And when I saw you…well, I thought it was the perfect chance to explore some of what I'd missed. To figure out who I am apart from Jason, who is afraid of oral sex."

"What?"

"Oh, not of me giving it to him. But he sure as hell never wanted to do it for me. Though, he did it for her. Bastard."

"Some men do not deserve for women—for anyone—to give them free rein over their naked bodies. You have to respect a gift like that. Cherish it. Bend it over a desk in the office."

She laughed. "I love that about you."

The L-word on her lips made his chest do something weird and tight. "What?"

"That you're this total playboy, and you own it. But that you do, you respect the gift. You've never taken advantage of me. You always make sure I'm satisfied."

"I don't have a lot of gifts, but I'm good in bed."

"That's not true."

He smiled. "I'm not good in bed?"

"That you don't have a lot of gifts," she said. Her expression went all serious and she smoothed his hair back from his forehead. "Tell me something about you."

"There isn't much. I'm from a rich family. Had a nice house. Anything I wanted. My first car cost more than most people make in a year. I think that led to my basically dissolute lifestyle."

"Serious relationships?"

"Nope."

"Brothers or sisters?"

He opened his mouth to answer, then stopped. There was no easy answer to this question. Say *yes* and they asked what she was doing. Say *no* and it felt like a lie.

"Yeah," he said, swallowing past the lump in his throat. Why was it still so hard to say? Ten years later it should be easier. And in some ways it was. He didn't cry about it at weird times anymore. But he still didn't like to talk about her. He preferred to just forget. Which was what he normally did.

"Younger or older?"

"Older." Jill had a birthday coming up. But she wouldn't actually be around to age. He was older now than Jill had been when she'd died. So he wondered if that was true, if she was technically older.

Shit, what a weird thought. This was why he didn't think about it. Jill wasn't any age now. Jill was just dead.

"What does she—"

He rolled over and kissed her, because it was way too intimate of a thing to have this discussion naked and in bed with the woman he was screwing. He didn't do connections; he didn't do sharing and hugging time. He wasn't about to start now.

"We were talking," she said, breathless.

"I know, but I want to do this instead."

"You always want to do this."

He laughed and ignored the uncomfortable weight that settled in his chest. “And you’re complaining?”

“Not really.”

He kissed her again. “Good.” Then again. And again until nothing else mattered but this. But the two of them and this bed and this moment.

And when they were done, she got up, got dressed, kissed him goodbye and left him alone in his bed. Just like he liked it. *Dammit.*

“If you like it so much, why are you so miserable?” he asked into his pillow.

Unsurprisingly, there was no answer. Because, like always, he was alone.

CHAPTER EIGHT

She went to Caleb's house every night for two weeks, and never stayed. And it was starting to bother her. Which was silly, because he'd made it very clear what his rules were. And she really, in many cases, didn't mind following his rules. Taking his orders…whatever.

But this was starting to feel sad. Every time she dressed to leave his house, it was worse and worse. And she was sleep deprived. She didn't manage to leave his place until the early hours of the morning, then she had to drive home, and try to settle down and go to sleep. She was getting an average of three hours' sleep a night and she was starting to climb the walls.

The alternative was asking to use one of his extra bedrooms so she could stay the night. But that seemed even worse.

Hey, I know I can't sleep with you, but could I crash on your couch? Oh, and thanks for the orgasms, by the way. Maybe tomorrow you can tie me up? Or perhaps I could interest you in some afternoon delight in a semi-public location?

No. No no no. She liked a little kink with her pleasure, it turned out, but humiliation was off the table.

At least humiliation in that context. Sexually, she'd

ruled very few things out. She was self-discovering, after all.

Though, none of this would be a problem soon. Because she'd finished the app. She hadn't told him yet. Which was silly, and immature, but the minute she told him…he would be done working in her office. Their affair time would be over. She wasn't ready yet.

Soon, but not yet.

It was a Saturday, so she hadn't seen him yet today, and the anticipation had her all sweaty. Well, that and the little gesture she'd come bearing.

She tightened her grip on the picnic basket in her hand—packed by her favorite restaurant—and pushed the doorbell, waiting for Caleb to come.

He wasn't going to like her bringing food. She could sense that already. He seemed to try and cut their personal interactions short. They saw each other in the office, he made noise about looking at her app, and in truth he'd had some very good ideas.

Caleb seemed to understand the client a little better than she did, which, considering the client was women who subscribed to a women's magazine, that was a little sad, but whatever. And his suggestions had been very valuable.

He was smart, even if he did do his best to play it down. She wasn't sure why he did that. The more she got to know him, the more confused by the playboy-reprobate-lazy-rich-boy thing he had going.

Because he was more than that, even if he tried desperately to not let her see it.

The door opened and she smiled widely, holding up the basket. "I brought food."

His gaze flicked over her, that perfected air of cool interest not fooling her for a bit. He wanted her, and he was dying to get her naked. She was confident in that. More than that, she could see it.

For some reason the veneer seemed extra false. Like being suddenly conscious of a painted backdrop in an old film, and then not being able to see anything else.

Caleb Anderson was full of shit. And she knew it. Had known it for a while, really. And yet it had only just become clear to her how false, how brittle, his playboy facade was.

"Can I come in or what?" she asked.

"Sure. What's in the basket?"

"Just food. Not handcuffs. Don't get excited."

"I can work with food."

"I'm sure you can work with anything," she said, walking past him and into the house. "But first, eat."

"All right, let's go to the table."

"I brought a blanket," she said.

"For?"

"An indoor picnic." Suddenly the idea seemed stupid. It had seemed fine while she was getting it all together. It had seemed like happy times, smiles and sex and floor. But now Caleb was looking at her like she'd grown a third boob and she was starting to feel like she'd made some grave misstep.

"Well, it'll hardly seem like a real picnic without the ants," he said dryly. "But hey, could be fun." His tone said it most definitely wouldn't be fun.

And now she just felt like some deluded, romantic idiot. She wanted to melt down into the cracks between the tiles and slither out.

"Let's just eat at the table," she said. "Better still, let's just fuck. That's what you like."

He put his hand on her arm and gripped it tight, drawing her to him. "What the hell?"

"You could not have made your disapproval of the whole thing more clear if you'd screamed and run from the room. It's just a picnic. Not a declaration."

"We'll eat on the floor then," he said.

"No. Now I don't want to eat on the floor."

"Too bad," he said, grabbing the blanket from her hands and stalking into the living area. He spread it out, awkwardly, and then sat, his knees drawn up, forearms resting on them.

She let out an exasperated sigh and went and sat down across from him, placing the basket in between them. "I hope you like seared tuna and fine wine."

"Who doesn't?"

"The same people who hate picnics indoors. And draw strength from the tears of children."

"So…me," he said, opening the basket and pulling out two wineglasses, and the wine bottle.

"I guess so. I hadn't picked you for that sort of person but, you know…"

He forced a smile and pulled a corkscrew out of the basket, jamming it into the cork. "Sorry," he said, not sounding any more genuine in his apology than he had in his sudden enthusiasm for the picnic. "It's not been the best day."

"Why?"

He paused, his eyebrows locking together. "No big deal."

"Then why are you acting like that cork has done

you wrong and you need to kill it?" She snatched the bottle from him and proceeded to pull out the cork, then poured them two healthy glasses of wine.

Caleb picked his up and took a much healthier first sip than she expected. "Because."

"Caleb…"

"Do we share now?" he asked, arching a brow.

"I think we share."

"Do you?" he asked, taking another long drink.

"I've confided my darkest most sordid fantasies in you and allowed you to carry them out. You tied my hands together and did dirty things to me, and I liked it. I'd say we share certain confidences, yes."

He looked down into his glass. "It's my sister's birthday."

"I…did you need to go and see her tonight? Am I interrupting something? Because I didn't know—"

"I've been to see her already. This morning."

"Oh. That's…did you go out to breakfast or…"

"No. I went to see her. I went…she's at Westwood Memorial Park. That's…" He cleared his throat. "I had a beer with her. I do that sometimes. She doesn't know, obviously."

Evie's heart crumpled up like a sheet of paper in an iron fist, the air pulled from her lungs. "Oh."

"I should have maybe said something when you asked about her. But…uh…I don't like to talk about it." He cleared his throat. "People don't know what to say. And usually, they can't say anything right. Whatever they say just kind of makes me mad, actually. Because they don't really know."

"I'm an only child," she said. "So you're right, I don't."

"She's thirty-six today," he said. "She was twenty-six when she died. It's been such a long time. You'd think…I never even plan to go out there. I spend all year not thinking about her. Not thinking about any of it, and then I end up there. Not the anniversary of her death—her birthday. It's always her birthday. And I just sit there, and I don't know what I'm waiting for. Or why I'm there. She doesn't know I'm there, so what's the point?"

The look on his face, the pain, the confusion, broke something in her. There was no point pretending she didn't care about him. No point pretending this was just sex. Not when his pain reached straight into her stomach and pulled out her guts.

Such a terrible moment to realize the strength of her connection to him, but it was unavoidable. Because she was seeing him clearly, and that forced her to see herself clearly, too.

She had no advice for him. Nothing to say to dull the hurt, the grief and whatever else it was he was struggling with.

It was big, and she could feel it. Something that she didn't feel up to. She didn't deal in real, grown-up emotion. She dealt in unicorn-themed apps, popsicle-fellatio art and a relationship in which "meh" had been preferable to acting like any kind of adult and improving her situation, because…habit, that was why.

She was a giant, immature ball of flail, and Caleb needed something. But she didn't know how to give it.

She hated that. She hated that she was failing him right now.

She put her hand on his arm, slid her palms up to his biceps, closing the distance between them. She just wanted to touch him. To let him feel like she was there. Like he wasn't alone. Because she had no insight, no answers, no moment of clarity to offer.

But she had herself. The whole ball of flail. She had it, and she wanted to give it to him. She'd been with Jason for ten years and never wanted to give herself to him. Sleep with him, live with him, say that she loved him, yeah, she'd done all that. But she'd never wanted him to have a piece of her. A connection that couldn't be compromised or shaken.

She'd never wanted to open herself up like that. Break off a piece of her soul and hand it to another person for safekeeping. She'd never really seen the appeal. She'd never known it was a thing.

But it was all she had to give. So she wanted to give it.

She leaned in and kissed him, and it felt like the first time her lips had touched his, even though she was sure their kisses numbered in the hundreds by now. But this wasn't about lust, or a list in an app, this was about him. About her. About how much she wanted to make him feel better. Feel something good.

He raised his hand and cupped her cheek, his touch gentle, tentative. It was a strange and new connection for them. She found it as exciting, as thrilling, as the others. As the intense, erotic encounters they'd had.

She parted her lips slightly, allowing him entry, giving herself to him.

When they parted he was breathing hard, his forehead resting against hers, his eyes closed. “That’s not the response I expected,” he said, his voice rough.

“Sorry,” she said. “It seemed like the best idea.”

“I’m not complaining.”

“I want to make it better,” she said. “I don’t know how.”

“I don’t either.”

“Can I just be with you? Or should I leave you alone?”

His hands came up and bracketed her face, his eyes snapping open, his dark brown gaze intense. “No,” he said. “I’m always alone. Don’t leave me alone. Please.”

“I won’t,” she said, kissing him again. “I won’t.”

She reached down and tugged his shirt up, pulling it over his head, sliding her hands over his perfect chest. Down his abs, down to the button on his jeans. No belt today, but it was just as well. This was about him.

Everything so far had been about her. About her fantasies, her exploration. Her figuring out what she’d missed while she’d settled for blah for all those years.

But this was about him.

Caleb, the man who’d had a lot of sex, the man who could always find a woman to go home with, but still always felt like he was alone.

“Is there something new you wanted to try tonight?” he asked, his voice rough.

She bit her lip and shook her head. “I just want you.”

“You don’t want to get out the app and—” She kissed him again, cutting off his words.

“No,” she said. “No app. No games. Think you can handle it?”

"You think I can't handle a little sex?"

She wasn't sure he could. Because she wasn't sure she could handle this either, whatever the hell it was they were on the edge of. And it was something. Something big. At least it was for her.

"We'll see if you can handle me," she said.

"You've come a long way, Evie, Evie James," he whispered, pressing his lips to hers.

She had, but not in the way he meant. If she had to put herself out there with a different guy, she would be as inept as she'd been that night they'd first met in the bar. The thing that had changed was the way she felt about herself.

It wasn't all false I'm-a-successful-millionaire-so-I-must-be-okay bravado. It was real. A desire to think that she could give something of herself and have it matter. And more, the need to demand more for herself. Better sex, better relationships, a real emotional connection.

She wanted it all, dammit. Because she was worth it.

"I have," she said. "Want to see how far?"

"Sure."

"The tuna's on ice."

"What?" he asked.

"The tuna. In the basket. So we can go…and it'll be okay. See? I'm still me."

"I like you like this," he said. "I like that you just say the things that pop into your head. I like that you aren't smooth."

"You don't think this is smooth?" she asked, sliding her hands over her breasts and down her stomach.

"Uh…there's no good answer for me to give here, so I am just going to kiss you. Talking is too hard anyway."

He leaned in and kissed her, tugging her up against his chest and drawing them both into a standing position without breaking it. Then he pulled her up into his arms, cradling her against his chest.

"Oh," she said, her hand resting over his heart. She felt slightly dizzy. It was cliché, but it was a cliché she'd never had before. Being carried to bed by her lover. It made her feel small and delicate, made her conscious of his strength.

And more importantly, it made her feel like he couldn't wait to have her.

Wow, that did things for her. For her ego, her libido…all the things.

He carried her down the hall and into his bedroom, where he laid her down on the bed, lowering himself over her, his arms on either side of her shoulders. "You're beautiful," he said.

He wasn't the one who was supposed to be giving. She was. She was the one who wanted to make him understand what he meant to her. What he did to her. How important he was. That he wasn't alone.

She'd had sex with Caleb a lot of times. Several times a night over the past two weeks. Honestly, they'd been like horny ferrets on crack. But they'd never made love. She wasn't sure she'd ever made love with anyone. No, she was sure she hadn't.

She'd never felt this desperate desire to meld bodies and hearts. To make the man she was with feel what was happening inside her, make him feel her emotion because she couldn't put words to it. She didn't know what to call all these feelings. And she was too afraid to try and name them. But maybe he could feel it.

Maybe he'd be able to recite it back to her and explain it in a way she could understand it, because right now it felt too big and tangled for her to ever get it completely.

And it was too scary. Way too scary to examine.

So she would touch him instead. Kiss him. Let him take her clothes off and touch her bare skin, while she gave him her bare soul.

She maneuvered out from under him and pushed his shoulders so that he was lying flat on his back with her over him. "Relax," she said.

"Impossible." He said, raising his hand and skimming her nipple with his thumb, his other hand resting on her backside, stroking her slowly, lazily. "With you, naked and perfect like this? Completely impossible."

"Well," she said, "you're going to have to. Because I want to have my way with you."

His eyes were like a glittering, black flame, his voice a feral growl. "Don't you know you've been having your way with me from the moment we met?"

She thought back. To the demands, to the hair pulling and the way he tied her hands so tight she was at his mercy. To the way he gave her everything she wanted, even when it was obviously something he'd never done, or wanted to do before. The way he got off on it, because she did.

He might have assumed a more dominant role in their sexual games, but he was right. It had all been for her.

"This is all for you," she said, pressing a kiss to the center of his chest. "I want to taste you. All over. I want to suck your cock until you're shaking with how much you want me."

His dark brows shot up slightly, his hand freezing on her ass. "Really?"

"Yep. I'm going to tease you until you beg. And then…then I'm going to fuck you. Do you want that?" she asked.

He swallowed hard. "Yes."

"Say it," she said, an echo of an earlier time. "Tell me what you want."

"I want you fuck me, Evie."

If she hadn't been so hot for him, she could have laughed. This was their version of making love, but hey, for her it worked. And hearing him say that to her, hearing him on the brink, just from her words? That touched her deep down, way past the physical.

"Anything for you," she said, and she meant it. She meant it so truthfully it shocked her.

She kissed his stomach, felt his muscles contract beneath her lips. She lapped at his skin, tasting the salt on her tongue, tracing the line of hair that ran down the center of his abs, before gripping the waistband of his jeans and tugging them, and his underwear off.

She put her hand over his length, the heat from his arousal burning her palm. Then she lowered her head and took him in her mouth, keeping her hand firm around the base of his cock.

He grabbed her hair, breath hissing through his teeth, and she took him in deeper, sliding her hand down between his thighs and cupping him, squeezing gently as she continued to pleasure him with her mouth.

She ran her tongue along his length until he shook, until he begged for more, then begged her to stop.

She waited until she felt the muscles in his thighs quivering, until she knew he was close. Then she pulled away and reached for his nightstand drawer. She took out a condom and opened it, slowly, then rolled it onto his shaft, squeezing him tight as she did.

"Tell me you want me," she said.

"I want you."

"No, tell me you want me," she said, straddling him, the blunt head of his cock probing her slick entrance. She teased them both with the near penetration, until she thought she would die.

"Evie," he said, his voice rough, broken. "I want you, Evie."

She slid down onto him, filling herself slowly, watching as the tendons in his neck stood out, as he ground his teeth to the breaking point, gripping her hips so tight like he was trying to anchor himself to Earth.

She put her hands on his face, held it steady as she started to move. "Watch," she said, her tone firm. "See how much I want you?" She lifted one hand and put her hand on her breast, pinched her nipple lightly. "See what you do to me?"

A slash of red ran across his cheekbones, sweat beading on his forehead. He wasn't the cool, disinterested playboy now. Not the distant order-giver. He was lost, and she could see it.

"Eyes on me," she said, and he obeyed, a shot of pleasure roaring through her.

She kept her gaze locked on his as she moved, as they both moved higher, closer to the peak.

"Caleb," she said, his name on her lips. Over and over again. "Caleb."

"Yes, baby," he said. "Just like that. Yes, Evie."

She rocked back and forth, moved faster, harder, her eyes on his face as he gave up control completely, his head falling back, his mouth open, his brows locked together. And it pushed her over.

She didn't bother to hold back the raw sound of pleasure that climbed her throat and tore its way out of her mouth. She shuddered out her climax, calling out his name, digging her nails into the skin on his chest as she was consumed with her release.

Then when it was over she lay down over his chest, her breathing fractured, her whole world fractured.

"Stay," he said, his arms coming around her waist, his palms warm and heavy on her back.

"Okay."

CHAPTER NINE

CALEB WOKE UP with a woman in his arms. That never happened. He never permitted himself that luxury. The intimacy of letting someone sleep with him. After all, they could smother you with a pillow while you slept, so it came back to trust.

He opened his eyes and looked down at the bright streak of red hair that slashed across his chest like a wound. A strange analogy maybe, but not inappropriate, since everything hurt. Since his chest hurt deep inside like she really had cut him open.

He moved away from her, untangled himself from her hold slowly, then sliding to the edge of the bed, sitting there with his feet on the floor and his face in his hands.

He'd told her about Jill. He never talked about Jill.

But it had been her birthday, and that was always the worst day. Because he had so many memories of her birthdays. They'd always spent them together. As a family.

Now, he didn't even call his parents that day. A day when everyone had gotten together, celebrated and eaten cake, had turned into a day where they never even spoke.

Jill was the brighter of the two of them, the most

ambitious. Poised to take over the family business. She'd lived for that stuff. Been so involved in everything. Their dad's favorite, for obvious reasons, and it might have bothered him if she hadn't been his favorite, too.

And it just seemed wrong, and cruel, that it had been Jill hit by another driver while cruising down the road they took between the office and home. That she'd been the one. It could have been the person in front of her. The person behind her.

It could have been him. He was in the passenger seat. And he'd been fine. He'd walked away. He'd walked away from an accident that had killed her instantly. His side of the car perfectly preserved, hers completely gone.

And he'd seen it. Seen that she wasn't there at all. He'd been sitting there, fine, unhurt, and she was just staring straight ahead, unseeing, unmoving.

Why was it her? Why, on such a perfect, sunny day, with nothing remotely sinister flashing up as a warning? Why was she the one in the path of a drunk guy who was wasted at six in the evening? Why was it her side of the car? Life didn't make sense.

Why was Jill gone when the world needed her? She was the sort of person who would have made an impact. Who had the resources and the drive. And he was…

He was the one who was still here. And he couldn't figure it out. Not then, not ten years on.

Even so, he wasn't sure why he'd spilled his guts to Evie, then clung to her like a needy child.

He'd begged her to stay, how sad was that?

He stood up and rubbed his hands over his face, and back over his hair.

"Morning, buttercup."

He turned and saw Evie, staring up at him, looking rumpled and sleepy and sexy. So sexy he wanted to climb back into her head, back into bed, back into her arms, and never get up again. The world sucked; he would rather spend the rest of his life in this bedroom with Evie. Spanking her and kissing her and being inside her.

The realization hit him with the force of a wrecking ball to the chest. He needed her. He'd known it was starting, but he hadn't done what he should have right when he'd realized it. He couldn't need her, because he had nothing to give back to her. He couldn't stay with her because…

She deserved more than he was. More than a playboy who did nothing but sit on his ass and spend his father's money.

You could be more.

Everything in him rebelled at the thought. He could do what? Step into the place Jill was supposed to occupy? The thought made him feel like he was on the verge of a panic attack. Jill, cool, composed, brilliant Jill's place couldn't be filled that easily.

And it certainly couldn't be filled by him.

You're assuming Dad would even want you to try. You're assuming Evie would want you.

Big assumptions.

Probably incorrect assumptions. And just as well.

"Morning," he said, his voice as broken and graveled as he felt inside.

She sat up, not bothering to pull the blankets up over her pale breasts, the morning light casting a golden glow over her bare body. “Did you sleep well?”

“Yeah.”

“Are you okay?” she asked, frowning.

He didn’t like that he was so transparent to her. BS was his game. He was better at hiding his feelings than this. He’d gone out the night of the accident, straight from the hospital, and picked up a woman, laughed, smiled, screwed her senseless. Then he’d given her a kiss, walked out of her apartment, got into his car, laid in the backseat and cried for two hours. Alone. Not in front of anyone. Not ever.

He’d done much the same most nights since. Minus the crying. He didn’t do that every night. But sometimes.

So why did it feel hard now? Why did it feel like he couldn’t hide this from her? Because she’d been able to tell something was wrong the moment she’d arrived yesterday. And he hadn’t been able to hold it in. He hadn’t been able to protect himself.

Just like now.

“I’m fine,” he said. “But I think you’d better get up and get ready to leave, I have some things I need to do.”

She frowned. “It’s Sunday and you don’t do anything.”

“Well, I have plans today.”

“What plans?”

“Maybe take a bloody hint, Evie. I’m not busy. I want you to go home.”

She jerked back like he’d slapped her across the

face, and he felt like he had. He felt like the absolute worthless bastard he knew he was. But the alternative was baring his soul and he was damn sure not going to do that.

"What the hell is your problem, Caleb?" she asked, sliding out of bed, naked, beautiful and making his legs weak.

"Look, this is why I don't have women spend the night. I want sex when I want sex, then I want to get on with my day."

"Oh don't hand me your bullshit and expect me to say *thanks.* That's not what we have."

"And you know that?" he asked, something dark and powerful driving him now. Something that tasted a lot like fear. "You know that because you've been with one other guy and had a long-term relationship? Wake up, baby, this is a game for grown-ups. And I thought you knew the rules."

"What? GTFO when you say and not a moment sooner? Hold you and make sure you aren't alone when you beg me to, but then don't get all needy?"

"Don't bring that up. Don't use it like that."

"Why? Because you get to conveniently ignore that it happened and then act like I'm overstepping? No. No no no." She started collecting her clothes. "I don't know what your problem is."

"This isn't what I do," he said, his heart raging. "I don't do fights and feelings and responsibility to another person."

"Too bad. I have feelings. I have feelings for you and I'm all up in your bedroom, so they're your problem."

"I didn't sign on for this."

"You did! You walked into my office so confident you were going to have another night with me. You took a job so you could be with me. You signed on. So don't give me your shit now that you're all scared."

Her breasts were rising and falling with her breath, her eyes bright and fierce. He'd never seen a more beautiful, terrifying thing in his life. She was going to ask things of him. Big things. He could feel it. And he knew he would let her down. Shit, he hated that he would let her down.

"Sure, that's it," he said, using every bit of nerve he had to turn and face her, stark naked, his mask firmly in place. He knew this mask. His Caleb mask. "It's that I'm scared, baby, not that I'm just not that into you."

"Fuck off," she said, tugging her clothes on, a tear spilling down her cheek.

Dammit. This was that open emotion of hers. Didn't she know what she was giving away? Exposed like this. Why was she doing it? Why could she do it?

Why the hell was he too afraid to do it?

"Nah, I think I'm done with the fucking, why don't you get out."

He watched her expression change, the color leeching from her face, like the blood had drained from her body. The funny thing was, he felt it in his chest, right where her hair had been, a slash of red over his heart. He felt it all bleed from him, as he saw it injuring her.

And he hated himself. But that was nothing new.

"Fine. Great. I'm out. Enjoy the tuna, asshole, it's still sitting in the basket in the living room. And I bet the ice pack didn't hold all night. Oh, and I finished the app, so I'll just send it all on to *Flirt* and you can never darken my door again. If you left any crap at your cubicle it will be on the street waiting for you, or stolen and sold on Craigslist by the time you get there. It doesn't really matter to me." She held up both hands, middle fingers high, then turned and started to walk away, then stopped. "You know what's stupid, Caleb? I just figured it out."

"What?" he asked, feeling like his body was slowly turning to stone, his head, his face, too heavy for his neck.

"The feelings. I knew I had feelings for you, but I wasn't sure what they were. But now…with all these feelings you've just given me with your complete dismissal of me, I know. I love you. I hope I don't for much longer."

She stormed out of the room and slammed the door behind her. And he listened until he heard the front door slam behind her.

And he just stood, rigid, heavy. A statue. He wanted to crumble. To give in to the unbearable pressure that was threatening to break him apart. But he couldn't. He just felt like his heart had turned into a hard lump of granite that was going to crack off the veins holding it in place and plummet through his chest cavity, blowing out all his other organs on the way down.

Which would be fine, really. Because it might mean a swifter death.

Which would just be pointless, because it wouldn't bring Jill back. It wouldn't fix anything. But then, his being here hardly did.

He didn't know why he was thinking that way. But he wasn't really sure why anything at the moment.

He'd looked it all up once. The thoughts he had. The desire to change places with his dead sister. Survivor's guilt, they called it. Which was stupid because he hadn't survived anything. He was just breathing still.

He'd gone from worthless asshole to greater worthless asshole because it had seemed like the thing to do. Because…because he didn't know why.

Because it had seemed like the thing to do. Because he hadn't known what else to do. If he could do anything else.

He did know one thing, though.

Evie was gone, and he didn't want her to be. But he didn't think he had the right to ask her to come back, either.

CHAPTER TEN

HEARTBREAK WAS THE WORST. It was worse than a cord wrapped around the wheel on your computer chair. Worse than a hangnail. Worse than when a fast food place put half a tub of mayonnaise on your hamburger.

This was what had been missing when Jason cheated on her. What had been missing when she'd ditched the man she'd shared her life with for ten years.

This was, apparently, love. Love blew chunks.

But at least she'd been right this time. At least she'd gone the whole hog. What did they say? It is better to have loved and lost than to be eaten by a velociraptor. Okay, maybe they didn't say that, but being eaten by a velociraptor was about the only thing that sounded worse than what she was going through now.

Either way, at least she knew this was the real deal. Cold comfort when you were lying facedown on your desk on a Monday afternoon feeling like you were going to die of heart failure.

There was a soft knock on her door and Raj and Cassie appeared. "Evie…we brought you a burrito."

"Thanks," she said, "but I'm not hungry."

"But it's better than just a burrito," Raj said. "It's a unicorn."

Cassie held it out and smiled hugely. It was a large

burrito on a tray, with a face made of olives and a jalapeño horn. “Because we finished ‘Unicorn Strike’ and it’s going to be a hit! And because you’re down. So I thought you needed a smiling burrito.”

“It’s…unique,” she said. “You can put it on my desk.”

“You okay?” Raj asked. “You seemed…”

“Sad?” she asked.

“Like you might cut one of our heads off, put it on a pike and roast it over an open flame,” Cassie said.

Evie frowned. “Have I been that horrible?”

“Pretty vile,” Raj said.

“Oh. Well. I’m sorry.”

Cassie shrugged. “We’re just worried. You weren’t like this when you and Jason the Horrible broke up. We were afraid something happened with the *Flirt* app. I mean, with that corporate stooge hanging out…”

“Caleb,” she said. “His name was Caleb.”

Cassie frowned. “Yeah, Caleb. He was really…” She got a dreamy look on her face.

“Yeah,” Evie said, scowling. “And no, everything’s fine with the app.”

“Well…good, then…I guess.”

“Happy unicorn eating,” Raj said, and he and Cassie scurried out of the room.

She didn’t mean to be a jerk. She picked up the fork that was on the tray and stabbed the unicorn in the back. Or maybe she did and she didn’t care.

She was fine without love. Or, she had been. Then Caleb had torn down a partition in herself she hadn’t even known she’d put up. And she’d suddenly had access to all this stuff. Desire, and bravery and this deep, deep emotion she hadn’t realized she was capable of.

What a bastard.

So now that she had access to all that stuff, all the good and bad things that went with it. That brave new Evie who wanted the whole world and felt like it was okay to demand it…well, now she just had to decide what she was going to do with it.

HE DIDN'T WANT to pick up a woman. He'd approached two of them tonight. With the full intent of taking one to bed. It didn't matter how he felt—like shit, incidentally—he knew this game. He could do it in the midst of grief. He could certainly do it after breaking up with someone.

No, it wasn't even a breakup. They'd never really been together. It had been just another of his physical-only affairs. It had been sex. Sex and only sex.

Liar.

Yeah, so what? He'd been lying to himself for years. It was what he did. It was right up there with breathing.

One of the biggest lies was that he liked to go out to bars. He hated it. He didn't want to be here. He wasn't sure he'd ever wanted to be here. He put his beer down on the table and called his driver.

He got into the car and closed the door, shutting his eyes.

"Home, Mr. Anderson?"

"No," Caleb said. "No."

"Where to?"

"Westwood Memorial," he said, and he really wasn't sure why. But Dave didn't ask why, so Caleb didn't even have to fake a reason, which was great. Because he couldn't think. He couldn't do anything but feel. Horrible, horrible feelings.

Why the hell was he going there twice in the space of a week? There was no answer there. He already knew that. There was nothing but stone.

Of course, since his heart felt a bit like stone, maybe that was fitting.

"Just stop here," he said when they got to the gates.

He walked through and took the well-worn path to Jill's grave and just stood, his hands in his pockets. "I'm sorry," he said. "I feel like it should have been me."

He said it out loud for the first time. "I don't know why it wasn't. And I don't know what to do about it."

There wasn't an answer. Of course there wasn't.

Though, he supposed that was an answer all its own. There was nothing he could do to bring her back. And he was still here. He was still here and he was wasting it, and suddenly he hated himself for it.

The stone was never going to talk back. It was never going to change. And this wasn't the place he needed to be.

No, he wasn't good enough for Evie. He was a broken mess.

But he wanted to try. He needed to try.

Because he had survived. And for the first time since then, he really wanted to live.

A BUZZING ON her intercom moved her from her slothful position on the couch. She got up and walked over to the front door and hit the button. "Yes?"

"It's me."

"What?"

"Caleb."

"I know but…why are you here?"

"Can you buzz me in?"

"Are you going to say horrible things to me again? Because if so, I think I'll pass." Her heart was pounding hard and she felt dizzy. She'd never expected to hear his voice again, and there it was. No mistaking it.

Caleb. And she still loved him. Damn his eyes.

"I'm not going to say anything horrible. At least, I don't think it's horrible. I guess…I guess the final verdict on that is up to you."

She buzzed him in and stepped away from the door, going back to the couch, her hands folded in her lap while she waited for his knock at the door.

When it came, she almost changed her mind. She almost didn't answer.

"Evie."

It was his voice again, and she couldn't not go to him. Even if she should ignore him. Even if she should throw live lobsters on him and hope they pinched dangly bits.

She got up and walked to the door, her hands shaking. Like ripping off a Band-Aid.

She flung it open and put a hand on her hip. "What do you want?" she asked, trying to play it cool. And suddenly very aware that the sweatpants, ratty hair and vague odor of cheesepuffs probably negated the cool facade.

"You," he said.

The word hung there, and she was sure she must have misheard it. But she didn't see how she could because it was so simple. Because it could hardly be anything else.

"What?"

"I want you, Evie. I was…I was being a dick."

"Well…yeah, but please define what you mean by *want me*. Do you want to have more sex with me? Because I enjoyed the sex, Caleb, but it can't just be that. Not anymore."

"It's not enough for me either."

"Well…what is?"

"I… Can I come in?"

"Sure." She backed away from the door and swept her hand grandly across the space. "Welcome to my home. Do not touch my *Lord of the Rings* stuff—it's mint. Now, tell me," she said, turning to face him, her heart in her throat, "what do you want? Don't play with me, Caleb, please. I can't take it."

"I don't want to play with you. I…I need you. I need you so much it terrifies me. Not just because of what it means to me, but because of what it means to you."

"Tell me about it," she said, sure her heart had stopped altogether.

"I am so screwed up. I don't even know where to begin. I've always been the lazy one. The player. The one who would never amount to much. But it was okay because there was Jill. She was smarter, more driven, more…everything. And then she died. I was in the accident, too."

"Oh…Caleb."

"I saw her die. Or…you know, I didn't even see it, I just…the accident happened. I was fine. I looked over at her…she was already gone."

"No, Caleb. I'm so sorry."

"For ten years I've wondered why it was her and not me. I've been stuck wondering that. Feeling like I wasn't worthy of this extra shot I got. Proving I wasn't worthy of it. I realized something tonight."

"What?" she asked, the word a choked whisper.

"It's not changing. It's done. It's done and I'm still wishing it wasn't, but it won't change anything. I have to go on. And I haven't. I never have. But…but this is the scary thing. I need you and I don't know that I'll ever be able to give you back what you need. I just feel like all I can do is take. I feel like…I'll let you down."

"Caleb." She took a step toward him, fighting to keep her emotions in check, just long enough to say what she needed to say. "It's okay to need me. It's okay to need other people."

"But I don't want to take from you."

"Caleb, someday I'm going to need you, and I know for a fact that if you love me, you'll be there. That's the way it works."

"But…I don't deserve any of this, Evie. I don't deserve you. I don't even feel like I deserve to be here half the time."

"But you have me. You have my love. You have life. It doesn't matter if you deserve it or not."

"But you…"

"Let me tell you something. I've had that bland relationship that was just there to be there. This isn't that. I love you, Caleb. And I knew it for sure when I felt how much losing you hurt. You make me a better me. Braver. You make me have more fun. You make me ask for what I want and you never make me feel like what I'm doing is wrong. I've had my work life down to a science for years, but I never knew how to demand something good in my personal life. Until you. You give so much more to me than you take, and hell, I don't know if I deserve you. But I want you to be mine anyway."

"Why do you love me?"

"Because I see the you that you don't want people to know is there. And I like him. The guy who put me first in bed, who talked to me about popsicle fellatio with a mostly straight face, and who makes me feel like my happiness, my pleasure, my desires are valuable. Actually, I don't just like that guy, I love him."

"I love you, too," he said. "And I've only ever said those words to family members. And not once at all in the past ten years. So know that they mean a lot."

She blinked back tears. "I do."

"Never doubt it."

"I won't. Also, I'm really glad you're back," she said, leaning in and kissing him, quick and hard. "Because there's still more on my list."

"Is there?"

"Oh yes," she said. "That was a list of fifty sex tips, you know? And we only did maybe ten."

"Are you propositioning me?"

She wiggled her hips back and forth, knowing full well she looked like a dork and not caring at all. Because Caleb liked it, and she knew it. "Hellll yesss."

"I think I'll go for it—I'm kind of a slut. But only with you."

"Good to know." She looked down, a smile curving her lips. "I'm very glad to see you wore your tie. I think you're going to need it tonight."

* * * * *

USA TODAY and *New York Times* bestselling author **Erin McCarthy** sold her first book in 2002 and has since written almost fifty novels and novellas in teen fiction, new adult and adult romance. Erin has a special weakness for tattoos, karaoke, high-heeled boots and martinis. She lives on the shores of Lake Erie in Ohio with her family, her cat and her stylish and well-dressed Chihuahua/terrier mix. Visit her online at erinmccarthy.net.

PERFECT 10

Erin McCarthy

CHAPTER ONE

OMG. Are you insane????

KATRINA PHILLIPS GLANCED at the text from her best friend, Samantha, and ignored it. She didn't have time for drama. She was on the subway and she was late posting the Deal of the Day for one of her clients, Mind & Body Yoga, on all of its social networking sites. She really should have at least gone through the tutorial on her new phone, but she'd figured it was a phone, not a plane. She'd had a dozen previous smartphones, each one simpler to figure out than the preceding model.

Except for this one. All her apps and contacts and data had transferred, but it seemed to be doing some sort of internal knitting together of every individual account she had, weaving them into one lumpy, messy pile of informational yarn. Which reminded her. She had to tell the knitting club she'd joined on a whim that she was quitting. She sucked at knitting.

Only she couldn't do that because she couldn't figure her damn phone out.

Her phone dinged again and it was a text from Bryan, a guy she'd gone out with twice who had agreed that they'd split the check for cocktails, then had managed to slide the change into his pocket when she wasn't looking, stiffing her five bucks. Why would he be contacting her after two months of mutual avoidance?

Bitch.

Well. Good thing he'd bothered to get that off his chest. Annoyed, she deleted the text. Only to have another one replace it.

Hey, baby, wassup? Long time no talk.

O-kay. That was Dirk, a hookup from the year before. Hot, funny, great in bed. Not one to call the next day, as she'd found out. Why would he be crawling out of the woodwork?

Along with James, whom she'd dated for two months.

And Seth.

And Michael.

The texts and emails rolled in, one right after the other, like a *This is Your Sex Life* retrospective, and she thought OMG was about right. This could not be a coincidence. Alarmed, she shifted on her plastic seat, the coughs of the other passengers and the rumble of the train louder than she was used to. She wasn't studiously ignoring everyone with her earbuds in as she usually did, because she couldn't use her phone. And had she mentioned she couldn't figure out her phone?

Why? She texted Samantha, suddenly very, very concerned.

Go to your profile.

Uh-oh.

It took her an agonizing minute to figure out how to bypass all the initial demands her phone was making of her. Honestly, it was worse than her mother and no, she would not like the GPS enabled right this second, she freaking knew where she was. But when she finally got to her profile and saw what exactly her glorious little piece of electronics had synced, she wanted a GPS to guide her to the nearest hole to crawl her hipster ass into and die.

Her BootyBook app had synced with her personal page.

Now every detail about every guy that she had logged in to her handy, and slightly tawdry, app equivalent of a little black book was now visible to everyone. Including ratings on their manners, clothes, conversation during the date, and yes, their penis size if she had hooked up with him. Along with whether or not she'd had an orgasm, the quality of foreplay, and her overall general impression of his sexual prowess.

OMG became OMFG.

Delete, delete, delete. Her hands started to shake, her armpits cranked out massive quantities of sweat, and her heart started to race so fast she wondered if a stress heart attack was possible at twenty-four. "Come on, come on," she muttered to her phone, evil little piece of shit that it was, and clicked and scrolled and pinched and read, trying to figure out how in the hell she could get rid of what she had just seen. Forever.

When she thought she'd severed the mysterious connection she refreshed the site and finally remembered to breathe. It was gone. She called Samantha. "Check and see if it's still there!" she blurted out without a greeting, her phone slipping in her sweaty hand. There wasn't air-conditioning strong enough in the world to prevent clammy palms in this situation.

"It's gone!" Samantha said, her voice triumphant. "Thank God. What the hell happened?"

"I don't know, exactly." Regardless of the fact that leaning against a subway window was never a good hygiene choice, she needed the support. She sagged backward. "But it doesn't matter how. It did and I seriously don't want to think about how many people saw it." Given the commonality of instant notifications on status updates, it could be a lot. Everyone on her friends list. Including her mother.

Her phone dinged in her ear. And then again.

Katrina smacked the back of her head into the window so hard she actually managed to garner a side glance from the man sitting next to her, no small feat in New York, where eye contact on the subway was a social no-no. "I'm going to die," she told Samantha.

The man looked away again. He so didn't care.

"I'll meet you at your place," Samantha told her. "I'll bring wine."

"Thanks." It was something.

"We'll strategize damage control. Don't freak."

Yeah, too late. "All right, thanks. See you in a bit. Bye." Tucking her hair behind her ear, Katrina bit her lip and gave her phone a sidelong tentative glance as it rested in her lap on her red skinny jeans, afraid to see who the latest texts were from.

Except one was from Drew Jordan, her best friend at NYU, her secret crush for four years, then her one-time lover after a boozy night at an art exhibit. Her throat caught as she frantically read the text, all too aware of what he must have seen.

Magnificent penis huh? I'm kinda speechless.

And with that, her humiliation was complete.

Because while there were quite a few BootyBook entries she remembered only in the vaguest sense, she distinctly recalled what she had written about Drew in the first flush of morning-after bliss when he had left her apartment. She had rated him a nine, skimping on a full ten because they weren't in an actual dating relationship and because she had coaxed him into bed only after many vodka tonics. For kissing she had given him a ten, along with the description "dreamy." His penis had been rated, well, magnificent, as he had noticed.

And she had written, "Now I understand what everyone is saying. Sex with someone you love *is* better. Happy sigh."

But that happy sigh had turned into weeks of misery when it became apparent that neither one of them knew how to deal with the sexual aftermath of crossing that line in their friendship. She had acted weird, texting him too much. He had pulled away. She had flaunted a guy in front of him at a concert. He said she drank too much. Then came that fateful day when she realized that he was avoiding her altogether.

And she had absolutely and utterly humiliated herself by drunk texting him that she missed him.

So really, in the context of that text, she wasn't sure she'd made it any worse.

God. Her life was over. No man was ever going to want to date her again.

AN HOUR LATER, Katrina felt as though she was on a QVC infomercial. But wait, there's more!

Just when she thought nothing could be added to her shopping cart of suck, yet another text or email came in, proving that it could always get worse.

"Who is James again?" Samantha asked.

"He's the guy who didn't have a condom and when I insisted he find one, he came back with a sandwich bag and said he could make that work."

"Oh, gross, that's right."

There was a moment of silence where Samantha contemplated the horror of that moment, and Katrina relived it. At the time it had seemed like possibly one of the worst things ever to happen to her. Oh, the naïveté. This was so, so much worse.

Spending the rest of her life dateless and sliding into crazy cat lady status one litter box in her apartment at a time was the veritable tip of the awful iceberg. Because apparently not only had her BootyBook information posted to her personal social media site, it had uploaded itself as a spreadsheet to her business page.

"How does that even happen?" Samantha demanded, popping the cork on their second bottle of pinot grigio. It was that kind of night.

"I must have hit the share button when I was setting up my phone and it uploaded to all of my accounts," Katrina said, wishing she had a shovel to bash herself in the head with. She'd even settle for a gardening trowel.

But this was Brooklyn, not her hometown upstate. There were no tools of any kind hanging around her apartment, unless you counted the guy who lived next door who went tanning three times a week.

The palms of her hand were numb from squeezing her hands into fists. "I don't remember setting it up that way, but you know how it is. You get efficient. You start clicking and connecting and the next thing you know, you're Facebook friends with your ex-boyfriend's mother. We're always just one tap away from complete and utter disaster."

Samantha pushed up the red frames of her glasses, her fringe bangs starting to brush the top. She was into the granny chic look, with Peter Pan collars and lots of floral patterns and blouses, and she was smart enough not to have a BootyBook account. "Trina, you need to do damage control."

"How do I do that?" she demanded, wanting her glass refilled but unable to get off her couch and walk the three steps to her pseudo kitchen. It was really just a three-foot space in the corner outfitted with appliances better suited to a leprechaun family, but she didn't cook anyway. She had created a makeshift island in front of the row of cabinets and the minifridge out of an old dresser, and Samantha was leaning on it, having poured herself a fresh glass of wine.

Katrina removed her purple scarf from around her neck and threw it on the coffee table. It was too tempting to strangle herself with it. She had already gotten several emails from clients demanding an explanation, and the truth was, she didn't have one. No one was going to buy that she had been hacked. The information was too detailed, and it would serve no purpose for a hacker other than to humiliate her, and that generally speaking wasn't their MO. No, everyone was going to know it was her screwup and hers alone.

"Well, you need to issue a statement, both on your personal page and your professional page. I mean, it worked for Kristen Stewart, right? She apologized within hours and RPattz was hers again. She's not unemployed, either."

"I'm not sure it's the same thing. And they didn't end up together ultimately anyway." But Samantha was right. Katrina sighed. "I guess I should do that before I get drunk."

"Yeah, let's not compound the problem. We'll write the statement, post it, then we'll go out to dinner and try to pretend none of this happened. You can leave your phone at home."

It was a plan, though not much of one. Katrina was debating using the phrase "sincerely regret" versus "deeply sorry" as her phone continued to blow up. In the end, she went for "deeply regret an unfortunate technical error that caused private data to appear in a public forum." She went on to say the information seen was neither accurate nor factual in any way, but merely an opinion based on personal observations and that she apologized sincerely for any embarrassment caused.

Awful. Plain and simple. "I'm done. Shitty damage control, but there you have it. I'm a social media manager. That's my *job*. But I just proved that I can't manage my own. Great endorsement for my business. Fabulous."

Samantha sat down beside her. "It was up for about three minutes. Probably none of your clients even saw it. Plus look at the bright side. If you ever had a moment where you wanted a guy to truly know how you felt, you just got them all clumped together."

Katrina raised an eyebrow. "That is supposed to make me feel better how?"

"And you know, it could be like a public service announcement. All those guys who thought they were the shit in bed now know the score. Maybe they'll be more sensitive, maybe they'll ask for sexual directions. Maybe they'll discover why clitorises matter."

"So I set off a wave of men in New York checking their prowess and embarking on a sexual odyssey?" She snorted. "Yeah, I doubt it."

Her phone dinged for the nine thousandth time. She sighed and glanced at the screen. "Shit, it's Drew again."

"What did he say?"

Heart thumping at a rate more appropriate for a hummingbird, she unlocked her phone and tapped on the message.

Want to talk to you. Working tonight. Can you come up?

"Omigod, he wants me to meet him at the bar tonight. He's working, but he wants to talk to me. What do you think that means?"

"That he wants to talk to you."

Katrina threw back her wine, taking down half a glass in one swallow. "Yeah, but why? I mean, what is there to say?" Other than that she was a fuckup? That was a fact; it didn't need to be discussed.

"Maybe he wants to talk about his magnificent penis. Maybe he wants to show you his magnificent penis."

"What should I say?"

Samantha looked at her as if she was first idiot on the command bridge of the USS *Moron*. "That you'll meet him. Look, we're buzzed, you've been pining over him for years, I say you go for it. It can't possibly be even more embarrassing than it already is."

That remained to be seen, but she was just masochistic enough to want to know what Drew would say to her. "Okay, but I'm cutting myself off from wine then. No more alcohol or somehow I'll end up crying in front of him. You know I'm a teary drunk."

"Oh, yes, I do know that." Samantha studied her. "What is it about Drew anyway? I mean, he's cute and all, and I can see why he makes your lady parts flutter, but you wanted to legit date him, didn't you?"

She had. For a minute, she reflected, thinking back to her years as an undergrad, new to the big city, feeling very pedestrian next to fellow students from Hong Kong and Hollywood and Istanbul. Students who were valedictorians, overachievers, with awesome style and raging confidence. She'd just been Trina, an A-minus student from the burbs with no particular skill but a drive to make something happen for herself. Drew was one of the first classmates she had felt completely comfortable around. He wasn't pretentious, or arrogant, and he had listened to her.

Many late nights had been spent in her dorm room on her bed, their legs stretched out, listening to music and talking about everything from childhood memories to how to pull off the ultimate catfish. It was a lot of little things and it was one big thing.

"When my father had a heart attack, everyone was all 'oh, I'm sorry,'" she told Samantha, whom she'd actually met the semester after that. "But Drew skipped class and went home with me on the train. He let me cry until I fell asleep on his shoulder, and he went to the hospital with me." She swirled the wine remaining in her glass and stared at it, a lump in her throat. "That's why I always feel like he's the one who got away. He's a good guy and we had a deep friendship."

"Then you definitely need to see him. Even if it never becomes a relationship, you should try to reclaim your friendship."

"You're right." Katrina tapped out a response. Sure. Be there around eleven.

Cool. :)

The smiley made her feel better. He couldn't be super pissed if he was using positive emoticons. What it meant beyond that, she had no clue, but she was only going to allow herself one minute to think it was that he wanted to repeat that magnificent penis performance.

She set the timer on her phone.

"What the hell are you doing?"

"I'm giving myself exactly sixty seconds to fantasize that Drew wants to be with me." She closed her eyes and remembered the sensation of his mouth on hers, kissing her with passion and intensity. By the time she got to his lips trailing down over her breasts and to her girl bits, the phone alarm squawked.

She opened her eyes. "Okay, I'm good."

Samantha pushed up her glasses. "You're a freak."

"Truth."

CHAPTER TWO

KATRINA STOOD OUTSIDE the Plaid Kimono, yet another of Brooklyn's fusion hipster bars that sprung up like weeds, and took a deep breath. She'd never been inside because she'd known since it opened about nine months earlier that Drew was a bartender there, and she hadn't wanted to run into him. She and Samantha followed a group of guys in skinny jeans and cardigans inside and paused to look around.

Yep. It was exactly what she was expecting. Pub atmosphere, a dark and dim interior, expensive modern decor with a slight hint of Asian influence. There was a band playing at the very far end of the room and there was a plethora of flannel and beanies everywhere she looked. The servers were wearing kilts.

The thought of Drew in a kilt made her secretly just a little bit aroused. Okay, that was a lie. A lot aroused.

"There he is," Samantha said, pointing. "He's at the far end of the bar."

"Don't point!" she hissed at her friend, grabbing her finger. "That's so obvious. Just be casual." The wine was wearing off and she was nervous as hell.

"This isn't like an accidental meeting. He knows you're coming." Samantha rolled her eyes and started toward the bar, weaving through the crowd.

There were no stools free, of course, because there were never any tables or chairs available anywhere. New York was crowded. It was something that still surprised Katrina sometimes even after six years of living there. So she tried to artfully lean on the three inches of bar top accessible between two groups of friends. Watching Drew move around behind the bar, shaking and mixing and washing, she fought the urge to sigh.

Back in the day, before the sex, she had spent a lot of time with Drew, hanging out in her dorm room or his, going to concerts, lying in the sun in Washington Square, and studying in the coffee shop. Seeing him, his head bent over as he rinsed glassware, made her realize how much she had missed him. Her heart squeezed.

Then she saw he was wearing a kilt, his muscular calves showing, and it was her vagina doing the squeezing. Holy amazeballs.

Was she drooling? She wiped the corner of her mouth, sure there was going to be saliva there.

Which was precisely when he looked up and saw her.

Their eyes met and held and he gave her a grin and a nod of acknowledgment. Moving down the bar toward her, he leaned forward and said, "Hi, Trina. Thanks for coming."

Coming? She wished.

"Sure. Listen, Drew, I'm really sorry about the whole post. God, it was just so stupid and awful and this day has been hell. Just hell." She felt her cheeks heat with an embarrassed blush.

He gave her a rueful look. “How does that even happen? Seriously.”

“I have no idea. All I know is that I single-handedly pissed off every guy I’ve ever dated and my mother has called me six times and left me a message suggesting I get STD testing.” She propped her head up with her palm and shook her head. “My mother thinks I’m a whore, I probably just ruined my business, and it’s possible than an actual sex tape would have been less mortifying.”

“Next weekend you can make a sex tape. You should have goals, you know.”

She gave him a long look. “Really? Thanks.”

He cracked a laugh. “Come on, it’s funny, you have to admit. But then again, you gave me a high ranking, so I have no complaints. You basically gave me an endorsement. Think of how much action I can get now.”

Lovely. Just what she didn’t want to imagine—him with a bevy of women wanting to test-drive his penis. “Excellent. I should charge you an advertising fee.”

Drew grinned. “How about I just get you a drink. What do you want?”

Him. “Pinot grigio.” One glass wouldn’t kill her.

He nodded and looked behind her. “Hey, Samantha. What can I get you?”

“I’ll have the same thing.”

“Coming right up.” He moved away and Katrina watched his plaid ass saunter off.

She didn’t feel better. Granted, she was relieved he wasn’t mad at her, but shouldn’t he be more…something? More curious? Instead he was just Mr. Casual.

As if they hadn't basically stopped speaking to each other for a year.

"He seems quite pleased with himself," Samantha commented. "He just got the ego stroke of a lifetime."

"It would seem." She wasn't exactly happy about it, either. He thought it was funny. Entertaining. She'd said she was *in love* with him and that seemed to have had zero effect on him. Fabulous.

When he came back with their wine, she was wondering why the hell she was in the noisy bar, getting pressed from all sides by purses and bodies angling for more space. Feeling exhausted and suddenly angry, she asked, "So, what did you want to talk about?"

"I don't want to get into it here. I'm done in half an hour. Can you hang out? We can go to my place."

Was that a trick question? She searched his face for clues as to what that meant, but he just looked serious. There was no telling if it was a good serious or a bad serious. Taking a sip of her wine to stall, she swallowed and licked her lips. "I'm with Samantha."

For a second she thought he looked disappointed, but maybe that was a delusion.

"Don't worry about me. I'm going to grab a cab home soon. I have to work tomorrow." Samantha gave her a smile. "Have fun."

"Cool. Okay, let me get back to work."

Katrina made a face at his retreating back. "What the hell does he want?" she asked Samantha. "I feel super stressed out. I'm sweating."

But Samantha was looking at her cell screen. "OMG, look at this. I just got sent a suggestion to like a page called Drew's Magnificent Penis Fan Page." She showed Katrina the request.

"Oh, shit." She groaned. "He's going to kill me."

"Maybe he started it."

Now that would be ridiculous. They both burst out laughing.

"I'm sending you this," Samantha said. "Look at the profile pic. It's a cartoon penis. This is awesome."

Katrina studied it, not nearly as amused as Samantha was. But even she had to admit that someone was creative. "The 'About Me' section says, 'Looking for a lady locker to store my valuables. Have a license to kill memories of bad sex.' Favorite song "Up All Night." Inspirational quote is 'To handle yourself, use your head…,' Eleanor Roosevelt." Katrina looked up at Samantha. "Oh my God. Who do you think did this?"

"It had to be Jason. That has him written all over it."

Katrina jumped when a hand slid across her lower back. Turning, prepared to tell off a douchebag, she closed her mouth when she realized it was Drew. "Oh, you scared me."

"What are you two giggling about? Funny animal pics?"

"No." Samantha held her phone up for him to see.

Drew's lips moved and Katrina's heart sank.

He didn't look furious. He looked irritated, but not bust-up-furniture angry. "Who the hell did this?"

"I have no idea. It was a suggested page for me."

Drew pulled out his own phone and he snorted. "Jason is a dick."

"Ironic choice of slurs," Samantha said.

Drew shot her a look. "He sent me a text taking

credit." He shook his head. "Let's head out. And thanks, Trina, for making my Thursday a little more interesting."

"You're welcome. I think mine would be classified more as suck than interesting, but glad to be of service."

Drew waited for them to go in front of him, his hand once again resting on Katrina's back and staying there the whole way to the front door. She wondered what that was all about, and tried to remember if he had touched her like that BS. Before Sex. She couldn't think of any time he had, but she felt like a neurotic 420 smoker yelling "What does it mean?" at a double rainbow. She was overthinking the hell out of everything.

Samantha gave her a wink as she hopped in a cab out on the street. Katrina waved, breathing in the warm night air. "God, it's gorgeous out. It was so hot today."

"I see the advantage of wearing a skirt," Drew said as they started down the sidewalk. "I thought I would hate this kilt, but I dig the circulation."

"It's a good look for you."

He smiled at her and something about the look on his face made her suck in a breath.

"Trina, I never meant for us to stop being friends. You know that, right?"

She nodded, a lump lodging in her throat. "Yeah, I know. I didn't mean for that to happen either. Or I never would have..." But she stopped talking, because she wondered if she had the option of giving back that one night, would she. Because even though she missed Drew's friendship, the truth was, it had been becoming painful to be around him, knowing her feelings went way beyond friendship. Not knowing how to tell him. At least the sex had kept her from endlessly hoping they could be a couple. That dream had been shattered instantly in the aftermath of sex.

"You never would have had sex with me?" he asked, crossing his arms over his chest as they walked.

Awkward. "It obviously wasn't planned, and I know I didn't handle things well."

"Sex happens. But it doesn't mean we should let it ruin our friendship. I miss you."

Oh, God, oh, God, he missed her and she was going to melt. Just puddle right at his feet. "I've missed you, too. I know we can't go backward, but I want what we had before we got naked."

"You mean, before my magnificent penis?"

Katrina made a sound of disgust. "You don't have to sound so smug about it. You should be just a little embarrassed that everyone we know now knows we had sex."

"Why would I be embarrassed? It's not like you're a troll."

Huh. This conversation was not going the way she'd hoped. "Don't flatter me so."

But then he surprised her by taking her hand and pulling her to a stop. He pulled her in close to him. "Hey, come here."

"What?" She could feel the blush starting in her cheeks again and she wondered when she was finally going to be old enough to stop blushing. It was like acne—it just shouldn't happen past middle school.

"It was a great night, you have to admit."

"I think I did. Quite publicly." It was distracting to be so close to him, his kilt brushing against her, his fingers entwined with hers. But it was good to hear him say he'd enjoyed it, too.

"And you're beautiful." He tucked her hair behind her ear.

The love she felt for him, that she'd been attempting to suppress with mixed success, came rushing back to the surface. "Thanks," she whispered.

"Now can you please tell me why I only got a five out of ten for the good dresser category? That was brutal. I may need therapy."

Way to ruin the moment. She rolled her eyes. "You have exactly two pairs of jeans and enough plaid to represent every clan in Scotland. I had to ding you somewhere or the app would have recommended I see you again."

She wasn't trying to be suggestive. She really wasn't. But the words just sort of hung in the air between them for a long, painful pause and she refused to be the one to speak first, because she would apologize or embarrass herself by sounding needy.

Finally, Drew said, "But an eight out of ten for kissing? I don't know. I thought we had a ten going on."

Interesting. And arousing. Katrina tried to play it cool, which was hard to do when her entire sexual history had been posted online and when he was wearing a kilt. But she gave it her best shot. "You misread. It was definitely listed as a ten."

"Let's find out for sure," he said.

Then he closed the gap between them and kissed her.

CHAPTER THREE

DREW KNEW FULL well Trina had listed their kiss as a ten. He'd taken a screenshot of his entry in her little BootyBook post before she'd taken it down. It was a good thing he got alerts on his phone or he might not have seen it before she yanked it, but it had so clearly been a mistake that he'd known it would disappear as soon as she realized it. He'd wanted the opportunity to read what she'd written about him a little more closely.

Which he had. Repeatedly. The kiss had been listed as a ten, but claiming it was only an eight was as good of an excuse as any to get his mouth on hers again. That night, the one and only time he'd been that close to her, he'd been drunk on vodka, and he wanted to repeat the experience sober. See if it was really as amazing as he remembered.

Trina was short, with lush lips, bangin' curves and soulful dark eyes that widened when she realized what he was about to do. Her mouth drifted open and she went up on her tiptoes. Clearly she wasn't going to stop him. In fact, her body leaned toward him, and when he dropped his head and covered her lips with his, she gave a little sigh of pleasure that kicked him in the gut and groin.

Damn.

She tasted like wine and willingness and it took

him about two seconds to decide he wasn't going to leave it at a teasing kiss. Not the way she was responding, not the way she felt. He teased his tongue inside to slide across hers, and was forced to grip the back of her head to hold them steady when she rocked against him. A simple kiss became full-on making out, mouths moving eagerly, tongues tangling, breath anxious as they tasted each other. Her fingers squeezed his waist and he realized that, without a shadow of a doubt, the kissing was definitely as hot as he remembered it being.

Vodka hadn't conned him.

Maybe it was because he knew her so well as a person or maybe it was just the unexplainable randomness of chemistry, but they could write a make-out manual, they were so in tune with each other.

Finally she broke off the kiss, gasping for air, staring up at him as though she wasn't sure what to say.

"Ten?" he asked, curious what she would say. Hell, maybe she had been still drunk when she'd updated her BootyBook post-sex. Maybe she wasn't feeling it this time around, and he was projecting his own desire onto her or some such crap like that. Though he would bet his favorite guitar she had. He just wanted to hear her say it.

"I'm not sure your ego needs any more stroking today."

He could think of something better than his ego he could stroke, but he wasn't about to push his luck. He'd fucked up last time. He'd rushed off out of her apartment before she'd been awake because he hadn't known what to say. It had been a dick move. A complete and total dick move that he still couldn't think back on without mentally wincing.

But he hadn't expected it to go down the way it had. Hadn't expected her to be willing to get naked with him. They'd been friends, just friends, for so long, he'd never seen it coming. He'd always known he wasn't good enough for her, the struggling sometimes-musician, mostly bartender, and it had felt wrong to take advantage of her drunkenness. But he'd done it anyway.

It had ruined their friendship. She'd been weird, he'd been embarrassed and plagued with guilt. Unable to see her without picturing her naked and fantasizing about his cock buried inside her. So there it went. A four-year friendship straight down the crapper because he couldn't keep it in his jeans when slinging back vodka. So lame. Utterly asshole lame.

But now he'd been presented with new information that was so amazing, so pleasing, so fantastic, he hadn't been able to think about a single other thing all goddamn day. He was going to make this work for him, whether her post about him had been exaggerated or not compliments of vodka-tinted goggles.

"Not all the attention has been positive," he told her. "I got two angry texts today from girls asking why I hadn't been that awesome with them." There was nothing like being called on the mat about why you apparently devoted more time to oral sex with someone else than you did with them. There was no delicate way to say that women were like mushrooms to him. He liked the taste of some and others he did not. It wasn't personal. Some people loved chanterelles, he preferred shiitake.

Trina had been shiitake.

"Really? Sorry." She frowned, as though she wasn't sure what he meant by that.

He shrugged. "But I also got a fan page devoted to my penis, so I'd say it's a fair trade."

She rolled her eyes. "Where are we going, by the way? If we stand here any longer, we're going to get mugged."

"This is a safe neighborhood." But he started walking, wondering if she would think it was weird if he took her hand. Yeah. That would be definitely weird. He opted out of being a creeper and crossed his arms again over his chest as they walked, the warm air muggy and heavy. "It's only two more blocks." He'd moved to this place after they had stopped talking to each other.

Trina fell in step beside him, but she sighed. "What are we doing, Drew? I'm sorry, but I have had a total shit day and I should probably be doing damage control for my business. I came out because you said you wanted to talk but I kind of have a headache and I can't handle any more stress."

He instantly felt bad. "I'm not trying to cause you stress. I'm trying to..." What was he trying to do? "Kiss you." That cleared everything right up. Not.

"You already did that."

So he had. What he really wanted was to know if she were at all receptive to the idea of her no longer needing BootyBook because the only guy she was going to be seeing was him. But he hadn't said that a year ago, before or after sex, and he couldn't just say it now. She'd run for the nearest bus stop and get the hell away from him. Then they'd at least been friends; now they were, well, estranged. He had to finesse the situation. "I want to give you a ten in every category."

Now she completely stopped walking altogether and looked at him as though she was twelve and he was a forty-year-old stranger offering her candy and a ride to see his puppy. "What?" He had to laugh. "Why are you looking at me like that? I'm not trying to sell you the Brooklyn Bridge."

Reaching out, he took her hand after all, and tugged her so she started walking again. It felt good to touch her again. Back before he'd seen her naked, they had touched all the time. Hugs, hand-holding, piggyback rides, hair stroking, shoulder rubs. They'd been comfortable with each other and he hadn't understood how quickly that could change by leaping into sex without a conversation about it first.

"So you want to practice how to achieve the overall perfect dating score? I think that is probably statistically impossible for any man or woman." She squeezed his hand. "Don't stress out about it. Plenty of girls will be absolutely thrilled to go out with you and I'm sure every chick who saw my post will be calling you."

That gave him pause. Was that what she wanted? Him to date a parade of women she was friends with? "What are you doing this weekend?" he asked, directly avoiding addressing what she said.

"I'm going to eat ice cream, drink wine, answer texts from angry men who now hate me, try to avoid my mother, and pray that my clients don't all walk. So really, with all that going on, I shouldn't stay out too late. I should head back soon."

They were in front of his building. Initially his thought had been to go from bar to kiss to bed with her, because when he'd seen her summary of dates with other men, he'd gotten jealous. No doubt about it. A hot wave of caveman possessiveness had washed over him and he'd wanted to whisk her off to his lair and stake a claim with his mouth and his cock. Show her that while Dirk may have been "fun, strong, and with an adorable pink penis," he was even better for her. He wasn't sure why he was better, he just was.

Wait. Because he wanted her more. That was it. He knew her. They were friends.

But then he'd realized he needed to play this right, smooth. Not just drag her off and nail her. "I'm sorry, I shouldn't have asked you to come out tonight. Let me take you home."

She stared up at him, her mouth opening to speak, then closing again.

"Can I see you tomorrow? I want to take you to dinner and then maybe swing dancing. I know how much you love that."

Now her eyebrows shot up. "You would go dancing with me? Mr. Cool Indie Musician?"

That made him frown. Is that how she saw him? Self-important? "I'm walking around wearing a kilt, Trina. I don't give a shit what people think of me. If you like dancing, I'll go dancing with you. Though for a dude who can play the guitar, I don't have a ton of rhythm."

"I think your rhythm is just fine," she said, voice husky, her tongue slipping out to moisten her lower lip.

Damn. She wasn't talking about dancing. Drew rethought the plan of sending her home. Maybe dragging her to his bed wasn't such a bad idea after all. "Sometimes my moves are all right," he murmured, tucking her hair behind her ear. She had thick hair that had been every color of the rainbow in the years he'd known her. Right now though, it was very close to her natural color, a honey oak, with some strands darker, others lighter. "Do you want to come up or do you want me to get you a cab?"

AGAIN WITH THE trick questions. Katrina had no clue what was going on in Drew's head. None of what was happening made any sense. She was standing on a sidewalk in front of his apartment and she couldn't tell if he was asking her to come up and check out his vinyl collection or come up and smoosh their bodies together.

It was tempting to find out, but honestly she wasn't sure she was prepared for either. But at the same time, if she just went home, she'd be up half the night wondering which one it would have been. The internal debate raged on and on as he waited for an answer and she started to panic because in either direction lay *madness*.

Her phone's insistent buzzing in her hand brought her melodrama to heel. "What time is it anyway?" she asked, using that as an excuse to check her screen. "It's midnight." Which changed absolutely and utterly nothing. But she did see she had seventeen texts. That was a new hourly record for when she wasn't actually engaged in a conversation. Those were all just for her, awaiting response. Yay.

"Lots of messages?" he asked, gesturing to her phone.

"Yeah, um, there has been something of a negative response to some of my comments. Imagine that."

Drew gestured to his apartment. "Come on. I'll

make you an iced coffee and I'll help you draft responses."

She laughed. "Oh, now there's a great idea. What would you say to this?" She held out a text from Bryan for him to read.

"I'm going to sue you for slander," Drew read. He looked up, alarmed. "Can he do that?"

"I don't know. Everything I said was true. He stole my change when I gave him a twenty for my half of the bill. So what would you say back to him?"

"That he's too cheap to pay for a lawyer so you're not worried. Damn, what a tool." Drew's expression was earnest, caring, sexy. "You deserve a hell of a lot better than that."

Yeah, she wasn't going home. She'd never been able to resist that face with its perennial five o'clock shadow, dimples, and pale blue eyes. She wanted to dip her tongue into that dimple, then ravage him. "I know. That's why I never went out with him again. That's why I used BootyBook, you know. Not to judge or vilify men. I use it remind myself that I do not want to answer 'hey baby' texts from the guy who asked me to smell his feet on our first date. Or the guy who, while a lot of fun and super good-looking, can't have a single conversation without mentioning another woman he finds attractive."

"Why would you need reminding? You should just delete all their numbers immediately."

"I never delete numbers. Each one is a cautionary tale." Katrina went through the door Drew held open for her. "Besides, it feels rude to be like 'who is this?'

which is what happens if you delete a contact and then they text you."

"Who cares? That's it. We're deleting every guy who's ever been a dick to you."

"No!" For some reason that felt threatening to her. As if she were erasing possibilities. Or more like wiping out any time she'd ever felt hope. It was depressing.

"Are you going to see any of them again?"

"No." But she knew that wasn't necessarily true. She was the type who couldn't say no. If she were bored, feeling fat, lonely, or depressed, if any of those douchebags asked to hang out, she might be vulnerable any given Friday night to say yes. Except for Bryan. He could suck it. But Dirk? Well, how horny was she? Just being honest with herself. But the days of being honest with Drew were over. She couldn't share any of that with him.

Was that what sex did? Destroy the ability to speak freely? Now there was a sobering and flat-out awful thought. "What floor are you on?" she asked.

"Third."

They jogged upstairs, Katrina wishing both that she had greater lung capacity and that Drew were in front of her so she could see his calves in his kilt. Not to objectify him or anything.

"Then why do you care if we delete them?"

He was back to that. Damn it. "Are you going to delete the two chicks who complained?"

Nothing. She turned around and saw he was checking out her ass. Hey, now. Was she giving a good ass impression or was he wondering how she managed to keep from toppling over backward because of its heftiness? He lifted his eyes. Good ass impression, definitely. He looked as though he wanted to bend her over the stairwell and take her right there.

Wow. "Please tell me you have central air." She was feeling overheated. Hot. Downright on fire.

"Are you kidding? Of course not. I have a window unit in my bedroom."

Fabulous. "You never answered the question."

"There was a question?"

She hit the landing on the third floor and paused, not sure which door to proceed to. Suddenly he was right behind her, hands sliding down her arms, lips close to her ear.

"Whatever the question is, you're the answer," he murmured.

Granted, it turned the heat in her panties up a bit, she couldn't lie. But no. Just no. "That line is a two," she told him. "I'm docking you in the sincerity category."

"What?" he protested. "I was totally sincere. And I didn't realize I'm on the clock already. I thought we were starting the quest for a perfect ten tomorrow."

"Only men with massive quantities of chest hair say things like that, and they really shouldn't. And you invited me up, so that means I'm free to gather information."

"Romantic recon?" Drew pulled his key out of the bag thing hanging in front of his junk and opened the door to his apartment.

"You're the one who wanted a do-over. Though I'm not exactly sure of what."

"I didn't say a do-over. That implies failure. We

had a great night together. You agreed we did. You can't take that back now." He held the door open for her, giving her a cocky grin.

She was getting a little tired of him having the upper hand in this situation. As she moved past him she reached out and cupped the man purse strapped around his waist. She knew there was a name for it and that it was part of the kilt, but she didn't know what it was called. "Don't wear this tomorrow. You need to have a beard and be able to throw a log to pull this off."

"It's my work uniform," he said, his teeth gritted. "Not my clothing of choice."

"I bet you sit around the apartment in this. It is really freaking hot in here." Katrina peeled off her short-sleeved sweater. "The kilt keeps you cool down there."

"Mostly I sit around my apartment naked."

"You do not."

He raised his eyebrows.

Oh. My. There was a visual. "I feel weird sitting on your couch now."

Drew cracked a laugh. "You don't have to take your clothes off to sit on it. Unless you really want to. I won't object."

"Nice." She rolled her eyes. "See, suggestive comments under the guise of teasing causes you to lose points."

"What?" Drew held out his hands. "For real? Shit. You're tough."

Katrina wasn't sure if she was having fun or not. She was pretty sure she was, because it felt good to tease and laugh with Drew. But at the same time, she wasn't sure what his end goal was. Sex, presumably, but for what purpose? Just to prove he was the Booty-Book champion? Maybe he was genuinely attracted to her? Because he wanted to sleep with her repeatedly?

She had no idea.

When he sat down on the couch and patted the seat next to him, she decided she didn't care.

CHAPTER FOUR

KATRINA SAT NEXT to him and pushed her hair back off her forehead. "So how have you been? Seriously."

"Fine. Little lonely." His hand landed on her knee.

Since she was wearing a skirt, that meant he was touching bare skin. "You haven't been dating anyone?" She knew he wasn't, or if so, it wasn't serious, because she hadn't seen any smiling couple pictures on his social media of him and someone she would have to hate on principle.

He shook his head, his thumb stroking over her flesh, softly, gently. He had calluses from playing the guitar, but she didn't mind. It just made her more aware of him, a slow tingling starting inside her. "Nope. The magnificent penis has not been out to play in a while."

"You haven't had sex?" She found that hard to believe.

"Just once since we did, and that was only because I was going to punch someone if I didn't release some of that tension."

Oh, my. That was interesting. It could mean any number of things. It was satisfying to know he hadn't been sticking it anywhere there was an opening, but at the same time, it meant he had to be über-horny and everything he was saying and doing was colored by that. It also meant there was no doubt what he wanted to do.

"I'm sorry to hear that," she said.

But he just shrugged. "It was my choice. It wasn't like I didn't have opportunities. Plenty of those. It just didn't seem…right."

"No?" Her nipples had hardened and without even realizing it, her knees had shifted slightly apart.

"I was waiting for something."

"What's that?"

He gave her a little smile. "You."

Oh, no he didn't. She felt everything in her sigh in a big heartfelt girl gush of emotion. She was so going down on him for that. But she wasn't going to give in that easily. "Yet I haven't heard a word from you in eleven months. And liking a status or a picture doesn't count as communication."

"That doesn't mean I wasn't thinking about you."

She was a tough sell. "But if I hadn't screwed up and advertised my ridiculous love life, you would have never texted me."

"I can't say if I would have or not. Doesn't mean I didn't want to, though. And when opportunity presented itself, I jumped at it." His hand had inched up under her skirt, officially in the "we have passed friends yet again" territory. "I'll never forget looking down at your hair spilling all over the pillow and thinking how lucky I was. Who wants a random hookup after that?"

Sold. She was sold. "Dial it back, Mr. Jordan," she said, but her voice sounded a little breathless even to her own ears. "That's overkill."

His hand went to the back of her head and he massaged his fingers through her hair. “No, it’s not. You chicks all say you want romance, and then when we bust it out, you roll your eyes.”

He had a point. “It makes me feel uncomfortable, because I feel like it can’t be legitimate.” So maybe she could be honest with Drew after all. It was surprising how easy it was to fall back into the friendship with him, as if a year hadn’t gone by.

“If it wasn’t legitimate, I wouldn’t say it. Learn to take a compliment.”

“So why haven’t I heard from you?” That was really the sticking point here. Because he was definitely saying that despite what she’d thought, his reaction to their night together had been positive. He hadn’t woken up horrified and wanting an undo button.

“Trina, just kiss me.”

She should push for an answer. She should seek immediate clarification of What This Was and Where They Were Going.

Instead she leaned forward and met his mouth with hers. It was even better than it was on the sidewalk because this time there was no hesitation on either of their parts. It was all hot, tangled tongues, excited sighs, and shifting on the couch to press bodies together. Drew reached a hand back behind his head and yanked his T-shirt off.

“It’s hot in here.”

Yes. Yes, it was. Katrina ran her hands over his bare chest, enjoying the definition and firmness of his pecs. Someone had been doing more than strumming chords in recent months. “You feel very nice,” she told him as his tongue dipped into her ear, setting off a chain reaction of shivering from ear to nipples to inner thighs.

"Right back at ya." His hand cupped her breast through her tank top. "Can I take this off?"

The sooner the better. So she gave her answer by pulling it over her head and tossing it on his coffee table.

"Hey. I wanted to do that."

Right. Suddenly Mr. Romance. "I left the bra for you. See what you can do with that." But first, she wanted to kiss him again. He tasted so good. Like a dessert she hadn't indulged in for a year. His scent was familiar, the feel of his hands over her nipples not. That first night had been all hot desperation and alcohol buzz. This was so real it felt surreal. She was acutely aware of every inch of him, every sound he made, every brush of his skin against hers.

Drew pushed her back until she was lying on the couch and he was over her, hands on either side of her, erection pressed firmly up against her thigh. It was a piece of cake to infiltrate his kilt from behind and she understood why men were so excited by the sight of a skirt. There was no boundary there. Boom. She was under and squeezing his ass cheeks. Even though he was wearing tight briefs, it was still a hell of a turn-on.

"Two can play that game," he said, his hand disappearing under her skirt.

And landing right between her thighs with ease, his thumb circling right over her clit. Whoever had invented the skirt deserved a pat on the back. Had someone actually invented the skirt? Did it have an origin? Katrina decided she didn't give a shit when Drew's finger slipped inside her panties.

She moaned. She didn't mean to. Moaning seemed a bit premature and showy, but it just spilled out before she could prevent it. He smiled down at her before giving her a deep, fervent kiss. Squeezing his butt harder, she raised her hips to meet his touch as he stroked inside her.

But just when she got going he pulled away, and her hands fell off his ass. So disappointing. But before she could complain or beg for him to touch her again, he started to kiss down the front of her, mouth trailing over her neck, pausing to brush over the curves of her breast, and then on down lower. Oh, yeah. She saw where this was going. She'd forgive him for his finger disappearing. His tongue dipped into her belly button, then he lifted his head, and lifted her skirt.

He got her panties down one-handed. Impressive.

Then he was doing things with his tongue that had her eyes rolling back in her head, and her reaching to hold on to something. She found his hair and gripped it.

"Drew," she breathed when he found a rhythm that had her panting and squirming on his couch.

He paused. "Yes?" His breath tickled across her sensitive flesh.

She hadn't meant for him to stop. It was just a general call of encouragement. "Nothing. Well, actually, that feels really good. Like, amazing good."

DREW COULDN'T BELIEVE he was here, again, with Trina. He hadn't expected to have another shot at it, and he hadn't really meant to get her naked tonight. He wanted the opportunity to show her what they could have, and he didn't mean just sex. But then she had been staring at him so intently and it had been so easy to slip a hand under her skirt.

Next thing he knew he was making a meal out of her, listening to her soft moans of enthusiasm drift over him, urging him on. But he decided he was going to make her come and leave it there for the night. Show a little self-restraint, even if it was a bit after the fact. What could show her more clearly that he intended to do it right this time than taking her home after giving her an orgasm?

When he gently sucked on her clit, then slipped his tongue lower again, she broke, calling his name tightly in a way that made his cock throb and his muscles tense. Yeah, he had to admit, he felt a wave of pride. That had been less than five minutes. Maybe he wasn't the only one who'd been living the celibate life. Trina's post with those details about other guys had been taken down before he could look, and he was glad. He didn't want to know what she'd been doing and with who. He didn't expect that she had been pining for him, but he'd just as soon not have any details.

When she quieted down, her grip on his head relaxing and her breathing slowing, he pulled away and kissed the inside of her thigh. "How was that?" he asked, feeling pleased and lazy all at the same time. As though now that he knew where he was going, he was in no particular hurry to get there.

"So good," she murmured.

Rising up on his hands, he gave her a smile before sliding her panties back in place.

She frowned in confusion. "But…"

"But what?" He smoothed her skirt back down over her thighs. Shifting on the couch, he moved up so he could kiss that grumpy expression away. She hesitated for a second, but then she kissed him eagerly, her calf locking over his. But when her fingers reached for him, trying to stroke over his erection, he broke off. He wanted to wait and he wasn't going to be able to if she got her hands on him.

She didn't say anything. She just lay there, her breasts spilling over the top of her bra, her chest flushed pink from wine and arousal. Those full lips he loved so much were pulling a pout. "We're supposed to be answering your many men," he told her.

"I'm not sure there is anything to say. I apologized for accidentally making it public, because seriously, my intention was never to embarrass anyone, but I'm not sure I need to apologize for telling the truth. Samantha says it could set off a wave of male self-improvement."

He somehow doubted that. Men didn't react well to being shamed. Hell, women didn't either. Even when people knew they were being asses, they didn't want to be called out on it. "Then we're back to the delete-the-contacts thing." He wanted that to happen. Immediately, if not sooner. There was no reason for her to keep the numbers of guys who were tools and didn't treat her the way she deserved.

Of course, according to that logic, she should have deleted his number. Why the hell had he brought this up?

"Fine."

Fine? That was it?

Katrina just stared up at him, and suddenly he felt that maybe he didn't know all he needed to know. He couldn't read her eyes, or her expression. "Good girl." Drew sat up and pulled her with him. He kissed the side of her head. "We should get you home. You had a rough day."

"I did." She reached for her tank top and pulled it on. "Thanks for not being pissed off at me about the whole thing."

"I'm glad I texted you." He was. Very glad he'd finally pulled his head out of his ass. "What time should I get you tomorrow?" He reached for his own shirt.

"You're serious about that? You really want to go out?"

She looked so doubtful and adorable he wanted to laugh. "Yes. Now let's catch the train before you're rolling into bed at three a.m."

"You're walking me to the subway?"

"I'm walking you to your *door*," he said firmly. "It's late. I don't want you going home alone."

"I can just take a cab then."

"No. I'm taking you home." It wasn't negotiable. He pulled his shirt on.

"I can take care of myself."

Trina was intelligent, driven, and way ahead of him in terms of her career and ambitions. She was also adorable, petite, and maybe a touch naive. All qualities he loved about her, but hell to the no was he letting her take the subway home solo. "How many nights did I walk you to your dorm at school? If it were up to you, you would have strolled around the Village by yourself at all hours of the night. My escort service is back in effect."

"I can think of better services you can offer," she said drily.

He grinned. "Oh yeah? Just let me put on a pair of shorts and we can go." He wasn't wearing this kilt out just for the hell of it. "What service would that be?" he called, stepping the three feet to his room and pulling on a pair of basketball shorts under the kilt. When he turned, Trina was in the doorway watching. He dropped the kilt.

"I just clicked like on your Magnificent Penis Page," she told him, her phone in her hand.

He'd almost forgotten about that. The look on her face made his still-half-hard cock swell. "So you're a fan?"

"You know I am, though the memory is getting a little fuzzy at this point." With that, she turned and walked away.

He followed, giving himself an adjustment as he went. His shorts felt too tight.

She was killing him and she knew it.

They talked about nothing in particular as they went outside into the warm night air and made their way to the subway station. Her arms were crossed over her chest, giving him no opportunity to take her hand, which he now decided he had every right to do. On the G train she yawned and leaned on his shoulder, so he put his arm around her.

This felt right. Friendship mixed with something more, a possible real relationship. He just hoped they were on the same page.

When she'd first moved to Greenpoint he'd been disappointed because it extended their commute if they wanted to hang out together. But now, he was grateful for the extra few minutes with her. At the door to her apartment she turned and smiled at him.

"Good night, Trina. I'll be here about seven, okay?"

She nodded, looking sleepy. "Cool. And thanks for rubbing one out for me."

Um. "You're welcome."

The door closed in his face.

Those weren't the words of a woman looking to be his girlfriend. He didn't think. Then he thought about the fact that the app she was using was called BootyBook. As in casual sex.

As in that's what he had been, and was.

Suddenly he didn't want a ten in her BootyBook log, he wanted the whole damn thing deleted off her phone.

Feeling frustrated, his balls decidedly blue, Drew went home.

CHAPTER FIVE

"You said what?" Samantha said, jaw dropping.

"I know, it's awful." Katrina put her hands over her face. "I didn't mean to say thanks for rubbing one out! It just appeared out of nowhere, like ninja words. I guess it was stress or something. It was all so overwhelming."

"Having a guy go down on you is overwhelming? If it's too much for you, I'll happily take your life." Samantha pushed up her glasses and shook her head.

They were sitting in a bagel shop, but Katrina was so disgusted with herself she couldn't eat. She was nursing a coffee and wondering why she didn't think before she clicked buttons on her phone or allowed words to leave her mouth. She was utterly unprepared for adulthood it seemed, even though the laptop in front of her with many, many emails indicated she still had a job, and the lack of money in her bank account proved she had adult-size bills. "It's just all so confusing. I tried to ask him what we were doing, but he just flirted with me."

And gave her an orgasm, but asked nothing in return, much to her disappointment. What had that been all about?

"I still can't believe he took me home. It was very…

mature. None of this 'see ya later' with a wave as the door hits me in the butt when I leave, like most guys post-sex. Of course, he didn't get any, so maybe this is all part of some elaborate chase."

"Why would he need to chase? You've already put out and you called him Grade A Awesome Sauce in your assessment, which he read. I don't think he feels like he needs to really work this one hard from every angle."

Good point. "So what does it mean?" Katrina chewed her hangnail and jumped when her phone buzzed on the table. She glanced at it, hoping it was Drew. Just James. Want to get together?

No. No, she did not.

"Maybe it means he likes you."

"That's ludicrous. He would just say that." Had he said that? "God, I don't even know. I just feel oddly manipulated."

"Which is ironic."

"What do you mean?" That made her feel more than a little defensive.

"You knew what you were doing when you and Drew went out after that art show. You wanted to sleep with him and you set it up so you did."

"That's called expressing interest in someone."

"How is this any different?"

"Because I don't know what he wants. Honestly, I think he's just trying to score a huge BootyBook endorsement so he can get ass."

Samantha gave her a look over her coffee mug rim as she lifted it to sip. "You don't really mean that."

She didn't want to mean that. She didn't think that was what he was doing. But after a night of tossing and turning and wondering why he hadn't really answered any of her questions as to what they were doing, now she was a bundle of neurotic girl doubt. It was awful. Suddenly she felt fourteen instead of twenty-four.

But whereas at fourteen she would have been hurt and done something as completely stupid as responding to James that she would go out with him in some vain attempt to make Drew jealous, she was not going to do that. Hell, what was she talking about? Fourteen? She'd done that a year ago.

"I honestly don't know what Drew is doing. But thanks for meeting me for coffee. Hearing how melodramatic I sound out loud is helping me rein it back in. Why am I expecting an answer before the question has been asked? Maybe I should just enjoy the fact that Drew and I are friends again."

"And you're getting oral sex, which is way more than I'm getting."

Katrina pushed her phone across the table. "You can have Dirk if you want. And James. I'm passing the wang, I mean the wand."

"You're donating your sexual leftovers to me?" Samantha threw a piece of her blueberry muffin at her. "I can get my own stable of men who shag me and don't call for three weeks, thank you very much. It doesn't require voodoo, just a vagina."

"You should copyright that—it's beautiful." Katrina grinned, popping the bite of muffin that had hit her in the boobs and tumbled to a rest on the fox on her sweater into her mouth.

"Trina, what does the fox say?"

"What?"

"Fuck you."

The muffin bite flew back out of her mouth as she let out an unattractive snort.

DREW IGNORED YET another penis joke from Jason and Samuel and concentrated on completing the set of squats he was doing. He was hot and sweaty and more determined than ever to both increase his muscle strength and win over Katrina that night. He'd read the screenshot of his entry, yet again, before meeting the guys at the gym for a workout, and while gratified that she had rated him high on all things sexual, and in conversation, she had dinged his clothes, his morning-after behavior, and his cuddling. Seriously. A cuddle rating. Who came up with that shit? Whoever had, it meant he had to cuddle her like a pro just to prove a point.

He'd also scored poorly for leaving a condom in her wastebasket (where was it supposed to go if not in the trash?) and for failing to use her name enough. So what he had learned was that he was a good lay, but far from the whole package.

Tonight she was getting the whole package.

"Did someone see an award-winning dick in here?" Jason asked, doing curls, wearing a shit-eating grin. "Because all I see is a pussy doing some squats."

Drew rolled his eyes at his friend. "At least the fan page you created was witty. That was not."

"You know your fan page only has eleven likes," Samuel said, wiping his shaved head with his arm. "That's pretty weak, my friend."

Samuel was that kind of ridiculously pretty guy with the kind of coloring that made female panties just drop as he walked by. He was fit, his skin was a rich café au lait, and he had startling blue eyes. He was also independently wealthy, with ginormous financial support from his family in the Middle East, but despite all the advantages he'd been born with, he was a good guy, and usually not so annoying.

On the other hand, Jason was usually annoying, but Drew was used to it. They'd been friends for nearly a decade.

"So you've been checking out my penis page, huh? I bet you're ten of those eleven likes. You probably made up half a dozen identities just to stalk my penis online." Grunting a little as he finished his rep, he dropped his bar and stepped back. "Beat that, motherfuckers."

"You're obviously sexually frustrated," Justin said. "You never lift with that kind of intensity." His friend actually looked impressed.

"I am sexually frustrated. I took Katrina home with me last night and we didn't have sex."

Samuel dropped the weight he was holding, hard. "Why not? I thought you've been half in love with her since like junior year in college."

"Seriously," Jason added. "We had a bet going back in the day how long it would take you to figure it out. Clearly I am the winner because I said you'd be too stupid to ever recognize it."

"Thanks for the vote of confidence." Drew sat down on the nearest weight bench and propped his elbows on his thighs. "Maybe one of you assholes could have mentioned it to me and I wouldn't have wasted two years."

"Mentioned what? If you're too stupid to figure out

you're in love with someone, that's not my problem." Jason scratched his beard and shrugged.

"It's only hard until it's not," Samuel said.

"What kind of wisdom bullshit is that?" Jason asked.

Drew didn't get it either. "I'm going to take her out tonight and I'm going to finish what I started a year ago."

"That's what I mean," Samuel said. "Don't make it so hard. Just go for it. Trina's a good girl, you know? She's always the first one to throw someone a party, the first one to bring a bottle of wine, the first one to offer a hug. Lock her in, man."

"Unless you're afraid of rejection. She did say you dress like a lumberjack and dropped your jizz-filled condom in her trash."

"She never said lumberjack, and if not the wastebasket, where the hell is it supposed to go?" It wasn't as though he'd turned it upside down and shaken it all over her bed.

"Flush it, dude," Samuel said, as if it were pure insanity to do otherwise.

"And then when her toilet stops up, the night will really be sexy. Plus she'll get slapped with a maintenance fine from her landlord." Drew stood back up and shook his head. "You guys are killing my hard-on. I'm hitting the shower. I have a hot date tonight."

DREW WAS AT her door at three minutes past seven. Katrina slipped on her strappy sandals that she couldn't afford but had bought anyway, and smoothed the front of her flare-skirt dress as she went for the door. She'd agonized over what to wear. It was August, hotter than hell, and she had no idea where Drew was planning to take her. So she had gone for summer fun, with a white halter dress with cherries all over it, very light and fresh, pinup-inspired, flirty, dressy enough but not too dressy. She hoped.

Odds were high he would be in jeans and a grungy band T-shirt, hair in his eyes.

But when she opened the door she realized she had been wrong. Very, very wrong. Holy hotness.

Drew was wearing a suit, a very trendy modern cut that showed his lean but muscular body. She felt her jaw going slack and her panties going damp. She hadn't seen him in a suit…ever. At graduation he'd worn khakis under his gown, and a plaid button-up shirt. He'd never looked quite so mature or polished. He looked as though he should be on the cover of *Rolling Stone* with a cigarette in his hand, smiling slyly while a headline declared him the new sexy voice in rock.

"Hi," she did manage to say. "You clean up nice."

He grinned. "I have my moments. No plaid in sight."

Holding the door open for him, she defaulted to teasing him, because it felt more comfortable. She was still feeling stunned and knocked off balance by how amazing he looked, and he didn't need to know that. "Maybe you're wearing plaid boxers."

But her strategy backfired. His hand dropped to his belt buckle. "Want to see?"

"No!" *Yes.*

Smiling, he leaned over and kissed her. "You look beautiful, Katrina. Tasty."

He hadn't called her Katrina in years. The fact that he did now unnerved her. What the hell was really happening between them? "I just need to get my purse. Or do you want a drink first?" Because maybe she did. Because maybe she needed a shot of tequila to calm her nerves right now.

Drew just shook his head. "I don't think I'm drinking tonight. I want to be fully aware of everything I do and say, and I want to remember every minute with you."

Hello. Who was this Don Juan Drew? She didn't know this guy. She knew the intensity he displayed when he was studying for exams, or when he'd been lost in the recording studio at school. Their final year he'd practically lived at the music lab on Mercer Street. But he'd never been all that intense with girls, not that she had seen. Unlike some of her other guy friends, Drew had never gone off the deep end over a girl before, during or after a relationship, that she witnessed.

This was a side of him she didn't recognize, that he'd clearly been cultivating since graduation.

She didn't know what to say to something like that. Men she knew just didn't speak to her that way. Most were either super-sexual in what they said or were so terrified their words would be misconstrued as a quest for a relationship that they were vague to the point of rude. It made her realize she'd been allowing men to treat her with something less than respect, though Drew never had. Men she'd been dating, if that was what you could call it.

"That's probably a good dating strategy," she told him, going for a light and teasing attitude. "I'm pretty sure every legit dating book or blog ever tells you not to drink when you're just getting to know someone. I should apply that theory more often."

"We're not just getting to know each other." His hand was in his pocket. "I just don't want my senses dulled. I want to feel you."

Oh, my. Without meaning to, Katrina swallowed nervously. She picked her clutch purse up and fluffed her hair with the other hand. "So where are we going?"

"There's a new upscale pizzeria that serves an amazing crostini with pistachio pesto. Is that okay?"

White dress. Sauces. It was probably a disaster waiting to happen, but she was pretty damn sure she would Dumpster dive with Drew if it meant she got to spend time with him. "I do love a good pesto sauce. I wore flat sandals so if we're walking I'm good."

"Remember in the Village you used to say you were going to buy a pink Cadillac online and just live in it once you found a parking spot?"

She laughed. "I honestly don't think there is a parking spot in all of Manhattan big enough to accommodate a Caddy. Especially not the way I parallel park. But it was a fun fantasy."

"And I wanted an Airstream so we could haul it on the back of your Cadi to Graceland and Nashville and then the mountains." He went out into the hall, a smile on his face as she locked the door behind her. "We had some plans, didn't we? I still have a sketch of the tattoo I wanted to get. A sugar skull with Elvis hair."

"I remember that sketch!" Trina laughed. "You never got it? Maybe that's a good thing."

"Hey. Don't be hating on the King."

"I'm not hating on the King, just the idea of mashing Elvis with a Day of the Dead face. It seems a little bit like a bad omen to me." The hot air hit them the minute they stepped outside and Katrina blinked against the sun, wishing she'd brought her sunglasses. "Oh, jeez, you're going to be boiling in that suit."

"I am pretty hot."

She laughed. "Modest, too. So how's the music going?"

They chatted as they walked, comfortable with each other, falling into old patterns of conversation as though there hadn't been a gap of a year. He told her about his latest gigs with his band, some good, some not so much. He talked about recording a demo and their lack of success in really making social media work for his band.

"Well, that's my area of expertise. Maybe I can help you guys out."

"How is everything going with your business?" he asked.

"Okay. It was better on Thursday than it is today. I did have two clients walk today after the whole BootyBook debacle." Even though she had been upset to lose her clients, she had been prepared for it and in a way was relieved the worst was probably over. She was geared up to regroup and move forward. "I'll just have to work harder and pick up some new clients. It could have been a hell of a lot worse."

"I'm sorry. That really sucks. But you're a savvy businesswoman. I know you'll recover and be in an even better position. And you might want to delete BootyBook, or just use it on your laptop, not your phone."

"Trust me, I will be using the website to log in, not the app. Less chance for a repeat problem. I have learned my lesson." She glanced up at him. "But seriously, if you can trust me not to totally screw it up, I can help your band. We can launch a media campaign."

"I doubt I can afford you," he said with a smile.

"I wouldn't charge you."

"I couldn't take up your time like that."

She was about to protest, but he took her hand, startling her into speechlessness.

"We're here." He held open the door for her, and he dropped her hand.

Katrina felt disappointed. She'd only gotten a five-second hand-hold. It had felt nice to be strolling down the sidewalk with him, looking like a real couple. Which immediately struck her as potentially problematic if she was enjoying the idea of being his girlfriend, at least in the eyes of everyone around them.

She hadn't learned a damn thing. She was still in the role of friendship, yet fantasizing about being more to Drew.

That knowledge wasn't going to stop her from sleeping with him, though.

Which certainly seemed to be his plan as well. He touched the small of her back, he touched her leg, he let their knees brush together once they were sitting down. He stroked her hand across the small table in the intimate restaurant and he moved his eyebrows up and down as he read the menu.

"Oysters. I should order those for you since they're an aphrodisiac."

As if she needed it. "Are you flirting with me?" she asked, feigning outrage.

"I'm not here for the bread." He took a bite of the

slice in his hand and looked at it in surprise. "Though this is damn good bread."

Katrina laughed. "You always did love your carbs. By the way, what have you been doing in the gym? You didn't get that buff playing guitar."

"I'm trying to keep up with Samuel. He looks like a goddamn underwear model. It's very hard on the ego. Though he doesn't have a fan page for his penis, so I do feel better about the whole thing."

"You look good," she told him honestly. "Really good."

Just like that, sexual tension sprang to life between them. His eyes darkened as he stared across the table at her. "Would you like to see more?"

"I definitely would." Crossing her legs to quiet the ache throbbing low in her belly, she reached for her glass of water and took a sip, waiting for him to say something more.

But he just gave her a sly smile. "Let's see where the evening takes us."

It was going to take them to bed, or she was going to smack him with his own magnificent penis.

Whatever game he was playing, whatever manual he'd read overnight on how to seduce women, was driving her nuts. There was no need for him to prove he could get the girl or improve his score. She could handle Drew peeling off her dress and going to town on her. She could not handle Drew on a mission to charm.

She had ordered a glass of red wine, because she could sip it slowly throughout the meal, unlike white, which tended to go down way too fast. Lifting her glass, she raised it in salute. “I’m looking forward to seeing all there is to see, Drew.”

His nostrils flared.

And she had the distinct feeling that they were heading into dangerous territory.

CHAPTER SIX

DREW WONDERED IF Trina had any idea how sensual and appealing she looked. She had always thought of herself as a little goofy, a little messy and klutzy. Yet he had always known those were just pieces of the overall package. She was also fiercely passionate, determined, fearless when trying new things, and gorgeous, with the most compelling and expression-filled brown eyes he'd ever seen.

He wanted to take her to bed for the entire weekend. He wanted to lose track of time and forget about the world around them.

The waitress dropped their pizza down in front of them.

So he'd already lost track of time. Either that or they had baked a pizza in three minutes. "Here, let me get you a piece," he said, holding his hand out for her plate.

She passed it to him. "Thanks."

Trina tucked her hair behind her ear and fussed with her napkin. She actually looked shy, which struck him as very unexpected, but very adorable. It wasn't a trait he associated with her. But given what he'd scanned of her recent dates before she removed them from her page, she hadn't exactly been hanging out with quality men. It wasn't hard to treat her with respect or a modicum of consideration. He was actually really enjoying himself.

"I had a guy tell me once that he wasn't going to pass the bruschetta because if women wanted equality they could get their own bruschetta. He said feminism extended to opening your own door."

Drew snorted. "Ah, pretentious irony at its Brooklyn best. The truth is, he's just lazy."

"Probably. And yet he wanted oral sex but refused to give it in return. I'm not sure how equality applies in that case."

"You had sex with him?" Drew paused in handing her plate back with a slice of pizza on it. He really didn't want to think about that. Not now.

"No. We were fooling around but then I saw where it was going—all about him—and I bailed. He got pissed and we never spoke ever again."

"Good." He got himself a slice. "I mean, I'm sorry if you were disappointed. Sorry it didn't work out."

She laughed. "No, you're not."

"No. I'm not." He was big enough to admit it. "A guy like that is not worth your time or effort. You'll always be the one compromising, and why should you?"

"That seems to be the modern interpretation of dating. Random texts, half-ass effort, constantly distracted by whatever new and shiny girl has a profile online. We're all trying so hard to be remote and cool. It's exhausting."

That was precisely why he hadn't really been dating. His focus was on his music and taking the next step in his career, such as it was. He'd been disgusted with himself after he'd left Trina's apartment before she woke up, and he'd realized he didn't want to be that guy. So if he wasn't prepared to put the time and thoughtfulness into a relationship, then he wasn't entitled to have sex with that woman either. Plain and simple.

"There's nothing remote about what I want to do with you."

She would interpret that as sexual. He was okay with that for now.

Before the night was over, she would understand that he didn't want to prove to women en masse that he was worthy of a chance. He just wanted to convince her.

Her phone had been buzzing repeatedly the whole time they'd been talking and he wanted to throw it out the window. Instead, he told her, "I do have one request though."

"What's that?"

"Power your phone off. Not silence it. Not turn off the wireless. Totally power it off and put it in your purse."

She looked panicked for a second at the thought. "But..."

"But?" he asked.

Then she swallowed hard and shook her head. "Sure. Of course. I'm sorry, I wasn't trying to be rude."

"I know. But you don't need a picture of our pizza. If it's good, we'll remember it." He wanted all of her attention on him. Selfish, but he wanted to be with her. All of her.

She turned her phone off and tucked it away. "I feel naked without my phone."

He grinned. "Then we're setting the right tone for the night."

TRINA HADN'T THOUGHT for one second that Drew would actually follow through on his suggestion they go dancing. Men dangled carrots, reeling women in, then had a very good reason why it didn't pan out. Usually one couched in bullshit that tried to make it seem as though they were really being thoughtful when they just wanted to do what they wanted to do. Which was never what she actually wanted to do.

Or again, maybe she was swimming in the wrong dating pool.

Because Drew seemed to have no problem peeling his jacket off and making every effort to learn the steps in the thirty-minute tutorial on how to swing. Dance, that is, not the other kind of swinging. He was terrible at it, but he concentrated, tried, and they laughed a lot. Dinner had been easy and intimate, sexual tension simmering below the surface of their conversation, but in an exciting way, not an uncomfortable way.

Dancing was just fun, Drew's expressions comical as he moved right instead of left, and collided with her on more than one occasion. "Holy crap, sorry," he said for about the twelfth time. "I was never great at that whole left-right thing."

Trina was flushed from dancing and from laughter and she decided that maybe she would have to force his lead without him knowing it. So she spun out and came back to him in a way that required very little effort on his part. Yet somehow he still managed to shift and clip her in the shoulder.

"And I suck." He let her hands go. "I think I need a little more practice. Like about seven hundred hours' worth. Open dance has started. Why don't you let one of these guys take you around the floor for a song or two?"

She stared at him, trying to decide if this were a trap or not. "You wouldn't mind?"

"Of course not. You love to dance. These dudes have some skill I don't, if not my good looks, so why don't I step aside and watch you do your thing?" He gave her a mock smarmy look. "And if your dress happens to fly up a little more than expected, this way I can see it."

She rolled her eyes. "I don't get that wild. There won't be aerial flips going on."

"Not this portion of the evening."

Okay, that made her laugh. Katrina gave him a kiss on the cheek. "Thanks," she said, sincerely. She meant for all of it. For being him. Her friend.

He looked slightly sheepish as she turned and looked for a partner. Four dances later, she had gotten some exercise, had some fun, been challenged by an exceptionally skilled partner, and needed a glass of water. She figured another dance would be pushing it anyway. Drew had been more than patient, so she thanked her partner and went to find him. He was talking to a woman in her sixties about the Caribbean.

Expecting him to be bored beyond belief, she was surprised that he actually seemed to be entertained by the conversation. Though Drew had always been the guy who could talk to anyone. He knew all the cafeteria workers in their dorm by name, he got friendly with all his professors, and he frequently gave yogurt to a homeless man in Washington Square Park who had no teeth but a brilliant smile.

After he introduced her, they chatted for a few more minutes, then the woman gave them a smile. "I'll leave you two lovebirds to your night."

Seriously? Katrina waited for Drew to say they were just friends or something that made it clear they were not a couple, but he just smiled and told her to have a great night. He put his hand on the small of Katrina's back and led her away.

"Can I get you a drink? They have a full bar in the corner or I can get you a soda."

"Water would be great, actually. I hope you weren't bored."

"No, it was fine. I enjoyed watching you and there are plenty of interesting people here to talk to. I was getting the 'I remember Brooklyn when' speech from different people."

"I guess the Brooklyn they knew is different from the one we know."

"Very." Drew asked the bartender for two waters, then handed one to Katrina. "But I wouldn't be making the kind of money I am if I was living in that Brooklyn, so here's to overpriced cocktails and thrift shops."

"What do thrift shops have to do with your income?" she asked, amused, sipping her water.

"The current trend of spending less money on high-end designer clothes equals more money for alcohol. After popping tags and scouring a sweater from the eighties, no one thinks twice about paying fifteen bucks for a drink. For which I'm grateful."

He had a point. "This is why I drink at home." Then she laughed. "Wait. That didn't sound right."

Drew gave her an amused look. “That’s a sign of a problem, you know.”

“I meant I enjoy a nice glass of wine at home with friends.” She nudged him when he still looked skeptical. “Be quiet.”

“I didn’t say anything. Speaking of which, if you’re done swinging.” He winked at her. “Want to head out? It’s a little loud for extensive conversation.”

“Sure. I’m done *dancing*. Where did you have in mind?”

“There’s a coffee shop a block west.”

He was moving them step-by-step in the direction of his apartment. They were firmly in Williamsburg now and only a few blocks from his place. She suspected it was no accident and she wondered why his place versus hers.

But this was clearly all planned, and he was pulling out the stops. He’d paid for her dinner and he opened doors, pulled back her chair. It was a date. Not hanging out. Not a hookup. A genuine “we are grown-ups and are on a date.” Weird. Totally weird.

Yet…wonderful.

At the coffee shop they sipped iced drinks and talked about anything and everything, sometimes about the past, sometimes about the present, and briefly about the future. Whereas back in school they had frequently talked about their dreams for their mid- to late-twenties, now they both seemed to be of a similar mind that the point was to enjoy *now*. Neither was where they wanted to be in their careers or goals, but where they were was solid. Positive.

"There's only one thing I'm missing," Drew said, lounging back in his chair, making his suit look both chic and casual at the same time.

God, he was sexy. He always had been, but seeing him as a man, so confident and self-possessed, had her feeling that she couldn't get him on top of her fast enough.

"What is that?"

"I'll tell you later."

"It's a secret?"

"Something like that."

"You know I hate secrets." She did. It always bothered her that someone was lording something over her. Why bring it up if you weren't going to share it? It drove her crazy. "What could you possibly be missing?"

He gestured to her coffee. "Come on, then. Grab your drink and let's go. I'll show you what I'm missing."

Oh. So he was talking about sex. Right? That's what he was talking about. He had said that he hadn't been having any. So now he was prepared to finish what they had started the night before.

Happy dance.

Presumably. "Are you going to take me to the animal shelter and pick out a hound dog?"

He laughed. "No. I can't have pets in my building."

Good. "Maybe someday when you move to Jersey you can have a dog."

"Bite your tongue. I'm not ready for the white picket fence anytime soon. If ever." They stepped out onto the sidewalk and he took her hand.

Drew invaded her space, his other hand going into her hair to urge her head toward his. “Come back to my place? I have cookies.”

She let him kiss her, enjoying the play of his mouth over hers. “Mmm. You do know me. I’m a sucker for baked goods.”

“I believe once you said you’d do literally anything for the oatmeal raisin cookies from that bakery on Fifth Avenue. Let’s put that statement to the test.”

Katrina was pretty sure her panties melted at his words. He had taken the train to the Village, on a Saturday, to get her cookies? Wow. Just wow. “You got me cookies?”

He smiled down at her. “Yep. Think how great they’ll taste with coffee tomorrow morning.”

The man was holding nothing back. She would give him that. She could flirt, too. Wrapping her arms around his neck, she smiled and pressed her breasts against his chest. “That was really sweet of you. I can’t even think how to properly say thank you.”

“I have an idea or two.”

“I’m open to suggestions.” Since they were clearly having a sleepover, she would be open all night to suggestions. Quite literally.

“Then let’s go before we end up making out on the sidewalk.”

“It wouldn’t be the first time.”

He laughed and pulled her arms down to take her hand and start walking. “You’re trouble.”

“No. Katrina.”

“You’ll always be Trina to me.”

As they walked, she didn’t notice the dog barking,

the sound of a honking horn, the smell of heat and food and exhaust fumes. She just noticed Drew.

Maybe uploading her BootyBook account was the smartest thing she had unintentionally done.

CHAPTER SEVEN

THE FIRST THING Katrina noticed about Drew's apartment was that he had cleaned. Everything was tidy and put away and it smelled like pine. There was a bottle of red wine and two glasses sitting on the coffee table, ready, along with various scented candles, which he immediately lit, leaving the room mostly dark, save one lamp in the corner.

She took her sandals off. He removed his jacket. They were standing next to the couch, and he took her cheeks with both of his hands and kissed her softly. The look he gave her took her breath away. It almost looked as if this was way more than proving a point about his finer qualities, or about having a do-over of their accidental night together. This look squeezed her heart and hardened her nipples. This look spoke of warm feelings and hot arousal and that nebulous future they had avoided talking about.

"Thanks for a great night," she told him truthfully.

"It's not over yet."

"I know, but I want you to know I appreciate the effort that went into it."

But he shook his head. "Everything is easy with you. No effort."

Oh, God, he was destroying her. She was aware of

how loud her breathing was, a sort of desperate and frantic increase in air intake as she stared at him, not sure what to say, how to act. It felt as though Something Was Happening. Something that might change tomorrow and a whole lot of tomorrows after that.

She didn't want to give it the Katrina Effect and mess it up.

So she took a calming breath and rested her hands on his waist. "So then maybe I should just say that I appreciate *you*."

"That works," he murmured, before kissing her again, deeper, hungrily.

She gripped the belt loops on his pants and tugged so that their hips collided. "I can think of a great way to appreciate you even more fully," she said, and unzipped his pants.

"You don't have to do anything but be you."

Katrina slipped her hand into his pants and stroked his growing erection. "I'll be me going down on you, how does that sound?"

"That sounds—"

But he didn't bother to finish the sentence when she gave him a naughty smile before bending over. She unbuttoned his pants and pulled out his thick length and gripped it firmly, stroking up and down over his smooth skin. "Yeah?" she asked.

"That sounds like a great idea," he told her. "It feels even better than it sounds."

"I bet it tastes good, too." She flickered her tongue over the tip of his penis and slid slowly down before backtracking. When she reached the head, she opened her mouth and fully enclosed him, taking a deep, long swallow of his cock.

The noise he made was very gratifying. As was the way his hands gripped the back of her head. "Damn, Trina, that feels amazing."

Their boozy night together, she hadn't really given him oral sex. She'd made one sloppy attempt but she'd been a little too buzzed and he had stopped her, clearly not into it. So maybe he wasn't the only one who had something to prove tonight. She could give him the kind of pleasure he had given her the night before.

So to serve that purpose, she decided her angle wasn't going to allow her free range, so she pulled back with the intention of going on her knees. But Drew tipped her chin up.

"Look at you," he said. "Shiny, wet lips. So sexy, so gorgeous."

He would have raised her back up, presumably to kiss him, but Katrina ignored his gentle tugs and followed her original plan. She dropped lightly to her knees and took him into her mouth again, her hands on his hips, holding on to his front pockets. Drew swore, and she took that as a positive sign, especially since he was suddenly gripping her head, hard, and carefully guiding her onto him.

Listening to his breathing, his low groans, she found the rhythm and the grip he responded most positively to and worked steadily on him, enjoying the knowledge that she could do this to him, make him so hard, so tense with arousal.

Especially when a minute later, he yanked her backward, breathing hard. "Stop."

She smiled up at him, wiping her dewy lips, feeling more than a little sassy. "You sure?"

"Positive." Drew pulled Trina to her feet, knowing he couldn't take another minute of that without totally losing control. "Damn, you are fucking amazing at that. I need a second." He kissed her hard and tucked himself back away. Reaching for the bottle of wine he'd thought to set out ahead of time, he swallowed hard and concentrated on not throwing Trina down on the floor and taking her on the threadbare carpet. He wanted this to last.

Uncorking the wine, he studied her. She looked pleased with herself, a naughty little smile on her face. She should be. "What are you smiling about?" he asked her, pulling his shirt out of his pants before filling both glasses halfway. He handed her one, trying to ignore the way his cock was throbbing.

She sipped it, then licked the rim of the glass. "Mmm. This is delicious."

After taking a sip of wine himself, he leaned over and licked the swell of her breast, rising above the perky cherries on her crisp white dress. "You're right. Delicious."

Even that little touch had her sucking in a breath, and Drew marveled at how combustible their chemistry was. Had it always been like this? Had they always been so aware of each other's skin, each touch, each brush of fingertips, each soft smile and random gesture? He couldn't say at this point. All he was certain of was that he knew Trina as he'd never really known any other woman, and adding intimacy, physical intimacy, to that seemed so logical now he didn't know why they hadn't done it earlier.

"Come lie down with me. It's cooler in the bedroom with the AC."

"Is this a plot to get me naked on your bed?" she asked with a tilt of her head and complete acquiescence in her eyes. She was as on board with this as he was.

"Yes."

"I was hoping you'd say that."

"Follow me to the air-conditioning where marvelous wonders await you, including the most magnificent penis you've ever laid eyes on." He shot his eyebrows up and down and grabbed the bottle of wine. "Free spirits to those daring enough to look." He walked backward toward his bedroom.

"You're insane." She followed him down the hallway, a smile on her face even as she shook her head. "But you are also very, very hot, I will admit that. And adorably ridiculous. It's a lethal combination."

"I don't want to kill anyone." That would be an end to all the fun. "But I'm assuming you're being facetious."

"Yes, smart-ass."

"Speaking of ass, I haven't had a chance to see yours yet. Trina, all I've been thinking about all day is every last piece of clothing gone from your body and me touching you everywhere." They had reached his bed and he set the wineglass and bottle down on the dresser. Then he moved behind her and lifted her hair to kiss the back of her neck, taking the zipper down on her dress. "I hope you weren't planning to sleep tonight."

"That's right. 'Up All Night' is supposed to be your theme song, isn't it?"

Damn Jason and his stupid penis page. At least Trina was finding it entertaining. "It's a rock star thing."

"Is it a circus penis or a rock star penis? I think we need some clarification here."

"It's yours. That's what it is." He nudged it against her backside just to prove the point. He wanted to add that he was hers as well, all of him, but he didn't want to scare her off. He really wasn't sure what Trina wanted out of their relationship. She'd never really indicated on BootyBook how she felt about him. She had just said the sex was good. Plus the minor criticisms that still rubbed him the wrong way.

Now wasn't the time to talk, though. Later. When she was sleepy and relaxed, they could have that talk that they should have had a year ago.

He dropped his pants to the floor as she turned around to face him. Unbuttoning his shirt, he watched her undo the tie around her neck, slide her dress off her shoulders and down over her hips, exposing her body to him. Her bra and panties were flesh-colored and sheer. The bra was there for support, obviously, but the panties were pointless as far as he could tell. Both were so sheer that he could see everything. Every inch of flesh, from her dusky nipples to the rich curls between her thighs, it was all right there for him to visually devour. She was gorgeous and his tongue felt two sizes too big, his cock pushing painfully against his briefs.

"Wow," he said with a total lack of eloquence. "That is the sexiest bra and panties I've ever seen. I feel like I walked in on you behind a shower curtain or something."

"I was wearing a white dress," she said, as if that explained anything.

Because it didn't. Not to him. Why did wearing white mean your nipples had to show? He reached out and touched one, unable to resist, just going back and forth across the front of it with his fingertip. It tightened beneath his touch, and goose bumps rose on her flesh above her breasts.

"Other colors would show through my dress," she added.

Oh, that made sense. "Ah. I see. In fact, I see a lot." He couldn't stop staring at her. His eyes swept down past her belly button to the apex of her thighs, then back up to the full roundness of her breasts again. He couldn't help it—she was just so sexy. He was glad she hadn't shaved everything down south, leaving him a little strip he was looking forward to playing with.

Lifting her wineglass to her lips, he tilted it so she could drink. She did, her eyes dark, mysterious, smoldering above the rim. When she pulled her head slightly away to indicate she was finished, he went in for a kiss, the rich warm fruitiness of the wine transferring from her full lips to his. Damn, she tasted good, felt good. They kissed for what felt like forever, and while he enjoyed every intimate tease of their tongues, every press of their mouths, he was working hard to keep himself under control. She'd already had him on the edge when she had been sucking him, and every sigh she gave, every brush of her nipples over his chest, had him wound tighter and tighter.

Stepping back from her, he took off his unbuttoned shirt and undershirt, then pushed down his briefs. He remembered he was supposed to be romantic, so he picked up a lighter and lit the half dozen candles he had set up. Thank God he'd been smart enough to lay it all out in advance, because he was too befuddled by her near-nudity to think about wine or candles. There were condoms under the pillow as well, so he sat down on the edge of the bed next to the nightstand.

"Come here."

"This is very impressive, Drew," she said, glancing around as the candlelight danced over the walls and furniture of his small bedroom. "I feel a little embarrassed that I was perfectly willing to sleep with you last night without any of this. I should learn to hold out more."

"Now is not the time to hold out," he told her, most sincerely, as she moved between his legs, her hands on his shoulders. He dipped his tongue into her belly button before peeling her panties down, exposing that tantalizing soft strip of hair. "Though please feel free to find every man lacking in comparison to me."

She laughed softly. "I shouldn't be taking advantage of you this way."

He looked up at her, surprised. "What do you mean?"

"You clearly want to prove that you're a perfect ten, and I'm letting you pull out all the stops. But you had me at hello last night."

"I want to do this." How did he explain that she was special? That he'd spent a year kicking himself in the ass wishing he had put more thought into his relationship with her before he'd gotten drunk and fallen on her like a hungry lion. He couldn't change what he had done that morning he'd left. He couldn't make the last year disappear. But he could show her that he had matured and that he cared about her. That she was entitled to his pulling out a stop or two. "You deserve a little wine and a scented candle, Trina."

"And dinner and dancing and coffee and cookies."

"I'm not sure any of that is even enough," he told her frankly. "If I could figure out how to give you more, I would." He took down her panties. "Hey, here's an idea." She was standing in front of him, perfect position. Drew leaned forward and tilted his head so he could flick his tongue across her clit.

The sound she made was so satisfying, he dragged his tongue over her again, slower, harder, dipping inside her just to see what she would do. The humming of pleasure got louder, and her fingers came out to rest on his shoulders. He opened her to study the soft pink contours of her body, enjoying the privilege of intimacy. He wanted to breathe her scent in, absorb her, drag moisture from her body at the same time his tongue dragged out those sexy sounds of ecstasy.

"Oh," she said, nails tearing into his flesh, hips rocking forward. "This is… I think…"

When she didn't complete sentences he knew she was really getting into it. Trina was rarely speechless. Gripping her ass with both hands, he helped her thrust onto his tongue. She was already going to come, he could feel it in the tightening of her thighs, the increasing desperation of her cries. When she did, he reveled in the sound, the taste, the feel of her orgasm.

As her tense grip on him loosened, Drew pulled back and looked up past the beautiful swell of her breasts to her gorgeous face. Her eyes were wide and she was panting. "Good?" he asked.

She nodded. "Very good, thank you."

Still watching her, suddenly in awe of what he felt for her, he reached under his pillow and pulled out a condom.

"You thought of everything."

"I tried." He ripped the package open with his teeth and rolled the condom on. "Sit on my lap."

"Like this? Facing you?" She looked daunted by the idea.

"Yes. I promise to do all the hard work."

Trina laughed softly and gave him a smile that made him realize that he was absolutely 100 percent in love with her. That for years the bond of friendship had slowly and steadily grown stronger and deeper until it was love that was too large to be contained by a platonic relationship.

"You always were able to talk me into anything," she said. Putting her hands on his shoulders, she raised herself onto the bed, one knee on either side of him.

He held her firmly by the waist and guided her down onto his cock. "Oh, baby," he murmured, eyes drifting closed when she sank slowly, thighs spreading farther. "I love the way you feel."

"Agreed. And you do have good ideas. I guess that's why I'm so easily coerced."

"So I'm always right?" he asked, raising her up on him before driving her back down by her hips. Damn, that felt so good, so hot. So deep. Her breasts brushed against his chest, that sheer fabric tickling him. "Is that what you're saying?"

"Don't get carried away."

"Take your bra off. Please." He wanted to feel every inch of her flesh against his.

"Hold me so I don't fall."

"I have you. I'd never let you fall."

One-handed, she undid her bra as he slowed down the thrusts of her onto him so she could ditch the last scrap of clothing between them. The minute it was gone and her hand was back on his shoulder, he went hard, groaning at the tight, wet sensation of her wrapped around his cock, the slap of their skin loud in the dark room. The candle flickered next to them, casting shadows across Trina's creamy flesh. Her head was thrown back, hair spilling over her bare shoulders. She looked luscious and sexy as sin.

Suddenly her head snapped forward and she went silent, breath caught, before she let out a cry, her body pulsating on his cock. He felt a rush of warmth over him and feeling her pleasure, seeing it, sent him rushing into his own climax. Yeah. That was a fucking ten and he dared anyone to say otherwise.

Holy shit.

He rested his forehead against her shoulder for a second, dragging in deep breaths, his cock still shuddering a little from the aftershocks of intense pleasure.

"That was amazing," she said.

"I don't think it's my penis that's magnificent so much as it's us together that is magnificent," he said, his voice gruff, throat dry. "We bring out the best in each other."

"Lie back on the bed," she said, her expression mischievous. "Let's see what else I can bring out in you."

TRINA HAD NEVER thought of herself as the type who got aroused by musicians. She'd never been a groupie and the fact that Drew played the guitar had been just part of who he was, not the reason she'd sought him out as a companion. Now she understood the appeal a little better.

She was curled up on Drew's couch in her panties and a T-shirt she had borrowed from him, while he perched on the coffee table across from her in black briefs, strumming his guitar. They had brought their wineglasses with them and it was some ungodly hour of the night. Trina was sleepy and satisfied, yet she didn't want to close her eyes and have the night end. She wanted to savor every moment with Drew.

He was softly singing as he glanced down at his fingers, and she realized she hadn't heard him sing very often. When she'd gone to gigs he'd played, he'd been plugged into an amp, and he only sang backup vocals. His voice had been drowned out by the drums, guitar, and lead singer. But here, in his living room, candles still flickering, the guitar quiet and melancholy, she could clearly hear his throaty and emotional vocals. This was Drew stripped down, quite literally.

It was amazing and powerful. It gave her goose bumps and made her fall even deeper in love with him, to see the intimacy of him and his guitar. To know that he trusted her with what felt like a secret in a sense. She couldn't have told anyone what the lyrics were, what message the song was conveying, but she did know she was transfixed by him.

When the last note drifted away Trina tucked her feet under her butt and brushed her hair back off her eyes. "That was beautiful. I didn't realize how interesting your voice is."

"It isn't particularly. But my guitar feels like another arm. I can't imagine life without music."

She couldn't imagine life without Drew. How had she just let him drift so far away from her? If he did that again, she wasn't sure she could allow it. She was fairly certain she would go stalker-girl on him. The question was how to avoid all of that altogether, because she was pretty certain psycho didn't sit well on her. It was like a bad outfit that wouldn't fit. She'd be terrible at it. She was too ditzy to be manipulative enough to make a nonexistent relationship work.

"Play something just for me," she told him nonetheless. So much for not being a demanding chick who wants too much too soon.

"Just for you, huh?" He was plucking chords idly, the musical equivalent of doodling.

The window behind him was open and the warm night air was sending his curtain fluttering. The night was mostly silent, which was amazing. The city did sleep at 3:00 a.m., it seemed. For the most part.

"Yes, just for me."

He smiled at her. "This reminds me of you."

Katrina got fluttery girl feelings for a second. Until he started playing and she realized the lyrics were quite clear in that the girl in the song hated the guy. Like a lot. Like in a way that involved lots of swearing and throwing of things.

"Very funny," she told him. So it was possible to sing and grin at the same time. He was achieving it, clearly amused with his joke.

He cut off mid-song, laughing. "No?"

"No."

"Okay, how about this?" He started playing a soft,

quiet melody, and Katrina felt her smile fall off her face. It was beautiful.

"What is this?" she asked.

"'Sweet Thing' by Van Morrison," he said between verses, his fingers moving easily. "That's you. My sweet thing."

Oh, God. She felt a shiver roll across her body, from her head, to her vagina, on down to her toes. That was the single most delicious thing any man had ever said to her. "Okay, you win," she told him. "That's a ten. Maybe even a twelve."

He laughed, but then he started singing again and for a few minutes she lost herself in his voice, his eyes. The way he looked at her…it was almost as if he felt the same way she did.

When the song faded away and he asked, "Do you think I could talk you into losing those clothes one more time before we crash? I suddenly find myself with an erection." He shifted his guitar to show her.

Her answer was to lift his T-shirt off her head and toss it at him.

CHAPTER EIGHT

DREW SPENT SUNDAY at work in a post-sex haze. Customers were rude, he didn't give a shit. His coworker Sara shattered a martini glass all over the lemon wedges. No big deal. He whistled and helped her clean it up.

"You're in a good mood," she commented.

"Yep." That was an understatement. Waking up with Trina had been lazy and damn nice. Sure, she'd taken off by ten, saying she needed to work. But he had taken advantage of her sleep-deprived but sexually satisfied state of mind to extract a promise to see her again. They'd settled on Wednesday, his day off.

He figured it didn't make him look as desperate to see her as if he asked her out for Monday, and the weekend was just too damn long to wait. It was a good compromise.

The confidence of Sunday cracked a little on Monday when he didn't hear from her at all.

On Tuesday, while she did answer his texts, she seemed busy and frazzled, though she did suggest he pick their activity since Saturday had been all about her.

Which he thought was hilarious and ironic. It had been for him, too, no doubt on that.

But he was more than willing to take the opportunity to spend as much time as possible with her, so he told her he wanted to go to the Brooklyn Museum, which closed at six. That meant they had to meet at three at the latest, which meant he was basically guaranteed a twelve-hour date.

Nothing awful about that.

She came to his place, then they went from there.

"I can't believe I've never been to the museum," she said as they waited for the train.

It was hot again, the day humid and full of random odors Drew preferred not to think about too carefully. "I've been once, that's it."

"When I was in high school I thought coming to New York would be like this huge cultural awakening and then I got here and realized I was too busy to take advantage of everything the city has to offer. Except somehow I always managed to find time to go to a club." She made a face. "What a waste of time."

"Not if you had fun." Drew was having the handholding debate again. Why the hell was this so hard? He'd opened the door to Trina thinking about nothing but giving her a long and deep kiss, but she'd immediately brushed past him with a smile, nothing more.

So he'd let it ride and now he was debating handholding? For the love of all that was sexual, why was he being such a neurotic loser? Based on that pep talk, he leaned over and slid his hand into the back of her hair. "Kiss me."

"Right here? There are people here." Her eyes darted around nervously.

"There are always people here. It's a big city." He enjoyed the way her eyes widened, the way she always gave in to him. She was already leaning forward, though she didn't allow him to linger over her lips.

"We're those people we used to roll our eyes at. Sucking face on the subway platform." But she was smiling, looking amused.

"I don't think that qualified as sucking face. I can do that next if you'd like."

"No, I'm good for now." She rolled her eyes at him and stepped forward as the train stopped.

Trina was wearing another one of her endless sundresses. Drew thought if he opened her closet it would be nothing but sundresses in the brightest colors imaginable. This one showed cleavage and he dug that. It made him want to suck on the tops of her breasts.

But he restrained himself and he asked her about her business, to explain to him the nuts and bolts of it, as the train lurched forward. When they were undergrads, she had been full of nebulous ideas, and he wanted to hear now she had taken her ideas from conception to actual application. Trina thought of herself as a bit scatterbrained, but he didn't see it. As she chattered on and on, describing her average workday and her plans for expansion, he thought it was clear why she had gotten accepted to NYU with a merit scholarship.

He had been great at school, but he hadn't found his practical niche postgraduation. "You should be proud of how much you've done in such a short time," he told her, and they jogged up the stairs back out onto the street. "I'm damn proud of you."

"I get impatient," she admitted. "I want everything, you know, now. Which is why things like the Booty-Book incident happen. I'm moving too fast, trying to tear through my to-do list. Sometimes I just need to slow down."

"I'm the opposite. I'm always wandering around needing a fire lit under my ass." It was true. He was more of a thinker and dreamer than a doer. "And now my damn student loans need to be repaid." He gave her a grin. "Whoops."

"Don't act like you're lazy." She frowned at him. "That pisses me off."

"Pisses you off?" he asked, surprised. "Why?"

"Because you've been busting your butt with your songwriting and your band, writing new material, recording, booking gigs. It's not like you've been lying on your couch for the last two years."

She looked so adorable and indignant, he was touched and amused. "You haven't seen the band perform. You might change your mind when you do." Not that he thought they sucked, but hey, there was always room for improvement. But the look she gave him was so furious, her mouth dropping open, that he started laughing and retracted. "I'm kidding! Jeez. You look like you're going to kick my ass on my behalf, which is kind of ludicrous."

Katrina tried to smooth out her features, realizing he was right—she'd been about to rage on him. "Well, what can I say? I happen to think you're working hard and I don't like you talking smack about yourself."

She actually envied his easy style, his ability to work hard but not go into manic mode, the way she did. They really were a good complement for each other. Or so it seemed to her.

"Got it," he said, reaching for her hand. "No smack talk or you'll make me regret I was born."

That made her laugh. "I'm not sure that makes any sense, but maybe I don't make sense."

He gave her a look that made her breath catch in the back of her throat. "You make sense to me."

And with that, he liquefied her insides. It was a talent he had.

He also seemed intent on spoiling her. He insisted on buying their tickets to the museum since it was his idea. "I'm buying dinner then," she told him.

"The hell you are. But who said we're going to dinner?"

Oh God, had she assumed too much? "Uh…"

He winked at her.

Damn him. She punched his arm.

"Ow." He faked doubling over. "Don't hurt me, I promise to be good."

"Jerk."

"I'm not allowed to agree with you since you said I can't criticize myself."

"You're a word twister."

"I've been called worse."

"No, you haven't."

He shrugged. "Everyone has had an angry ex or two, right? Or a random crazy dude on the street screaming obscenities."

"Those don't count." Trina wandered next to him to the first exhibit. "But I might know a thing or two about angry exes." She was hoping the worst was behind her with the BootyBook fallout, but there was really no telling.

There was an Egyptian artifact in front of her, a statue of a cat. "What do you think people will say two thousand years from now when they find our leftovers?"

"They won't think anything because they won't be able to see it. Either the technology won't exist to view our current technology or the actual chips and hard drives will have eroded to the point they're useless. There will be nothing to tell people about who and what we were."

"That is a terrifying thought."

But Drew lifted her hand to his mouth and kissed the backs of her knuckles. "Why does it matter what happens a thousand years from now? I think today is enough to satisfy me."

That was one of the many things she liked about him. He was so easy, so calm. She smiled at him. "You're right. Yet here we are staring at this freaky-looking cat."

"Good point."

They strolled through the museum and talked for another hour and a half. It was interesting and entertaining to renew her friendship with him, even as sexual tension simmered below the surface all the time. But a year had matured them both, and she really liked what she was seeing and hearing. It was even better to be with him now than in the past, and she would never have expected that.

When they went to eat at a burger joint by Prospect Park, Drew talked about his music and she felt the passion she had always sensed from him, but there was a business savvy now that was new. She offered him some suggestions for how to get buzz for the band, and he was receptive and enthusiastic.

"I find the way your brain works fascinating," he told her. "Your thoughts move so rapidly, I can barely keep up."

"I think out loud. Stream-of-consciousness style." Trina put her hand on her stomach as they left the restaurant. "That was so good. I ate too much."

"Want to walk in the park?" He took her hand again, and again, it amazed her how natural that felt. "It's the Central Park of Brooklyn," he added with a goofy expression.

She laughed. "Is that the official slogan?"

"Actually, I think it is. But it's cooling down and it is, you know, leafy there, so it might be a refreshing place to take a walk."

Trina was amused. "So we stroll around the park for an hour, then take the subway back to Williamsburg? Why don't we just walk to Williamsburg?"

"Because that would be insane." Drew paused on the corner while they waited for a light change and leaned in to give her a kiss.

Every time he did, it still caught her off guard. It made her shiver, even in the sweltering heat.

"You coming home with me?" he murmured. "After the park."

She liked that he seemed to understand she needed reassurance or a guide as to what they were doing. As far as she was concerned, they could skip the walk. "Yes, for a while. I do have to get up in the morning since I cut short my workday today."

"Then let's kill the park idea and go back now."

His eyes had darkened and Katrina knew that look. Her inner thighs recognized it as well.

"We could do that."

Then he surprised her by turning to the curb and sticking his hand up. "Taxi! And turn your phone off. You're not taking any calls, texts, IMs, PMs, tweets, emails, or alerts."

Katrina laughed. "Fine. I can do that."

Twenty minutes later they were back at Drew's, and for some bizarre reason she felt awkward following him into his apartment. They'd been here before, had done this now more than once, and yet walking through the door she still got a tingle in her vag that seemed to permeate her entire body and make her incapable of not acting like an idiot. The minute sex was on the table she felt a shivery anticipation that made her twitchy. But she wanted to take the lead this time, to show Drew that she wasn't just along for the ride, expecting him to entertain her both in bed and out.

So when he paused to open the window in his living room, she came up behind him and wrapped her arms around his middle and playfully bit his shoulder.

"Hey." He tried to glance back at her, his hands coming up to wrap over hers. "What was that for?"

"I just wanted to taste you," she said.

"You can do that better with my shirt off."

"Good point." Katrina took that as an invitation. She took the hem of his shirt and pulled it up over his chest. He helped her by lifting his arms, and on tiptoes she took it up over his head.

Then she took her time exploring his abdomen muscles, his chest, shoulder, running her fingers lightly over his flesh, while she moved slowly around the side of him. She repeated her tiny bite but followed this one up with a kiss as she trailed her tongue across his collarbone. She kissed his neck and ran her lips across the stubble of his beard growth before covering his mouth with her own. She would never get tired of kissing him, of the way their mouths molded perfectly together.

Some men kissed with loose lips, but Drew always found that sweet spot between too much and not enough pressure. They were a perfect fit, and she wrapped her arms around his neck and tried to express what she was feeling with her touch. Making out was something she didn't do very often anymore and as they stood there, kissing with moist lips and hot breath, she wondered why. It was amazing how just that contact, face to face, mouth to mouth, could feel so intimate and draw out such heightened awareness of her whole body. Her nipples tightened and her inner thighs ached. As they teased each other with their tongues, she wanted to shift her leg, to grind against him, to mimic sex, but she resisted.

His hand had gathered the fabric of her dress at her waist. He made a sound of impatience, then reached down to cup her ass. "Sometimes these dresses you wear make life difficult," he murmured, nuzzling into her neck.

He had managed to completely draw the skirt up and lay his hands on her panties. She shot him an amused look of disbelief. "I'm not sure how, since your hand is now under it. Looks to me like it saved you a step."

"You're right. I'm sorry, am I being too forward?" He winked at her.

"Yes. I'm not that type of girl." It was hard to say with a straight face but she managed it, giving him a sweet kiss. Then she stroked across the front of his jeans. "I'm *this* type of girl."

His eyes narrowed and he gave a low groan. "I happen to like that type of girl."

"Good." Katrina gave him a sly smile. "Show me your room."

"I do have a cool record collection."

"I can't wait to see it."

He took her by the hand and down the short hall. Katrina's nerves had evaporated. Kissing Drew was so natural, despite the fact that their relationship had been a platonic friendship until the night of vodka. While the idea of having sex still made her feel unsure of herself, kissing had the opposite effect. It calmed her. In the doorway of his room, she reached up and cupped his cheeks, wishing she had the balls to tell him that she loved him, as a friend and as a man. But she didn't. She would just have to try to show him.

She gave him a soft kiss, then stepped back and took her dress off over her head. "Come lay down with me." She wanted to feel her skin on his, explore his body slowly, touch all his hardness.

He climbed on the bed behind her and they lay down facing each other. Drew had shucked his jeans quickly and they were a tangle of warm limbs, his hands brushing over her back, her ass, her waist. They kissed again and again until they were both breathing heavily and Katrina was shifting restlessly, distracted by the liquid heat between her thighs. Distracted by how easily Drew could arouse her.

"You're so beautiful," he murmured as they broke apart.

His stare was so intent that she felt something shift inside her, something she didn't understand. Something that felt important. "I…"

She wasn't even sure what she was going to say. There weren't really any words to describe the fullness in her heart. So instead she shifted her thigh over his.

In seconds he had her panties down her legs.

When he pushed inside her, his mouth covered hers and she felt every stroke inside her, every sweep of his tongue, in all its intimate intensity. Her fingers gripped his shoulders as she arched her back to take him deeper. It felt right.

And when he thrust her against him to meet his rhythm, she came in an easy and languid orgasm.

"I like your room," she told him.

"You haven't even seen the best parts."

Oh, yeah.

AN HOUR LATER Drew stared down at Trina, breathing hard, hot but satisfied. He didn't want her to go home. It would be a few days, maybe even a week before he saw her again and he wanted to be selfish and keep her there. Her cheeks were pink as she stared up at him, panting, lips swollen from his kisses.

"Oh, my," she said.

"I know, right?" He nuzzled her ear. "I could do that again."

"Yeah?"

"Definitely. But only if you promise to spend the night."

"Drew..."

The way she spoke his name, drew it out on a sigh, he knew it wouldn't take much coaxing to get her to stay.

"Please." He kissed one corner of her mouth. "Stay." He kissed the opposite corner. "With me." He kissed her directly on the lips, his hand sliding over her thigh.

"You don't play fair."

"I play to win." While Drew stroked over her clit with his thumb, causing her to shiver, he used his other hand to dispose of the condom. It pleased him how quick Trina was to respond to him.

She had just had an orgasm not five minutes earlier yet she was already lifting her hips toward him, eyes rolling back.

"I have more cookies for you."

"You got me more cookies?" Her eyes widened. "Oh...oh, yes."

He wasn't sure if that was for the cookies or for his finger dipping inside her, but either way, he enjoyed the look on her face and the delicious sounds she was making.

So much so that he reached for another condom.

A minute later, he was replacing his finger with his cock and stroking them both to a loud and satisfying ending.

DREW SIPPED HIS coffee as he leaned his back against the kitchen cabinets, and watched Trina eat her cookie slowly and enthusiastically, making little sounds of appreciation the whole time.

"This is so good. It's an orgasm in my mouth."

"I'd like to experience an orgasm in your mouth," he told her.

She rolled her eyes, but there was no bite to the gesture. She looked happy, rumpled, sleepy. She was wearing his shirt and leaning over the kitchen counter across from him so that he could just see a glimpse of her sexy little butt peeking out from under the hemline. He couldn't believe he was even awake before noon. They'd been up until four and he'd been damn grateful for all the hours he'd been spending in the gym. Muscle strength and stamina had been quite helpful in their entertainment.

But despite finally falling asleep so late, he had snapped awake at nine. Trina had heard him reach for a glass of water and she had given him the cutest smile ever, so he'd felt compelled to cuddle and kiss her repeatedly. It was only now that he remembered he was supposed to be making sure his cuddling was per Trina's BootyBook standards.

He no longer cared about that. It felt natural to cuddle her, so he had. She hadn't seemed to find any fault with it, either. Then he'd made them coffee and even though he had offered to make her some eggs, she said she was good with the cookies.

"What are you doing today?" he asked.

It was the wrong thing to ask. Immediately she pulled a face. "I need to work for a couple hours at least. How about you?"

"I have to work at the bar tonight." Reality. It sucked. He really wanted to spend another three or four days easily hiding in his apartment with Trina. "Do you want to take a shower?"

But she sighed. "I should probably just go home and shower there."

"Sure. Of course. No rush, you know."

"I'm done with my coffee. Guess I should go be responsible." She yawned and padded out of the kitchen and back into his room. He stood there in his underwear, holding his mug and feeling suddenly morose. The sucky thing about a great night was that it had to end at some point.

Especially when she came back out dressed, her phone in her hand. He could hear it buzzing over and over as texts and emails and notifications rolled in. She was frowning. He felt deflated.

"Everyone wants a piece of you, huh?"

She sighed and looked up at him. "Apparently."

He wasn't going to ask her again to delete the multitude of douchebags she seemed to communicate with. He'd already mentioned it twice. Now he would just look pathetic. She'd also laughed but hadn't really ever let him see the texts or draft replies as they had discussed.

"I hope it's nothing important."

"I guess I'll find out." She gave him an absent-minded smile. "I should head out."

He put his coffee down. "Let me get dressed and I'll walk you to the subway."

"You don't have to do that. You've already been amazing."

She was dismissing him. He felt it hanging between them. She wanted out of there, away from him. She was done for the day, night.

Regardless, he pursued it, keeping his voice casual. "It's no big deal. I could use the walk to wake up a little better."

But she was shaking her head. "Don't worry about it." She leaned over and kissed him, cupping his cheek.

Drew covered her hand with his. "Text me when you get home."

"Okay. Have a good afternoon." She smiled at him.

Then she left and he was standing in his underwear in his stuffy apartment, the remnants of an amazing night scattered all around him with the dirty wineglasses, her half-eaten cookie, and the nubs of the burned candles.

He suddenly had a bad feeling that he wasn't getting a perfect score as she studiously entered her data into BootyBook on the ride home.

Hell if he knew what he'd done wrong.

KATRINA PUT HER hands to her cheeks to feel how flushed they were as she waited for the train. God, what was wrong with her? She'd barely been able to look Drew in the eye after what was undeniably the best date of her life. But then he had been looking at her and she'd thought he would want his apartment back and his day to himself and so she'd gone to get dressed.

Turning on her phone had been like a bucket of cold water tossed in her face. She'd only had a few work emails, and she set social media posts up in advance so she hadn't compromised her business by going radio silent. It hadn't even been the many stupid and charmless attempts at flirtation from various guys who had been made aware of her again by her BootyBook flub.

It had been the realization that overnight a dozen women had liked Drew's Magnificent Penis Page. Most had made comments too, and indicated that they either had personal experience with his penis or would like to. Just like that, Katrina felt insecure and wondered what was really going on. Had Drew really been celibate as he'd said? For a guy who hadn't been having sex, he didn't exactly seem out of practice.

Nor had he said one word to her about her online confession that sex was better with someone you loved. Not once had that come up in their conversations. Why wouldn't he ask what she had meant by that? Or did he not care? Was the whole thing just a way to hone his skills of seduction?

She didn't believe that. Couldn't believe that.

Yet she hadn't been able to prevent herself from bolting exactly the way she'd said she wouldn't, and the very same way he had a year earlier. Well, she had said goodbye, which he hadn't done, but still, she was acting completely insane and she needed an intervention.

She called Samantha.

"Oh, my God, why are you calling me this early? Did sex blow?"

"No. It was amazing." She tried to speak softly but as the train roared down the platform and screeched to a stop, it was impossible. "It was mind-blowing. Mind-blowing sex."

The guy next to her glanced her way. Maybe she had spoken a little too loudly. But it wasn't as though she'd given him a walk-through of oral sex with Drew, so he could just mind his own damn business. Which was yet one more step in her complete morning overreaction.

"I don't know why I feel upset, Sam. Why do I feel upset? I mean, Drew was like rock god meets Romeo meets porn star and yet I feel like I'm having a heart attack. Like I'm literally having a heart attack." Katrina had heard people describe a panic attack and she was thinking this had to be what they felt like. She was clammy, her breathing shallow, and she was wringing her free hand in her dress skirt.

"Okay, calm the fuck down. What happened here that is bad?"

"I had always had a crush on Drew. I have always cared about him. But last night, I fell in love with him." That was it. She had fallen completely and irrevocably in love with Drew Jordan.

Everyone around her was on the train and the doors were already closing and she was standing there, stunned. "I'm in love with Drew."

"Okay." Samantha sounded puzzled. "So why is that a bad thing? Did you tell him that? Did he tell you to suck it or something?"

"No. I didn't tell him." The thought renewed the heart attack fear. "I sort of did already. I had that comment in my BootyBook post."

"That wasn't a confession of love," Samantha scoffed. "That was post sex gushing. Everyone knows the difference. He didn't take it seriously, I'm sure of it."

"So what am I supposed to do?"

"Um, tell him. Hello."

"But..."

What the hell was wrong with her? Was she such a complete and total wimp that she couldn't be honest with Drew?

There was nothing to lose. A week ago they hadn't been speaking.

If she said nothing, chances were high they would repeat what had happened last time, if on a less dramatic scale. There wouldn't be a fight but they would simply drift apart, stop communicating.

"How do I tell him?"

"You open your mouth and say 'I love you, Drew.'"

Katrina said nothing, chewing her lip.

"No? Well, you could use social media. You could post on his wall or his penis page. Or you could send a text."

"Send a text. You are suggesting I tell a man I love him for the first time via text."

"No, I'm suggesting you tell him in person. You're the one who's being too chickenshit to do it."

Nice.

"Fine." Katrina impatiently waited for another train since she'd missed hers. She needed a shower and a change of clothes, then she was going to do this thing, damn it.

CHAPTER NINE

"YOU COULD JUST put that you're in a relationship with her. She has to confirm it before it goes live. So if she does, you're golden. If she ignores it, you know where you stand."

Drew looked at Jason and wondered how he could possibly say anything like that with a straight face. "What are we, fifteen?"

"You're kind of acting like it." Jason reached over and plucked a fry off his plate. "And you're off your feed. That smacks of unrequited love to me."

"Thanks for the support, dick." Drew's chest hurt. He rubbed it. "I don't know what else to do. I mean, I had all the right moves, I thought. What do women want?"

"That is a mystery." Jason stole another fry. "What was she doing when she left? Did she look upset?"

"She was checking her phone."

"Bingo. Someone said something or did something."

"Well, that's helpful." Drew rolled his eyes and sat back in his chair. His burger looked disgusting. He really wasn't hungry at all.

"At least you know it wasn't anything you did. That's my point." Jason licked his fingers.

"Gross. Use a napkin."

"I suppose I should take the penis page down."

"Why?" Drew couldn't care less one way or the other and it wasn't like Justin to abandon a joke.

"Chicks are posting some suggestive stuff on it. I can't imagine Trina is digging that."

"No, I guess not." Or maybe she didn't care at all.

He was in love with her and she didn't care.

Fabulous. He picked up a fry, bit it, and discarded it.

KATRINA HAD TEXTED Drew, which was something of a cop-out, but she wanted to see him. So she very maturely told him she'd forgotten her bra at his place, which she hadn't.

When she got to his apartment, sweaty and agitated, he opened the door wearing his kilt. He was ready for work. Which meant she had about ten minutes if she was lucky to open her mouth and spill her guts out onto his carpet.

"Hi." He gestured for her to come in. "I'm sorry, I don't see your bra anywhere."

"I didn't actually forget it," she said, sheepishly. "I came back because I never say what I mean and I want to say what I mean even though I'm terrified of what you'll say when you hear what I have to say."

He looked utterly mystified, which anyone would after that ridiculous speech. "Okay."

"When I wrote on my BootyBook entry that sex with you was better because I was in love with you, I meant it."

"What do you mean?" He stood there, the door still partially open behind him.

"What do you mean, what do I mean?" Now she was mystified. How could he not understand that?

"I never saw that. Where did you write that?"

"In the entry log. I thought you saw it and it freaked you out or maybe you thought I didn't mean it. I do mean it."

"I never saw that. But you're saying…"

"I love you! That's what I'm saying." Jeez freaking Louise. This was harder than she'd even imagined.

But his face cleared. "Really? Like for real love?"

"I'm not faking it, if that's what you mean." Her whole body felt flushed.

"Oh. I had no idea you were going to say that." Then suddenly his face split into a grin. "I love you, too. I have, you know, for a very long time."

Thank God. Relief surged through her, followed by elation. "No, I didn't know that." Then she couldn't help but ask, "For real?"

"For real." Drew stepped forward and took her face between his hands. "Trina, I want to be with you. I am sorry for the way I left last time."

"I'm sorry for the way I left this morning. But I saw all these notifications and I wasn't sure what you were thinking…. I didn't know if I was an experiment or what." It sounded dumb saying it out loud, but dating was so damn complicated and every guy seemed to use double-talk and having everything online was just a total nightmare for a woman as in love with a man as she was with Drew.

"No experiment. It was just me trying to show you that I've matured. That I care about you. That I want a real relationship, built on friendship and love. With *you*."

Well. Okay, then. She couldn't prevent a smile from spreading. "Excellent."

He kissed her softly. “So this is a real relationship. We’re going the distance.”

She kissed him back, wrapping her arms around his neck. “I’m deleting BootyBook immediately.”

“Thank God. And I’ll make Justin take the penis page down.”

“Perfect.”

It was. Everything was perfect.

* * * * *

Award-winning author **HelenKay Dimon** spent twelve years in the most unromantic career ever—divorce lawyer. After dedicating all of that effort to helping people terminate relationships, she is thrilled to deal in happy endings and write romance novels for a living. Her books have been featured in *Cosmopolitan* magazine and E! Online. HelenKay loves hearing from readers, so stop by her website at helenkaydimon.com and say hello.

EVERYTHING YOU NEED TO KNOW

HelenKay Dimon

For my beautiful, smart and fierce niece,
Jennifer.

Welcome to the working world.
This one's for you!

CHAPTER ONE

Subject Report on Ryan Peterson: Spent entire date talking about Ryan—yes, he refers to himself in the third person. When he drove me home and I refused to sleep with him on the first date, he urinated on my front porch. Run from this blowhard. —Member 121

Need to Know admin staff: Confirmed blowhard.

JORDAN MCADAM LOOKED across the conference-room table at Ryan Peterson and fought the urge to roll her eyes. An "oh my God, shut up!" comment begged to escape her lips whenever he opened his mouth, which was every ten seconds.

The guy's personality consisted of being pompous, loud and loaded. That last one appeared to be his only positive attribute. Not to Jordan. No, she'd dated enough powerful Washington, D.C., types to place the entire metro area in dating lockdown. She'd limit her choices to a pool of males from at least two states away from now on.

Day Four in Ryan's presence. She'd confirmed the major complaints about him by the end of the first afternoon, but had yet to find one redeeming quality to include in the follow-up report for her website. When she'd started Need to Know, she'd known the dating world could be physically and emotionally dangerous for women. She never dreamed it resembled an apocalyptic wasteland populated with guys in business suits who possessed zero social skills when it came to handling strong women.

After reading the comments website members had posted about their dates, Jordan no longer worried about her relatively solitary existence. If her choices came down to Ryan, or that guy Ted who one member said spent most dates sending hate texts to his ex, or if she had to pick any of Ryan's or Ted's businessmen friends, she'd continue to limit her bedroom activities to Mr. Fancy, her bright purple vibrator.

Ryan leaned back in his chair and tapped his gold pen against the lined legal pad in front of him. When he exhaled, his stomach relaxed, pushing over the top of his black belt, which was never a good look on a man, money or not, and certainly not on a thirty-something. "The meeting this afternoon is important."

As if she cared. She'd taken the temp job to double-check the website reports on Ryan, since they seemed so out there for a grown man. "Yes, sir."

"I need to make a good impression." He made the comment while he coughed without covering his mouth. "Nothing can go wrong."

As far as she could tell, the only chance for success hinged on Ryan skipping it. "I understand."

The rumors racing through the employee cubicles over the past few days hinted at management problems. Something about a silent partner wanting out and money being tight, despite Ryan's bright red might-as-well-advertise-you-have-a-small-penis convertible parked in the coveted space right by the elevator in the downstairs garage. Then there was the expensive office suite on K Street, D.C's power-broker row.

Ryan sure did like to play the game.

He spun his chair around and stared out the eleventh-floor window to the busy street below. "You'll need to stay late this evening. Ryan needs this deal done."

There was the third-person thing again. In her view, *Ryan* needed medication. And a reality check…and maybe a few hours with a financial planner before he dragged his daddy's once-successful construction firm into bankruptcy. "Of course, sir."

Ryan grinned at her over his shoulder. "Maybe you can find us some dinner."

Right, because that was within her job description as a temporary office assistant. No wonder his regular administrative assistant quit two weeks ago. From what Jordan could ferret out during coffee in the office kitchenette, the woman, Victoria something, ran from the building after being asked to send yet another morning-after "we're over" email to a woman Ryan managed to date more than one time.

The guy was a raging dick, but Jordan had to deal with him only through the end of the day. He'd asked her to remain on next week. She'd lied and said she had another temp job lined up.

"I can order something for you to eat." As in, for him only, or him and the two businessmen who were due any minute. She'd rather choke up stomach lining than sit across a table and listen to Ryan talk about Ryan. Because, really, how sad was that little act?

The low rumble of voices in the small reception area outside the conference room and near her desk grabbed her attention. Anything not to look at Ryan another minute.

She moved closer to the doorway and glanced out. There, by the love seat and looming over the bad-bachelor glass coffee table and the stack of six-month-old magazines, were two men in matching dark suits. The black-haired, broad-shouldered one with his back to her suddenly turned around and met her stare for stare.

She didn't need a member's report from the Need to Know website or a business degree to identify him. Forest Redder, millionaire businessman and commercial real-estate powerhouse...whatever that was...and an integral part of every business and political power circle in town. Objectively good looking, all six-foot-whatever of him but—thanks to the rich-boy effect—not her thing.

The blond with him, Wendell Strong—Wen to everyone who knew him—had a could-sell-yachts-to-the-poor smile. That was even less her thing.

After seeing the names on Ryan's schedule that morning she'd done some investigating on both men. Their friendship stretched back through private schools and country clubs and wherever else rich people congregated. Neither man's name had made it onto her website yet, but being two of the city's most eligible bachelors in their thirties, reports and requests for information from the Need to Know community were inevitable.

Her goal for one year in business was a thousand active members paying monthly dues and, in return, getting the dating information they needed. She had eight months to go and with or without those two on the website, she was almost halfway to her membership goal.

She stepped into the reception area and closed the conference-room door behind her. "Gentlemen, may I help you?"

"We're here for a meeting with Ryan Peterson." Forest didn't break into a smile or even move. "Do you know where I can find him?"

Something about the commanding tone and presence made her feel as put together as an unmade bed. She tugged down on her pencil skirt, then stopped, because letting this guy throw her off stride was just not going to happen.

"Mr. Peterson needs a few more minutes." She had no idea if that was true, but she doubted this Forest guy had to wait for much, so she thought experiencing a little delay would be good for him.

"Are you his assistant?" His gaze dipped down and traveled over her for the briefest flash.

The last time she fell for a look like that, she ended up dating a guy who was about to get married. Not to her—not that she knew that going in. Funny how he'd forgotten to mention the fiancée and expensive wedding, complete with pre-nup and newspaper notice. Thank goodness her friend and web assistant, Elle Parker, saw that little gem or Jordan might still be the unwitting other woman to an idiot who deserved a nasty case of bedbugs.

"I'm just the temp." She stepped farther into the reception area. Next came the awkward gesture in the general direction of the floor lamp. “Have a seat.”

“We’ll stand.”

Of course they would. Heaven forbid this Forest guy do anything to stop the circus show dancing around in her stomach. “You’re early.”

Forest glanced at his watch. His eyebrow lifted a second later.

Yeah, that wasn’t annoying or anything. “Right. Well, if you’ll excuse me a second…”

Before he said anything else, she bolted back into the conference room. Ryan sat in his big black leather chair, spinning the seat back and forth like a spoiled child. No wonder the business his family had built for decades had been flushed into a downturn only two years after Ryan took over the reins.

“Your appointment is here.”

He waved a hand at her. “Send them in.”

She turned around when he started the tie straightening and hair combing with his fingers. Pulling the door open again, she peeked into the reception area and saw Wen and Forest. They hadn’t moved at all. No talking. No shifting. They just stood there staring at her. Wen also smiled, but Forest skipped over that part.

“Mr. Peterson can see you now.” She stepped back and gestured for them to step inside the conference room.

Wen gave her a nod as he passed. He really did have the six-foot all-American-boy thing down. She could imagine him in khakis on a polo field as his two perfect blond-haired children ran by.

Then Forest slipped past her. His shoulder brushed against hers and the fresh scent of soap fell over her senses.

He had the cleaned-up-businessman look, but underneath she sensed something rougher. Something not so proper.

Now that *was* her thing and the surprise kick of interest did not make her happy at all.

"Excuse me." His bright-eyed gaze drilled into her as he walked by.

At five-eight, she was hardly ever in a situation where men towered over her, but he did. All firm and lean and…

"Ms. McAdam?"

Something about Ryan's smarmy tone and stupid smirk sucked all the sexuality right out of her. She could feel her body dry up with every syllable he uttered.

She plastered a smile on her face and swallowed back the icky taste that filled her mouth whenever she glanced in Ryan's general direction. "Yes, sir?"

"Join us and take notes."

Wen waved her off. "I'm not sure that's necessary."

Jordan took that to mean this meeting was not exactly going to go as Ryan hoped. That almost made her want to stick around. "I can wait outside, and if you need me—"

"I want her to stay," Ryan said, as he looked at the other gentlemen. "I'm sure neither one of you will have a problem with that."

Never mind that she did.

"Fine." Forest delivered his command and sat in the seat directly across from Ryan. "For now."

Looked as if she could add *bossy* and *demanding* to the list of characteristics she silently compiled about this Forest guy. Usually the gruff, commanding type turned her off, but there was something about him. Something half annoying and potentially half interesting. She didn't intend to investigate either half any further.

Ryan nodded to the chair to his right and she dropped onto it. His smile stayed in place as he slid a pad of paper over to her. She started taking notes, even wrote out a nice header and remembered the date. Then she had to fight off the urge to doodle.

"We have a problem," Forest said as Wen joined him on that side of the table.

Ryan nodded as he leaned back in his chair, trying to give off a sense of security and failing badly when the sweat collected on his forehead. "I understood you had all the information you needed to move forward with our partnership on the new waterfront deal."

Jordan's head popped up. She listened, because information was her real business. She didn't care about dictating or notes or commercial real estate, but anything that brought money into D.C. connected to power and politics. If new players moved in, she needed to know them and be prepared to see their names appear on her website.

After Forest nodded, Wen started talking. "We thought we owed you an in-person meeting, mostly because of our historic relationship with your father and this firm."

"A very positive relationship." Ryan sat up again. "One I intend to continue."

Forest cleared his throat and all movement in the room stopped. The clock ticked on the wall behind Jordan, but she didn't dare turn around and glance at it. Not when every inch of Forest, from his straight back to the slow way he moved his fingertips across the tabletop, commanded attention.

"And therein lies the problem," he said.

Therein? Jordan knew that wasn't a good sign. Whenever the "'twas" and "furthermore" comments came out, all hell was about to break loose.

Ryan must have figured that out, as well, because the skin around his mouth tightened and the sweat raced out of him now. "What do you mean?"

"You are not your father." Forest put a beat of air between each word.

And that certainly stopped the collective breath of the room. Her pen dropped against the pad with a soft thud. The tick in Forest's jaw mesmerized her. So did his long, lean fingers and the way he braced them on the table in front of him.

Wen took a white envelope out of his inside jacket pocket and slid it across the table to Ryan. "The financial audit raised some concerns."

Ryan glanced at it, then at her, then back to Forest. "Clearly, we've all experienced some negative cash-flow problems over the last few years in this financial market."

Forest didn't even blink. "I haven't."

As far as comebacks went, Jordan thought that was a pretty good one. As someone who got laid off from her job when the financial world went wacky and the large law firm she worked for—the same one that everyone said could *never* go under—broke apart then shut its doors, she had some empathy for job loss and rough times.

But she'd picked herself back up again. Worked exactly three days at a department-store fragrance counter until she accidentally sprayed a wealthy regular customer in the face with some rancid-smelling perfume. Yeah, it had nothing to do with the lady directing Jordan to clean up after her little yapping dog who'd pooped in front of the luxury-night-cream display.

But now Jordan had Need to Know. She'd come up with the idea and made it happen. As fast as she'd predicted, it was making money and she was determined to keep it that way.

"I don't understand what you're saying." Ryan swallowed hard enough to make his throat bobble. "I thought we had a deal."

"We said we might be able to make a deal work and enter into a contract, pending an audit and other reviews of your management style and compatibility with our structure."

Jordan was pretty impressed with Forest's statement. He'd managed to use all those words and barely say anything. The man could be a lawyer. Then she remembered that was one of his degrees. Score one for overeducated people everywhere.

Forest pushed up to his feet and Wen joined him. "I don't see a partnership happening."

"Wait... I..." Ryan's sputtering continued for a good thirty seconds. "What other reviews about me?"

Oh, Jordan could think of some. No fewer than four women had filed reports on Ryan and not one of them had a decent thing to say about the spoiled-kid-turned-businessman. Thanks to his father's heart attack, he sat in the Big Boy office chair, but it was clear the company's management staff was pressuring the family to put someone else in charge, which was why Ryan needed this deal. Which also explained why his face had turned an odd shade of purple.

Instead of answering, Forest turned to her. “Maybe now would be a good time for you to leave us.”

Fine with her. She had a date with a glass of wine and a pair of pink fluffy slippers. Her plan was to grab the few things off her desk and keep walking until she hit the metro. “Of course.”

Ryan stood with a jerk, and his chair crashed to the floor. “She doesn’t work for you.”

She actually didn’t work for anyone but herself, and that’s just the way she liked it. No strings. No crappy boss.

Forest slowly turned to face Ryan. “I doubt you want a temp hearing the rest of this conversation.”

With that, the air visibly rushed out of Ryan’s chest and he leaned hard into the table. “Right.”

That was her cue to take off and she was grateful. Without another word, she headed for the door. She hesitated when her fingers touched the knob. A quick glance over her shoulder clued her into the reason for the tickling sensation at the back of her neck. Wen and Ryan talked in hushed tones with bowed heads. But not Forest. Nope, he stared right at her. Green eyes, dark look and concentrated focus.

Her hand shook as she fumbled with the door. There were few certainties in life, but she knew without any doubt that Forest Redder could mess up her plans. She ran out before that could happen.

CHAPTER TWO

Subject Report on Cam Matthews: When check came, he said dinner was on me. Then he said, "that's real equality for you." —Member 14

Need to Know admin staff: Confirmed payment.

FOREST CLAMPED HIS back teeth together to keep from shouting. He still thought about making a lunge for the keys jangling in Wen's hand. After the messed-up excuse for a meeting with Ryan that lasted forty-five minutes longer than planned, Forest's patience had expired.

He'd voted for delivering the bad news via conference call. Wen was the one who'd insisted they visit Ryan in person. As far as Forest was concerned, that meant Wen was solely to blame for the wasted work time and having to listen to a grown man swear, grovel and cry. The last part made Forest's head pound. It also got him up and out of the conference-room chair in about two seconds. He didn't need to be a part of that sort of nonsense.

He and Wen made it off the elevator and halfway to the guest spot in the underground parking garage before Wen started talking again. "That went well."

Leave it to Wen to try to find the positive in a heaping pile of negative. "Not for Peterson."

"I meant for us."

"Then, yes." But Forest wasn't convinced that was true, either. Now they had to double back and restart the process with a new construction team. He wanted the project moving. The preparation meetings were pissing him off.

Their shoes clicked against the pavement as they snaked through the lines of parked cars. The steady beat echoed around them. Forest tried to concentrate on the hammering, but the face of Ryan's temp kept edging into his mind. He'd caught only her last name—McAdam.

Not that he cared.

Sure, the long wavy brunette hair was hot. The slim skirt and pink shirt that skimmed her body all worked for him. And the face, round and pretty with big brown eyes… Okay, maybe he cared a little, but no way was he making a play for her.

He'd have to know her name. He could find it out easily enough. A few well-placed questions and a call or two to temp agencies would do it. But he vowed to let it go. Last thing he needed was a fling with a woman who made a living working in offices where he might have business meetings. That promised a bunch of awkward post-sex conversations.

No thanks. He'd settle for some heavy-duty sex fantasies about those spiky high heels and what she hid under that black skirt instead, then move on.

Wen stopped at the driver's side of his sleek two-seater. "Word is, without our business, Ryan could be out of his own firm."

A topic that didn't involve Ms. McAdam's long legs or high, round breasts. Yeah, Forest could handle this. "Last I checked we weren't a charity."

"He might have bigger troubles anyway." Wen clicked a button and the locks chirped.

"Such as?" Forest got in, checking his cell and barely listening as he mentally planned the rest of his day. A quick dinner, then back to the office to plow through the stack of paperwork on the corner of his desk.

"Need to Know."

It took a second for Forest to realize his second in command had gotten into the car and stopped talking. He hadn't bothered to turn on the engine. He just sat with one hand balanced on the wheel and stared.

Forest stared back. "Excuse me?"

"Need to Know."

Forest wondered exactly how many minutes of conversation he missed while unlocking his cell. "Repetition isn't helping."

"The website."

The last threads holding Forest's patience ripped apart. He turned in his seat and sent Wen a get-to-it-now scowl. "What the hell are you talking about?"

"Didn't you hear the guys at the club talking?"

His least-favorite place. Forest didn't fit in with the "in" crowd and he was more than fine with that. "I go there for business lunches because I have to. The rest is pure bullshit and not how I ever want to spend a day."

Wen smiled as he put the key in the ignition and the sports car roared to life. "Because you suck at golf."

Something else that didn't bother Forest. "I wear that as a badge of honor."

"Anyway, it's a website." Wen put the car in gear and eased out of the spot.

At this point in the post-meeting process Forest usually dove into his work emails or his schedule. Small talk during car rides was one of the many things he had no interest in. Just like golf and charity events and Monday holidays.

But Wen acted like whatever he was saying mattered, so Forest didn't turn off his attention just yet. "What is?"

"Need to Know. Stop frowning at me and take a look." Wen slipped his cell out of his suit pocket, hit a button and handed it over.

"You're showing me a member-login screen."

"For an anonymous site where women post information on their dates with D.C.'s business and political elite."

Now, that sounded a bit more interesting than anything Forest had heard today. He rested his cell on his thigh and reached for Wen's. Forest tried the site's home link and contact screen. It all struck him as some big puzzle that led nowhere. "You can't access it without signing in."

"But word is getting around. Some of our business associates are being named on it, and not in flattering ways."

"It sounds like tattling, more in line with something a preteen girl would do than an adult woman." Forest glanced up and realized the car hadn't moved. They sat idling in the middle of a lane, a good thirty feet from the security gate at the parking exit. "Drive."

"You're not getting this."

Not for lack of trying. He used his own phone to search for information about the site while he poked around, but after a quick check he couldn't track it back to a name. "Enlighten me."

"The women have to be approved for membership. They're vetted and then once online they post about their dates, rate the sex, even comment on a guy's body and breath. They talk about whether a guy is financially viable or known for cheating." Wen lifted his hands off the wheel and smacked them down again. "I'm telling you, nothing is sacred."

Forest tried to imagine the whining the men at the clubs must be engaged in over this. Now, that made him smile. "Cheating isn't sacred. Any man who is stupid enough to do it should get caught, but I get your point about the rest. Question is why anyone is paying any attention to some random site."

"Because women can't be too careful."

Forest shot his friend a sideways glance. "Come again?"

"It's the site's motto or tagline or whatever you call it." Wen drove up the ramp and handed the ticket to the attendant in the booth. "You know what I mean."

Forest bookmarked the site on his cell and handed the other phone back. He vowed to investigate the site further. Kick back at his desk at home and pry into Need to Know's inner workings. Just for a bit of fun and distraction. There was something about taking the pieces apart, examining them and putting them all back together again that intrigued him.

Talking about it didn't. "I'm ready to end this conversation and get out of here."

"Sure, because you're not on the website."

Forest shook his head. Clearly he was alone in wanting to end the discussion. Still… "How can you know who's on it and who isn't if you can't get access to it?"

"I asked Bernadette."

"Jay's secretary?" The thought of his chief financial officer's assistant spending hours of valuable work time talking about a guy's size and bank account sent the temperature in Forest's head spiking.

"I overheard from my assistant that Bernadette is a member of the website and appears to be sworn to secrecy, but she confirmed that neither of us is on there." Wen snorted as he drove over a bump and out into the bright sunshine. Light pounded on the front window and the summer heat filled the car. "Some of our associates aren't so lucky."

Forest ignored the steady stream of cars on the street in front of them and the honking of horns as some moron tried to make an illegal left in the middle of rush hour. "I think you need more work to occupy your time. I'll get on that tonight."

"It doesn't bother you? The site I mean." Wen glanced over at Forest, then away again. "And I've got enough work. But thanks."

Everything about the day bothered him. Ryan's idiocy. The way Ms. McAdam's hips swayed when she walked, and the fact he kept noticing. "No."

"What if one of your dates posts something negative on there? Do you understand what that could do to your social life?"

That was just about the last thing on Forest's mind. "I'm fine."

"I know you well enough to know you'd tear the city apart if your name goes up on the site."

"You assume the information would be negative."

Wen barked out a laugh as he turned right and moved into the flow of traffic. "Two hundred bucks says it is."

Pissing away money didn't make sense to Forest, but this was a bet he could win. "Five hundred says it's not."

"Of course, you may get to hold on to your money anyway even if I am right, since we won't be able to verify what's on the site to know who wins."

"I'll handle that."

Wen's attention left the traffic for a second only. "You think you can get in?"

Forest found his first smile of the afternoon. "I know I can."

AN HOUR LATER, Jordan stood at the breakfast bar separating her kitchen from the small family room of her condo. She kicked off her high heels and nearly groaned in relief when her bare feet hit the cool tile floor. Working from her couch in her yoga pants qualified as the best part of being self-employed. She cursed every minute she had to slip on a suit and three-inch pumps and head outside.

But she was home now, having dragged her body through waves of humidity on the four-block walk from the metro to the condo. She glanced through the window at the far end of the open room and spied the top of a building on the George Washington University campus two blocks over. She loved living downtown and ten floors up. The lights and the steady hum of life below worked for her.

When the sun finally went down and the traffic below slowed, she'd throw open her balcony door and plop down on the chair she set up out there. The space spanned only a few feet, but was wide enough for her to lounge with her feet balanced on the metal railing as the D.C. summer heat enveloped her.

A face appeared in front of her. Blond-haired and entirely too cute to be believed with those big blue eyes. Elle stood there, dressed in comfortable shorts and a sweatshirt, thanks to having the air conditioner cranked up on this hot early-September evening.

She reached across the counter and grabbed a wineglass and a bottle before taking off for the couch. "How was your day with the urinator?"

Jordan followed with a glass of her own, because this definitely was a red-wine night and no way was she letting that bottle out of her sight. She also brought the cell phone, because heaven forbid she be without it or not check the site's stats for more than ten seconds at a time.

"Ryan refrained from peeing on my desk before I cleaned out and left, so I guess that was a triumph."

With an expertise that was impressive for a twenty-two-year-old English-literature grad student, Elle had the bottle open and the wine poured in one grand sweep. "Are you done at that office?"

"Definitely." Jordan cradled the glass in her hands and let the rich scent of red wine wind through her and relax each muscle. She sank back into the overstuffed chair and balanced her aching feet on the oversize ottoman that sucked up too much of her eight-hundred-square-foot condo but was too comfortable to give away.

"Did he play a game of chase you around the desk?"

The very idea of that made Jordan's lunch curdle in her stomach. "He was too busy getting his butt handed to him."

The glass stopped halfway to Elle's mouth. "Is that code for something?"

"Forest Redder."

Those blue eyes went all soft as her look turned gooey. "I've seen pictures of him in the paper. That guy is delicious."

Jordan was withholding judgment and ignoring the fact she'd performed a lengthy internet search on him on her phone on the commute home. "You should meet the live version. Very potent."

"Holy shit." Elle's voice took on a breathy quality. "You saw him in person?"

"Saw, talked to." Jordan dropped her cell on her lap and tipped her head back. Closing her eyes felt good until Forest's face swam in front of her and she had to open them again. Last thing she needed was a movie of that guy, X-rated or otherwise, running in her head. "Anything on him in the database?"

"You know there's not. You have every last scrap collated, double-checked and memorized."

And that's what bugged her. There should be reams of reports on Forest. "There's no way he sleeps alone."

"If not, no one is talking."

Jordan sat up a bit straighter and shifted to face Elle. "How is that possible? I know about the guy a building over who likes to wear Spanx under his suit so his stomach looks smaller, so—"

"How exactly?"

"—how can I not know about one of the most visible bachelors in the city?"

Elle swished the liquid around in her glass and shot her wine a naughty little smile. It took a minute for her to run through her entire he's-hot facial expressions, but she finally got around to her point. "There are rumors."

Wait a second.

Everything inside Jordan stopped. She doubted she had measurable blood flow at the moment. "No way is that guy gay. I'd bet most women hand him their panties when they first meet."

Not that the comment applied to Jordan.

Elle was a neighbor and best friend, despite the four-year age difference. She was also the only person on the planet who knew what happened behind the scenes at Need to Know and about Jordan's ownership of it. Elle reviewed everything that came in on the site and took care of coding and proofreading. She also did some background checks.

Right now she looked two seconds away from launching into a serious cross-examination. Elle may have dropped out of law school in favor of something she termed "more Arts and Science-y," but those killer questioning instincts appeared to be alive and well.

She curled her legs up under her and leaned on the couch's armrest. "I think I'm unclear on what kind of meeting this was with Forest. Explain."

"The kind where Ryan tried to negotiate, but got outmaneuvered by Forest. The guy barely spoke and still led the discussion and demanded attention." But Jordan knew that part. It was the private intel on Forest she wanted. "Now back to the rumors."

"Confidentiality agreement."

Jordan downed a healthy portion of the wine with a hard swallow. "What?"

"You heard me."

"Are you trying to wow me with your legal knowledge?"

"The rumor is he has his dates, the ones that stick around for anything longer than a few nights, sign a confidentiality agreement."

"I... Wait..." Jordan wondered if maybe she drank too fast. "What?"

Her gaze searched Elle's face for any sign of amusement, but all Jordan got was a raised eyebrow. When the discussion was just between the two of them, Elle tended to spit out any information she had as fast as she could. She loved the gossip-oriented part of the site. Thrived on it. And Elle had never gotten her facts wrong. Jordan depended on that.

Still, this sounded insane. "Oh, come on. An agreement?"

Elle reached for the bottle and refilled Jordan's glass. "I'm just repeating what I've heard."

"That's a level of control bordering on crazy. Like, I want to call him a therapist right now." Well, maybe take a second to strip him out of that suit jacket first, just to see what he hid under there, but then straight to a therapist. Jordan was comfortable with that order. She wasn't as happy about how every crumb she collected about Forest intrigued her more, even this bit of weirdness.

Elle shrugged. "The rich do strange things."

"Testify, but what woman would sign an agreement for a dinner date? Is he that special?"

Elle smiled behind her glass as she rubbed the rim over her lips. "Well, are you still wearing your panties or not?"

Jordan intended to keep them in place whenever Forest was around, but… "Good point."

"Word is he's dark and mysterious. Maybe a woman is willing to do some out-there things to climb between the sheets with him."

Jordan decided her dear friend had a point. "But hire a lawyer to review a legal document?"

"I guess he likes full command over mattress time."

Forest. Bed. Naked. Shoulders.

Interesting. "Now you're just trying to make my head to explode."

Elle held up her free hand. "Hey, just passing it on. I heard he likes to be in charge in the bedroom."

"From?"

Elle's glanced drifted toward the television. The same one that was turned off and had been ever since Jordan got home. "Just here and there."

Ignoring her vow to forget about Forest almost as soon as she made it, Jordan set her glass down in the coffee table with a clink. "Let me get this straight. We run an anonymous website with hundreds of members, and our sole job is to collect and verify information on the eligible and not-so-eligible but possibly cheating males in the city, and somehow you have information on Forest Redder but no verification to put it on the site."

"What do you want me to do? No one is willing to write a status report or file a request for information on him."

And that was the key. "Yet. But they will. We'll get him."

Jordan regretted the phrase as soon as she said it.

Probably had something to do with the way the light in Elle's eyes flared. Or the knowing smirk.

"Are you saying you want more information, maybe for a personal connection?" Suddenly Elle seemed to have no trouble giving her boss-slash-friend full-on eye contact.

"He's not my type." Not totally true, but Jordan hoped it would fly.

"Hot and sexy with bedroom skills to make a grown woman moan and beg for more is not your type?"

So, no flying. "I started the site because I wasn't exactly finding that type of guy."

"Burke Landow is an ass."

Her most recent ex. Now, there was a subject guaranteed to suck the sexiness out of any conversation. It also had Jordan reaching for her glass again. "Oh, hell yeah. Agreed."

"Most men don't lie about being engaged. He's not the only type of guy out there."

Jordan shot Elle her best are-you-kidding-me frown. "I'm wondering if you've read over the Need to Know site lately."

"It's one of my favorite ways to spend an evening."

"What about that professor? He had solid reports on the site for charm, but no word on sex. Can you fill in the blanks?" The lack of information on something so vital, the fact no member had made it past a few dinners with the guy, raised Jordan's antenna. But Elle thought he was cute…never mind that's how the truly weird ones lured you in.

"Yeah, there was nothing on sex."

"You made it to date three, right? I would think that

means you have better things to do at night than read." When Elle had gone out on the first date, Jordan had felt a tiny kick of jealousy. She wanted to be attracted to the scholarly buttoned-up type, but she had the misfortune of loving a bad-boy streak.

Now, combine buttoned-up and naughty, and her control went on the fritz. She didn't know how any sane woman walked by that type without giving a second look.

Of course, the seeds for her feelings on men were not a secret. She hadn't spent time in therapy, but she knew. Not that she couldn't use an expert now and then, but she feared after a few hours of talking about her upbringing she'd need a lifetime pass.

Her mother liked men. Liked men the way little kids liked cookies. To say mom overindulged would be an understatement. The way Jordan figured it, her front seat to her mom's dating life should have made her prim or promiscuous. It was a miracle she didn't head for either extreme.

"There will not be a fourth date with the professor." Elle kept her head down and her focus on the stem of her wineglass.

No eye contact, cryptic—not good signs, so Jordan poked around a little. "Why?"

Elle smacked her lips together and made a strange sucking sound. "Shaved."

Between the noise and the word Jordan decided she missed a sentence. Maybe more than one. "Excuse me?"

"He doesn't have any body hair."

"You're saying—"

"None. I thought he didn't have hair on his legs because he was a runner, like it was some athlete thing. But, nowhere."

The visual image that flashed through Jordan made her a little dizzy in a forget-about-eating kind of way. Also made her wish for a temporary case of blindness. "Wait, you mean, not anywhere on his body? Like, really none."

"Yep."

And—boom—there was the weirdness thing.

But for some reason Jordan couldn't let it go. "Legs, arms and—"

"Nothing around his dick, either." Elle started nodding and didn't stop. "He shaved or waxed his private parts. Head-to-toe smooth like a baby. Try to imagine that."

Jordan doubted she'd be able to *stop* thinking about it. "So, he basically looked like a Ken doll?"

"With a tiny dick. Exactly."

Figures. "How tiny?"

"I don't want to talk about him anymore."

Jordan understood that. She had a line of forgettable dates behind her, but at least they all had the normal amount of body hair. She never dreamed she'd have to worry about that. Now she would. "Well, congratulations. He tops the guy I dated who stole my underwear."

"Since that guy took your bikini bottoms only and a pair at a time, then stored them in a baggie in his freezer, no you still win the Creepy Dude prize."

Jordan had blocked the freezer part. Huh, it all came rushing back now. "He was one giant nut bag."

"One of many."

"You do realize the last three guys I dated can be

described as the guy-who-only-talked-about-his-dog, the guy-who-stole-my-underwear and the guy-who-lied-about-being-single." And how depressing was that list of potential mates? "Maybe I should spend a little more time *reading* the site before I say yes to a date."

"Or maybe a few nights with someone like Forest 'Hot Between The Sheets' Redder is the answer to your troubles."

No way was Jordan diving into that conversation. She decided to start a new one and hope Elle somehow uncharacteristically came along. "So, did you get all the new status-report information entered?"

"Are we done with this topic?"

"I'm not sure how we even started it."

Elle nodded in the direction of Jordan's lap. "Did your mom text today?"

Jordan scooped up her cell and entered the unlock code. The thing had buzzed three times during the commute home. Jordan tensed as she read the most recent text. The stiffness eased out of her shoulders when she realized this one was G-rated. "She's going dancing and will text tomorrow with a report."

"Lucky you."

Not that Jordan had a choice but to hear the after-date tale. Her mom texted every day and overshared. This week the topic was a guy named Lin. He'd taken her to the Bahamas to relax, though why her mom needed rest was a mystery. She didn't work, unless you counted hunting down new men to marry as a job, which her mom did.

Elle gripped the armrest now. "Back up a second."

"I don't want to think about the Ken doll, or my

mom, or my mom with a Ken doll." The last one made Jordan want to discontinue her phone service.

"Forest. You're saying you're never going to see him again?"

"Not unless I get a temp job in his office or otherwise need to confirm a report, which sounds like—with all his rules—can only happen with the approval of the Supreme Court."

"Think of working with him as an opportunity for desk sex." Elle smiled as she said it.

Jordan knew she'd have that on her brain all night now. "Back to work."

"Did you bring me dinner?"

Finally, a safe topic. No men, no mom, no underwear and no hair. "Already ordered. After all, we're celebrating."

"What?"

That one was easy. "Me never having to work for, let alone think about, Ryan Peterson again."

CHAPTER THREE

Subject Request for Nick Asher: Rumor is he likes to get drunk and pick up bridesmaids, even if he's not invited to a wedding. Anyone have any information? —Member 339

Need to Know admin staff: Pending.

EARLY SATURDAY EVENING Jordan stood at the open bar and drank a silent toast to the bride, the newly minted Elizabeth Savory-West. Jordan could almost picture the personalized stationery. It would probably be in the same bright pink as the bridesmaids' dresses.

Jordan had a harder time figuring out the bride, since Jordan had never actually met her. She stood now and watched Elizabeth swish around in her fluffy white dress, surrounded by tens of thousands of dollars' worth of pink and white roses and her thirteen bridesmaids. Because that was a rational number. Jordan could barely come up with thirteen people she'd want at her wedding, never mind acting as bridesmaids.

She scanned the Highwater Observatory, the fancy room housing the reception. It was one of three ballrooms at the tony hotel on the edge of Georgetown. Jordan had to fight the urge to grab her phone and figure out how much the room rental cost. Something with skylights and "observatory" in its name couldn't be cheap. Add in the paneled mahogany ceiling, glitzy chandeliers and rich golden fabrics and you had a very expensive few hours of dancing and cake.

She didn't know one person in the room. That's what happened when you crashed a wedding to scope out a groomsman. Word was Nick Asher enjoyed sleeping with bridesmaids—any bridesmaid—and sometimes skulked around weddings looking for sex partners. Sex, as in having it, then sneaking out before the hotel-room bill was paid.

He was a real classy guy, this Nick. Just went to show money couldn't buy manners.

Right now she watched him move, circling a petite brunette and following her as she walked out the towering doors to the terrace. Jordan guessed it was time she got some fresh air, as well. She pivoted around one of the fancy columns at one end of the room and came eye-to-mouth with a guy.

At least it was a hot mouth, and the rest of the face… well, damn.

"How do you know Bitsy?" Forest stood there, dressed like James Bond, all sleek in a tux that fit him as if some dude stripped Forest naked and measured him for it.

Jordan felt all the blood leave her head. It had to be a reaction to the impressive outfit. No way was she responding to him. "What?"

"Bitsy."

Clearly the rushing sound in her ears drowned out part of the conversation. “Is that a person or a thing?”

“She’s the bride.”

Jordan decided this would teach her not to do more investigation on the bride and groom before crashing a wedding. She’d gotten a tip about Nick being a groomsman and showed up without any planning. It was a hotel, after all. Not exactly a security-protected event.

But none of that solved the six-foot-something problem in front of her. Damn, she couldn’t see anything past Forest’s broad shoulders. That couldn’t be normal.

She waved her hand and gave a chuckle. “Oh, sure. Bitsy.”

He shifted as he folded his arms over his chest. “No one calls her that.”

Shifty bastard. “Why did you?”

“To see if you knew her or were even invited to this event.”

“What makes you think I’m not supposed to be here?” Other than that being the truth, of course.

“You’re not talking to anyone.”

Jordan snorted before she could stop it. “So?”

He put his palm against the column behind her head and leaned in. “You were hiding behind the post and ducked when the bride walked by. You’re not giving anyone eye contact and I haven’t seen you talk or eat or even sit down, probably because you don’t have an assigned seat.”

“Yeah, that’s not creepy or anything.”

“What?”

“Your stalking problem.”

The corner of his mouth lifted but just as quickly

flatlined again. “You’re not exactly engaged in normal wedding-guest behavior.”

“Clearly you don’t go to many weddings.” Jordan had been to seven for her mother alone, so she considered herself a bit of an expert. And, really, hiding was the only way to get through them.

He held out his hand. “Okay, let’s see your seat-placement card.”

He sounded ridiculous saying that, but she bit back a laugh, mostly because of the ball of anxiety racing up her throat to choke her. “Were you invited?”

A young girl barreled by them and knocked into Jordan. The girl was off with a muttered apology. Jordan’s balance took a bit longer to settle out.

With quick reflexes, Forest reached for her arm and pulled her closer to his side even as the fingers stayed wrapped around her elbow. “Elizabeth’s father works in my accounting department.”

“Well, of course he does.” All of these rich, powerful folks knew each other. It was some weird exclusive club where admittance required stacks of cash.

Jordan decided right then she was the unluckiest person alive. First she buys a condo and gets laid off from the law firm the next week. Now, this. Him.

Her cell buzzed in her purse, reminding her of the one other problem she dealt with on a daily basis. Her mother and her active social life. The same mother who had just been dumped in the Bahamas by a guy named Lin after he found her searching through his wallet.

Mom thought he overreacted, because she was only checking his identification. But she did snag two twenties from the guy's wallet "to teach him a lesson" or something like that. Now she was in the resort lobby, trying to find a new "friend" or she'd need airfare to get back home.

Jordan dreaded the call and the possibility of having to send more money, but when her mom called, Jordan answered. Not having a dad, her mom was all she had.

Keeping the stalling to a minimum, Jordan held up a finger and opened her small bag. She grabbed the phone and scanned the lines of text. Looked like Mom landed on her feet. Again.

Forest glanced at the cell. "Everything okay?"

"My mother."

He frowned. "Is she in trouble?"

The explanation would take hours and Jordan would need many glasses of wine to get through it, so she went for a shortcut. "She's on a date with a man named Felix."

"Is that good?"

That should be a simple question, but almost nothing was simple when it came to Gloria Winchester. "For Felix?"

Forest's frown deepened. "What?"

"We'll have to see what Felix thinks a week from now."

"I don't understand."

"Not important." Jordan dropped the phone inside and snapped the purse shut again. "You were telling me how you know everyone in town. Please continue."

"Speaking of mothers." He nodded at an older woman across the room standing next to the wedding cake. She wore a sleek gray dress and had her hair swept in an updo.

Jordan had no clue who she was, either. "Were we?"

"We can go say hello to the mother of the bride," he said.

The music played and people danced. A few others roamed around the tables and gathered by the uncut cake. Jordan blocked it all in an attempt to sound as if she belonged here. "I've never met her parents."

With a hand still on Jordan's upper arm, Forest swung around and pointed to the bride as she smoothed her hand over her bump of a stomach again and again. "To Elizabeth then."

If Jordan's suspicions were correct, the potentially pregnant Elizabeth. "She's busy."

His fingers clenched against her arm. Not tight and not threatening. To others he probably looked loving. To Jordan it sent a clear do-not-move signal.

He stood close enough for his breath to brush across her cheek. "I will wait here and run through every member of the wedding party until you admit you crashed this event."

The closeness. His scent. It all combined to suck air out of her lungs. She had no idea what that was about. Sure, on the surface the guy looked good. Probably even had the normal amount of body hair. She could admit to him being objectively non-ugly, but she knew better than to think his looks provided any insight into the rest of him. Personal experience had taught her all about his type and that should kill any appeal.

Should.

"I was next door and came over to see the room. A friend is thinking of having a wedding here," she said, reaching for another lie.

"Who?" His hand brushed up and down her arm this time.

The mix of the demanding tone and soft caress messed with her head, but she stayed on track. "How is that your business?"

"Ms. McAdam—"

What little air she managed to force into her body all seeped out again. She actually felt her shoulders slump. "How do you know my name?"

"Does that scare you?" He seemed far too happy about that possibility.

Shithead. "Of course not."

"Dance with me."

Oh, hell no. She was wheezing and stuttering and there were still a few inches of space between them. Getting closer? Not a good idea. Not when her usual common sense appeared to stumble in his presence.

"I'm fine here," she said, feeling the exact opposite of fine.

"I insist."

There was demanding and there was jerky. Only the smooth delivery and dark good looks kept this guy on the right side of the line. Just barely. "Does that bossy thing usually work for you?"

"Almost always." This time his mouth hovered over her ear as he nodded to the woman headed right for them in the big white dress. "Look, there's Elizabeth. Ready to say hello?"

Jordan turned, edging her back toward the bride and angling Forest toward the mass of swaying people. "Fine, one dance."

A few steps and she went into his arms. A palm

pressed low on her back and the fingers of his other hand entwined with hers. His firm yet gentle touch and the mint on his breath had the tension across her shoulders easing. His steps were sure, as if he danced around his office each night.

Knowing his upbringing, Jordan assumed he'd gone to cotillions and polo matches and a bunch of other rich-kid things. With or without lessons, the guy knew how to hold a woman.

Damn him.

Forest looked down at her. “Are you still working for Ryan Peterson?”

She fought off a nasty shiver at the appalling thought. “It was a temp position and is over.”

“You sound torn up about that.” Forest guided her around the floor and away from the more obvious flailing couples out there who stomped and turned and took up more than their fair share of dance-floor space.

“He's a little...” Jordan searched for a word that didn't start with *ass*. “I'll say different.”

Forest treated her to a huge smile. “What about that the thing where he calls himself Ryan?”

“Right? What is that?” She tightened her hand on Forest's shoulder. A sexy warmth radiated off him, inviting her to trace his muscles with her palm. She beat back that temptation with an invisible stick.

“He has the maturity of a ten-year-old,” Forest said.

“You're being kind.”

Forest pulled her in closer. Only a whisper of air separated their bodies and his lips pressed close to her hair and couples passed by them. “Where do you go next?”

The steady beat and gentle sway mesmerized her. It took a second for the words to come together in her head.

She still didn't get it.

She pulled back and searched his ridiculously handsome face for the answer. "What?"

"Your next temp job." He led them to an open space on the dance floor and put his back to the crowd. "I'm assuming your office gives you a new assignment as the old one finishes."

For a second she forgot why she was even at the wedding and what she was supposed to be doing. Hunting down information and providing it to others was her *real* job and, as predicted, being close to Forest messed up her thinking…a lot. "Yes, but I have the week off."

"Are you looking for full-time employment?" His gaze dipped to her mouth and lingered there. "If so, I could pass your name on to my human resources department."

A vision screamed through her head. Her straddling him on his big leather chair for that desk sex Elle referenced. And the sex would be great. Jordan would bet all the money in her savings account on that.

But the vision blinked out as quickly as it had appeared when she realized his offer ventured a bit too close to her mother's M.O. of getting close to men in exchange for money and engagement rings. She'd known this guy for about ten minutes and he was offering her a job. He didn't mention strings, but there were always strings. Her mom taught her that.

The whole scene made Jordan wonder if she did inherit the using-men gene after all. Still, he was a temptation….

She glanced around, trying to see if anyone noticed the sudden heat on her cheeks. Backing up came a second later. She needed to keep her chest from pressing against his and wondered when *The Longest Song in History* was going to be over so she could dash out of there. "You don't even know me."

"I figure anyone who could work for Ryan without dropkicking him out the window has some skills."

She thought that should be a résumé line, as well. "That's an interesting employee threshold you have there."

"You could say I have a gift for reading people."

This guy knew how to say just the right thing at the right time to throw her off. It was as if he reeled her in and then tried to shock her. Maybe she should thank him for the wake-up call, but she was more concerned over this supposed superpower he claimed to have. "Really? What do you think you know about me?"

He looked her up and down, as if sizing her up. "Intelligent enough not to blow your temp job and strong enough to refrain from telling Ryan to get his head out of his ass, though that had to be tempting."

Relief crashed into her. Nothing to do with Need to Know or checking into her background. She could handle this. "All true."

"I'm thinking you're a little down on your employment luck."

Well, now, she didn't care for that at all. She glanced down at her royal blue sheath. "Is that a comment on the dress?"

"Definitely not. You look spectacular. Certainly impressive enough to turn heads and get offers, but not so out of the park with a flashy red dress or something similar that would stick in everyone's minds if they played the 'who was the lady in that dress' game later."

That was exactly the look she was going for, but still. "How romantic."

"I think it's all carefully crafted. You know how good you look and how to dress and picked a step away from all-out smokin' on purpose, but I have no doubt it's easy for you to get there fast." The heat in his eyes mirrored his words.

She blocked out the good parts and went with her new insight into his personality. "I'm guessing you think everyone is always working an angle."

His hand swept over her shoulder. "Aren't they?"

Time for a surge of self-protective control.

She stepped back again, shutting down all possibility of touching his impressive body even as she memorized how he felt for when she was alone in her bed tonight with Mr. Fancy. "The song is over."

"Well, Ms. McAdam, we have a few options." He nodded toward the reception area outside the ballroom and the hotel beyond. "For one, you could join me for a drink."

Or she could run like hell. "I don't think that's a great idea."

"Ms. McAdam—"

A thought flashed in her brain. "What's my first name?"

His mouth opened and closed, but no sound came out.

She put a finger behind her ear and leaned toward him. "Hmm?"

He actually treated her to a little bow. "Touché."

For some reason the idea of this in-control dude not knowing her full name tickled her. So did the little-boy-caught-doing-something-naughty look on his face. "Meaning?"

"I was never given your first name."

Score one for strong women everywhere. He might demand a confidentiality agreement, but he had to know the woman's name first.

"Then, *Forest*, it would seem you really don't know everything."

The expression morphed back into confident businessman. "But I could find out. I thrive on a challenge."

Okay, that sounded more like the half-bossy, all-demanding guy she expected. It must have killed him to admit he didn't know something, but he sure never came off as weak.

Which meant it was time to run. "I'm going to take myself out of this game and leave."

"Do you think that will stop me from finding out your name?"

Her legs refused to move. "You're sounding creepy again."

"You know you have the control. I appreciate women and know what the word *no* means."

She long ago learned not to take men at their word for that sort of thing. "If you say so."

"Ask around."

She was. She did. No one said anything bad or anything at all. "What makes you think I'm interested?"

"Call it a hunch." He winked at her. "Until next time, Ms. McAdam."

Then he was gone.

CHAPTER FOUR

Subject Request for Anton Betz: He broke up with me because his mother just died. Any advice on how to navigate this? —Member 37

Response from Member 258: He broke up with me more than a year ago...because his mother just died.

Need to Know admin staff: His mother is alive.

FOREST SAT AT his desk and turned his pen end over end, tapping each tip against the desk blotter as he stared at the note he made at the end of last week's chain of phone calls—Jordan McAdam. Exactly five days after leaving the wedding, he discovered her full name. Getting her attention took another four days of planning, but today was the day.

He arrived at the office just after seven and two hours later he knew where she went to college, her job history and her current address. The receptionist at Jordan's temp agency switched from chatty to oversharing without much prodding. Forest made a mental note to warn Jordan about that issue.

He spun his chair and stared out over the Potomac

River through the wall of windows behind his desk. From his office on the Georgetown waterfront, he could glance to his left and see the famous Watergate and look across to Virginia. Expensive real estate in a historically protected former warehouse turned sought-after office building. Forest knew every inch of the place because he'd developed the property, leaving the top floor of the four-story structure for Redder Investments headquarters and carving out the best view dead in the middle for himself.

With all the information and resources at his disposal, he'd expected to locate Jordan sooner. He refused to see the unexpected delay as failure. It wasn't as if he could ask Ryan what service he used to hire his office temp, though the guy did call often enough. Basically, every single day. He'd started with begging and now had entered the threatening phase. Not exactly a tactic that worked with Forest.

A sharp knock had Forest turning his chair around again in time to see Wen stroll in. He shut the door behind him while performing the same combination of frowning and head shaking he'd perfected more than fifteen years ago as captain of their prep-school lacrosse team.

Forest didn't find it any less annoying now. "Problem?"

The frown deepened as Wen walked over and unbuttoned his suit jacket. He dropped down into the chair on the other side of the desk a second later. "You forget to tell me something?"

"You probably need to be more specific." But Forest knew. His plan depended on Wen, even though Wen didn't know that yet.

"I have an office temp sitting outside my door this morning."

So, Jordan had risen to the challenge. Forest expected as much. Still, a wave of satisfaction spilled through him and he didn't try to beat it back. "Yes."

"Care to tell me why?"

Forest wasn't really prone to explaining his actions, not even to his best friend of more than twenty years. He didn't plan to start now. "No."

"Let's try it this way." Wen exhaled and the chair creaked as he eased it into a balance on the back two legs. "My assistant has been assigned to some sort of project that, up until twenty minutes ago, I'd never heard of, which is strange since I'm a VP here."

Forest glared at said VP until the front legs of the chair hit the carpet again. Then Forest jumped back into the conversation, or more appropriately, *waded* in, since he didn't go in very far. "True."

"Did I miss a meeting?"

"No."

Wen rolled his eyes. "You care to explain what's going on? Maybe use more than a one-word answer this time."

"Not really." Forest couldn't help but smile as he fired that one off.

The tension that had been building on his friend's side of the desk whooshed right out again when Wen started laughing. "Smartass."

Forest sat back, prepared to duck any questions Wen lobbed his way. "As I've told you for years, I'd rather be a smartass than a dumbass."

"I'll refrain from responding to that," Wen said. "But, really, what the hell is going on?"

The man was entitled to an explanation, edited as it may be. "Penny is working with the design team for the next week. She has the background and I know she'd eventually like to make the leap into that department, planning interiors and all that. I thought this might be a good time for her to try."

"Interesting." Wen's smile didn't falter. If anything, it became more pronounced.

Forest didn't care for that at all. "Is it?"

"Please, don't let me stop you." Wen swept his hand out in an exaggerated flourish. "Keep providing this illuminating explanation."

Yeah, not good at all. "With Penny gone, you needed a temporary assistant."

"And?"

"That's it. Now I've explained." Forest brushed a nonexistent piece of lint off his sleeve to signal his general disinterest in the conversation.

"You skipped over the biggest part of your riveting tale."

Forest's head came up. Yeah, Wen's stupid smile hadn't slipped an inch. At times like these Forest wished Wen didn't know him so well.

Wen finally shook his head. "You're annoying as hell today."

"Feel free to leave. You might want to take a look at the title on the door as your ass hits the hallway."

"So, this is about Jordan."

Jordan? Since when did Wen call her Jordan? She'd been in the office less than an hour. "Excuse me?"

"You think I didn't notice you drooling over her back

in Ryan's office?" Wen scoffed. "I've seen you in action with women, including girlfriends and your fiancée."

"Former fiancée." Stella was very much an ex and would remain that way forever unless he lost his mind, and even then Forest had left orders for Wen to shoot him first.

"Point is, I know the look. You saw Jordan and your antenna went up."

"Now, there's a disturbing image." Almost as annoying as the thing where Wen kept calling Jordan by her first name.

"Imagine how I feel having to watch you."

"All I did was get you a temp."

Wen's eyebrow inched up. "*You* did? Last I checked, you barely know my assistant's name."

Damn it. "Human Resources did."

"Uh-huh. And the temp in question just happens to the very hot brunette we met at Ryan's office a week ago."

Forest waved that one off. "Coincidence."

"Yeah, stick with that response. It's totally believable."

"She needed a position and we had one open." Never mind the fact she turned down the position the first time HR made the request to her agency last Friday. It wasn't until Forest personally called and insisted on Jordan—like, pointed out any use of the temp agency in the future depended on this assignment being filled as requested—that she suddenly became available.

He could hardly wait to hear how Jordan's office made that happen and what they promised Jordan to get her to show up today. And he would, because he intended to spend some time getting to know Jordan.

He had no idea what it was about her that tugged

so hard at him. The D.C. metro area wasn't exactly at a loss for pretty brunettes with shapely legs. But this one caught his attention in a way that kicked his ass. He hadn't expected it and sure didn't want it.

He blamed the wedding setting. Something about seeing her there, skulking around and evading questions, intrigued him. So did the fit of her body against his when they danced.

The way the energy thrummed off her and fire lit in her eyes as they exchanged verbal jabs. So fucking hot.

No doubt she would be wild in bed. He could sense it. He sure as hell had played a fictional movie of it in his head enough times over the past week. Those legs wrapped around his waist and—

"In other words, you wanted to see her naked, so you stuck her in my office space."

Forest almost jumped out of his chair when Wen's voice screeched through his thoughts. It took two throat clearings before Forest trusted his voice. "What did you just say?"

"You do not want her here for business. Well, not Redder Investments business. Personal business."

"If that were true, I would have put her outside my door as my temp. Close to me in my private office suite." And the idea did have merit.

"No, you're more subtle than that."

In this case, just barely. "Not usually."

"So, you don't mind if I ask her out."

The words bounced off the cherry bookshelves lining the wall. It took a second for the noise pounding in his head to die down, and a few minutes longer for Forest to wrestle the heat burning through him back under control. "She works for you, so yes. I would mind. She is off-limits because I'd prefer not to be sued."

Wen barked out a laugh. "Damn, I've never seen you this transparent before."

Forest had more than enough of Wen's amusement for one day. "And you should get back to your office before I find someone else to fill it."

"I agree." Wen stood and rolled his shoulders back, generally making a show of heading out.

Forest knew that battle ended too easy, and when Wen spun around again, Forest hated being right. "Damn," he mumbled under his breath.

"I'm just wondering how long it will be before you make up a reason to come visit me today."

"I do own the company." Though, at the moment Forest didn't feel as if he was in charge of anything.

"But you've never used it as a dating service before."

"I'm not now." But the comment struck a little too close for Forest's liking.

This was *not* about finding a date. This was about getting to the heart of the mystery that was Jordan. And if that included sex—and it better or he might lose his mind—that was just a bonus.

Wen's stupid smile came roaring back. "I'm betting I see you by noon."

CHAPTER FIVE

Subject Request for Wen Strong: Is his ladies'-man reputation for real? —Member 71

Response from Member 9: Dated him last year. He's smart, charming and amazing in the sack. He also heaves at the thought of commitment. Sex—yes. Anything serious—no.

JORDAN SENSED HIM before she saw him. People buzzed in and out of the double doors of the executive suite all day. She'd spent hours answering the phone, scheduling and copying the information Wen needed for this and that, all while watching out for Forest.

The entrance to his Big Boy private office sat directly across from her on the other side of an open lounge area. He'd stepped out several times to head for other offices and a conference room off to her right. He never looked her way. Never came over. Never went into the office behind her to see Wen.

But all that was about to change.

She spied Forest's charcoal-colored suit as he stepped into the lounge and headed her way. He walked with his head down and fiddled with his watch. The movements were brisk and determined...and when he lifted his head and pinned her with his green-eyed gaze, a rough breath shook her chest.

She blamed the reaction on the strange case of bouncing nerves she'd had since the temp office called with this assignment for the first time last Friday. First of three times. Seemed her presence had been specifically "requested" by someone on Redder's HR team.

Yeah, right. More likely that she got in the last word with the guy before she left the wedding and it gnawed at him until he tracked her down.

Because that wasn't nuts or anything.

Either way, he'd won because her temp coordinator threatened to keep her off any other assignments if she said no. For now, she needed the position. It provided her with extra cash and the perfect ruse to collect information for Need to Know.

But there were other temp agencies in town, and Jordan would find one as soon as this job ended, but she would not be run out thanks to Forest. She'd leave on her own terms—ticked off and spitting mad for being pushed around—and not look back.

Speaking of looking, this time he didn't duck or ignore her. He walked straight for her desk, never breaking eye contact. He'd somehow managed to clear the place out as he moved, because the busy activity dropped away and people disappeared, leaving behind just the two of them.

He'd waited until almost five o'clock to wander over and make his stand. Whatever control game they were playing, he seemed to be winning it. She hated that.

He stopped right in front of her, all big and imposing, and treated her to a curt nod. "Ms. McAdam."

The deep voice rumbled around her. She had no idea how he made it echo and bounce, but it left her a little breathless. "Mr. Redder."

He didn't budge as he nodded in the direction of the closed door behind her. "Is your boss in?"

"Wen?"

If possible, Forest's mouth flattened even further. "You can call him Mr. Strong."

Looked like Mr. Tall, Dark and Demanding preferred to draw a bright line between management and staff. That matched with his overbearing, suck-the-air-out-of-the-room personality.

The guy certainly knew how to suck the interest right out of her...almost.

"He said to call him Wen," she pointed out.

"And the second Wen owns the place, he can make that decision. Until then—"

"You're in charge." Yeah, she got it. Forest didn't exactly allow for gray areas.

"Exactly."

She shifted in her chair, keeping her legs tight together to keep her foot from tapping, and her fingers linked to stop any fidgeting. Something about him had her insides jumping and a soft fuzz slipping over her brain.

Usually the buttoned-up suit implied a certain personality type. One she wanted to avoid as much as possible—alpha, annoying, desperate to move up the ladder and looking for a quick lay. She'd tried that type and gotten smothered under a pile of lies.

Forest appeared to be the exception. She wanted the package—all six-feet, put together, commanding presence of him—to repel her. That wasn't happening. Maybe if he kept talking that would do it. It wasn't as if she was doing all that great with the other male types. Then there was the issue of the bad-boy streak she sensed running under Forest's surface. Yeah, if she tapped into that, her control could be a problem.

"And no," she said, picking up a lost thread to the conversation. It was either that or let her mind wander, and danger lingered in that direction.

He frowned down at her. "Excuse me?"

"Mr. Strong is still not back from his two-thirty appointment."

Still, Forest didn't move. He stood there with those broad shoulders blocking her view and dimming the lights around her. Another neat trick.

She knew she had a few choices. She could play it cool, ignore him and hope the weird uptick in her heart rate that happened whenever she saw him soon knocked it off. She could walk out and not come back, which was damn tempting. Or she could hit the unspoken issue zapping between them head-on.

Since she had nothing to lose, she went with the third option. "May I speak with you a minute?"

His face went blank. "Sure."

"In private."

A smile twitched at the edge of his mouth, then disappeared. Looked like Forest already marked this round in his "win" column. Honestly, the size of his ego astounded her.

He gestured toward the closed door. "We can use Wen's office."

She preferred an open space. Private or not, locked

rooms spelled trouble. Still, no way was she backing down from this fight, not when she pretty much started it this time around. "If you insist."

"I do."

Before common sense could step up and slap her, she slid out of her chair and grabbed her cell. She needed it nearby because it sounded as if the Mom-Felix connection had already taken a nosedive. This week's love troubles almost made Jordan wish she could forbid her mom from leaving the country.

Jordan walked the few steps to Wen's private office. She could feel Forest's presence behind her as she opened the door, not touching, but just inside her comfort zone. His scent wrapped around her and his reflection cut through the Georgetown skyline mirrored on the wall of windows behind Wen's desk.

She took in the plush leather chair and thick carpet. The space was done in blue, as if to match the painting to her left and its splashes of color. It looked like a mish-mash of streaks to her, but she guessed it cost more than all the furniture in her condo combined.

Rather than spend more time admiring the décor, she launched into her verbal attack the second she heard the door click shut behind them. She spun around and her balance faltered when she saw a short three feet spanning the distance between them. Man, the guy snuck up without making a noise.

But she needed to focus. Smelling him was not going to make that happen. "What is this about?"

His face tightened in a frown. "Excuse me?"

"Tell me why I'm here."

Forest folded his arms across his chest. “You wanted to talk with me.”

He just never stopped testing. “You know what I mean. In your building. Working for you.”

“You don’t technically work for me.”

The man could make a nun reach for the nearest weapon. “You’re parsing that line pretty thin, aren’t you?”

Forest exhaled then, in the way men did when they found women tiresome. “Wen needed a temp and you appeared to be out of work, so I thought the fit made sense.”

Forest even gave her eye contact as he lied his impressive butt off. *Nice try.* “Even after our conversation at the wedding and my comments about not wanting the job, you talked to someone at my company and demanded I be the one to take this position.”

“I *asked* for you.”

She wondered if he knew they were saying the same thing. Seemed his asking sounded a lot like ordering and she’d bet he was well aware how people jumped at his serious tone. “My temp coordinator threatened to fire me because of your call.”

His arms dropped to his sides as a bit of his stern control slipped. “What?”

Huh, that almost looked real. “Fired.”

“You’re serious?”

She shifted until a few more inches separated them. Not that it helped. She needed an entire football field of distance to keep her wits around this man. “What’s the end game here, Forest? Or am I required to call you Mr. Redder, since you’re the Big Boss?”

"Oh, I definitely want to hear you say Forest when we're alone." His voice changed. Actually dropped and roughened as it licked at her senses.

Whoa.

"Let's go back to the part where—"

"Yes." Pivoting away from the sound of his voice and the way it made her stomach do a strange little dance was a good idea. She needed focus and to tap into that deep well of anger inside her. She shifted until she stood at the side of Wen's desk with Forest in front of it. "Fired, Forest. I had to obey your command or risk losing my job."

He held up his hand in what looked like a pledge. "Okay, wait a second. The firing part was not on the table."

"Sure sounded like it to me. Probably because the coordinator actually used the word *fired.*"

The skin pulled taut over Forest's cheeks and stress showed in every line of his face. "I never threatened that and would never threaten that. You were supposed to be offered a bonus for taking this assignment."

As soon as the flicker of positive feeling ignited in her consciousness, it vanished again. With this guy's help, she could easily turn into her mother. A bonus here, a television there. Find a guy, grab the heirloom diamond and head for a quickie wedding in Vegas before the fighting started. Jordan had lived through that cycle too many times to get sucked into it now.

Forest did this and the temptation to kick him in the shins hit her hard enough to knock her breathless. "So, you're paying for extra services now, like I'm some sort of special on the menu?"

"No way am I saying yes to that." He rested his fingertips against the desktop.

She tore her gaze away as soon as she realized the gentle tap of his fingers mesmerized her. "That's smart, because you know what that sounds like, right?"

His hand flattened with a thud. "None of this is coming out right."

"No kidding."

"One more time." He made a dramatic scene with a loud exhale. "Because it was last-minute, and because I was insisting, I said I would pay more and your boss said she would pass that on to you. That's it."

If he was making it up as he talked, he managed to sound pretty convincing. Still, the heavy-handed thing needed work. "Uh-huh."

He shook his head as he took off again. In two steps he met her at the side of the desk and stared down into her eyes. "Look, I'll talk to your boss. Straighten all of it out."

The grim expression, the body language—it all struck her as the actions of a man struggling with a smack of guilt and need to atone. She might have found the whole scene a bit more chivalrous if he hadn't been the one to cause the mess in the first place.

Her cell picked that minute to buzz. She tightened her fist around the plastic and felt it dig into her palm. For a second she thought about ignoring it.

Forest's gaze bounced from her hand to her face. "Do you need to get that?"

"It's my mother."

"How can you tell?"

With a few swipes of her thumb, Jordan verified the sender. Saw something about needing money to rent a yacht and looked up again. “It’s almost always my mother. Sometimes friends. Every now and then a date. But usually my mother.”

His shoulders tensed. “Date?”

“That was a general statement.” And why she felt the need to point that out she had no idea. It would be better if he thought she was taken. That might kill off whatever odd attraction kept zapping between them.

Of course, with her luck, he might be the need-to-steal-her-away type. Jordan’s least-favorite type on the planet after the hairless asshole who stole bikini underwear, if there was such a combination type and she guessed there was.

“Well, is she okay?” Forest asked.

Jordan loved her mom, but there was just no way to answer that one quickly. “Depends on your definition.”

“Excuse me?”

She noticed he liked that phrase. “She thinks she prefers Felix’s friend John to Felix.”

Forest shook his head. “Should I know what that means?”

“I’m not all that thrilled I know.”

“We seem to be having a communication issue.”

As far as she could see they had a much bigger problem. Even at this distance she could feel the heat of his body and pull of something inside him tugging at her. “You know what this is about, right?”

“The ‘this’ is what in that sentence?”

Because the guy couldn’t say “huh” like everyone else on the planet. He had to add ten extra words. “The chase.”

He blew out a long breath. The head shaking came

a second later. "Okay, I thought I'd caught up, but you lost me again."

"You have a certain reputation with women." She took a step back and her thigh slammed into the edge of Wen's desk chair. A harsh breath hissed through her teeth as pain spiraled to her hip. But when Forest reached out for her, she shook her head. "I'm fine."

"You sure?"

The man was all but chasing her around the desk, kind of proving her argument, but she decided not to point that out. "Don't try to throw me off. We're talking about your reputation."

His eyes narrowed. "Which is?"

Sex God. "You get the women you go after."

"Where did you hear that?"

Like she was going to stroke his ego and repeat all the gossip. "Doesn't matter."

His head rolled to the side as he groaned. "Damn it, not that stupid site."

"Uh..." The brakes slammed on in her brain. "What?"

"You think this is a game to me?"

"Go back to the website comment."

He shook his head. "Answer the question first."

Need warred with curiosity. He'd mentioned Need to Know, not by name, but she got the idea, and she wanted to double back and poke around there. See what he knew and assumed. Her defenses rose as fast as her urge to stick up for all her hard work. But she continued to fight for focus. "I'm a challenge to you."

The smile came out of nowhere. So did his hands. One skimmed over her shoulder to the side of her face. "You are that."

She never thought he'd admit it. And the touching… not good. Not when her defenses against this guy, maddening and bossy and all, were stuck on permanent sputter. Hell, one caress and her insides took off on a spell of shivery nonsense.

Just the thought of that had her anger spiking again. "You thought you could spin me right off that wedding dance floor and into bed, and since that didn't work you're making a second run."

Her hand went to his with the intention of pushing him away. That pushing thing didn't happen. She just stood there, hand on his, engaging in a staring contest that had her heart hammering hard enough to echo in her ears.

His gaze searched her face and he leaned in closer. "You should see someone about your low self-esteem."

Right, she was the one with the confidence problem.

"I left without falling into your arms and now you're sniffing around." She meant to yell the observation, but it came out as a breathy whisper.

"So, now I'm a dog in this scenario?"

The laughter in his voice brought that kicking instinct winging back. She broke the contact then, ducking away from his hand and ignoring the warm tingle in her skin from where he'd touched her.

Anger. Yes, that was the only way to ensure her skirt stayed down and his lips stayed over there. "You're interested because you heard no from a woman and you expected to hear yes."

Forget that he hadn't actually spelled out his interest and she hadn't actually said no. She'd run from that dance floor. Found her purse, grabbed it and kept moving until she hit the parking garage. Between the banter and the pressure of his palm against her back during that dance, her control had teetered and stupidity loomed. She'd almost said yes to that drink, and that "almost" panicked her.

She'd made a vow months ago—no more D.C. power elite types. Ignore the impressive ties and the sweet talk and unbury the truth so other women wouldn't go through what she had. If men lied, women had to arm themselves. She wanted to lead the way on that charge and her site could offer that protection. Not only for her, but for other women—even the ones like her mother who fell for a series of men with big bank accounts, moving from relationship to relationship and failing at every one of them.

But hard as she tried, she couldn't manage to shove Forest into the forget-'em category.

Even now he closed in, until the tips of his polished shoes touched her scuffed ones. "For the record, I was interested long before the wedding."

Her stomach took off on another flip-flopping extravaganza. She backed up until she stood behind Wen's desk chair this time. She balanced her hands against the top for leverage.

"We've met exactly twice." And then there was the part where she wasn't his type. No money, no power, no country clubs to her name.

"The first time was enough for me to know."

No way was she letting that comment derail her from asking for clarification. "Are you denying the love of the chase?"

"If you're right that this is all about winning you, we

should take care of that right now. Experiment with a little catching, so I can show you the chase is not all I'm after." But he didn't move. He stood there, as if willing her to come to him.

No way was that happening. But much more time with the door closed and she'd have to climb over the desk to keep from touching him.

And refraining was the right move. She sensed that to her bones. "You think I'm going to have sex with you in Wen's office just so you can work me out of your system?"

The door shut with a crack. "I'm really hoping the answer to that question is no, or there will not be enough bleach in the world to get me back in that chair."

She hadn't even realized anyone came in until she peeked around Forest and stared into her temporary boss's eyes, bright with amusement. "Wen. You're here."

Forest finally backed up, but the grumbling didn't cease. "He's Mr. Strong."

She fought the urge to roll her eyes. If she wasn't so busy concentrating all her energy on staying upright, she might have done it. "Is that the point?"

Forest shrugged. "Just making my position on the matter clear."

Wen stepped up until he stood next to Forest. "I thought I knew what you two were talking about, but now I'm not so sure."

"Let it go," Forest said.

Wen's gaze went from Forest to Jordan and back again. "I wish I could, but right now I'm trying to figure out if I got back too late or too early."

Since she had trouble catching her breath, there was only one answer. "Both."

"Ms. McAdam and I were talking about some unfinished business," Forest said.

Thanks to her renewed vow to keep him off-limits, it was going to stay that way. "On that note, I think I'll go back to my desk now."

Running and hiding. Something about Forest had her favoring both options.

He nodded. "Good idea."

His quick agreement had her wanting to stay, but common sense won out. She slipped around Forest, never meeting his eyes or Wen's. It didn't take their law degrees to know she'd play a huge role in their upcoming conversation. Since she didn't want to hear even a peep of that, she headed for the door and kept going.

CHAPTER SIX

Subject Request for Clark Widener: He claims he and his wife are separated and that he lives downstairs because a divorce is imminent. Anyone have any information? —Member 8

Need to Know admin staff: Living arrangements unconfirmed, but several members state he's been making this claim for two years.

THE WOMAN KNEW how to stage an exit. Forest had to give her that. She also looked damn fine in the thin skirt and the slim pink shirt. It had taken all his willpower and Wen's untimely entrance not to open those tiny white buttons with his teeth.

Wen made a tsk-tsking sound as he rounded his desk. "Well, you made it past noon, but—"

"Do not finish that sentence or you're fired."

Wen dropped into his chair with an exaggerated sigh. "A reasonable response. Not overblown at all."

"I'd be in a better mood if you hadn't come back to the office today." Maybe then Forest would know what Jordan tasted like. Man, the wondering was killing him.

"I predicted this."

"We're not having this conversation again." He

shifted his weight. He hoped moving around, getting a little oxygen, would get the blood flowing to his head instead of his dick.

Wen leaned his head back. "Fine, but you know this thing with Jordan is a mistake, right?"

Hitting on a temp, spending even a minute of his valuable workday chasing her around a desk. None of it fit with his usual behavior, but Jordan had Forest tied up. Hell, maybe it really was the chase. If so, he needed to catch her soon.

At least he got one thing right. "The important point here is to note I did beat your noon deadline."

"But it still looks like you're sleeping alone." Wen shook his head and sent out a pitying look as he made the comment.

Forest was not ready to concede. "For now."

And he hoped to change that unfortunate situation very soon.

JORDAN MADE IT home from the metro three hours later with her feet relatively intact thanks to the comfort lining in her stacked heels. Her control wasn't as lucky. Her thoughts raced back and forth from a common-sense, hands-off policy for Forest to a maybe-she-could-try-him-just-one-time insanity.

No doubt about it. The man turned her mind to goop.

She dumped her briefcase on the kitchen counter and reached for the wineglass already sitting there. There were some benefits to having her best friend as an assistant. In addition to the skills of Elle's cousin in setting up a system of proxy servers and rotating IP addresses to ensure the anonymity of Need to Know, Elle enjoyed good wine and liked to share.

Jordan smiled as she walked over to join Elle in the family room. "Is it sick to say I need this?"

"I'd ask how your day with Mr. Hottie went, but I think that comment says it all." Elle paged through a stack of reports as she lounged on the couch.

Kicking off her heels, Jordan kept going until she stood in front of the balcony door. A warm puff of air hit her in the face when she opened it.

"That's President And CEO Hottie to you." Jordan swirled the wine in her glass. "He's really a controlling jackass."

Elle dumped the papers on the table and leaned back against the cushions. "I see."

"Yeah, don't do that."

Elle held up her hands. "I only said two words."

"There was a wealth of judgment behind those four letters." And the smirk…and the way Elle sat there all eager, practically vibrating with enthusiasm, with her legs folded under her and her attention on full alert.

"I'm still trying to figure out why you agreed to take this assignment when you know Forest makes you edgy."

That was a damn fine question. Jordan decided to evade it. "I was threatened with—"

"No. We both know you could have said no and found another temp firm." Elle set her glass down on the table with a clink. "Correct?"

Usually Jordan loved how insanely smart her friend was. Not so much today. "It would have been a pain and could have caused a delay in obtaining some of the site confirmations."

This time Elle crossed her arms over her stomach. Even snorted, which somehow, coming out of her cute blondie face with the pert nose, sounded adorable. "Try again."

Jordan gave in. After all, what good was having a best friend if you couldn't share your potential idiocy with her. "Okay, maybe I was curious about why Forest was so eager to have me there."

"Come to any conclusions about that?"

"I'm a challenge." And if the electricity kept zapping between them, a soon-to-be-naked one. "I'm probably the only woman he's met lately who didn't fall at his feet and strip her shirt off."

"I'm trying to picture that scenario."

Jordan had to fight to do the opposite. "You know what I'm saying."

"You want to." The glass went to Elle's mouth again. "Fall at his feet, I mean."

"I didn't say that." Technically, it was more of an on-her-knees-and-then-jump-into-bed thing. Jordan doubted there would be much falling or waiting if she ever got Forest in a clothes-off position. Nope, she'd be very much awake and active.

"It's okay, you know." Elle's voice had dipped to a whisper as she shifted the glass between her palms.

"What?"

"To want him. Flirting with a guy, taking it farther, makes you a sexually healthy woman, not a victim."

"Going from one powerful man to the other is not something a smart woman should do. I had his type. I'm done with that. Maybe a nice guitar-playing playwright would work." Jordan swallowed hard enough for the wine to scrape and burn against the sides of her throat. "Do you know a lot of those?"

Hairless or not, Jordan couldn't work up even an ounce of interest in that type, but she could learn. Maybe. "Any on the site?"

"In this town? No." Elle grabbed the spreadsheet sitting on top of her stack of documents. "In terms of new reports, I have four legislative aides to congressmen, a maritime lawyer, and a guy who owns a new French restaurant on Capitol Hill."

Nope, no uptick in heartbeat or even a blip of interest. "Is the restaurant any good?"

Elle snorted. "You're saying you'd date for food?"

That struck a bit too close for Jordan's comfort. "I do have an excellent role model for that sort of thing."

"Don't do that." Elle leaned forward on her elbows as her eyes narrowed. "You're not your mom."

That was the fear. It bubbled right under the surface, but never fully left Jordan's mind. "I know."

"Hey, it's me. Don't brush this off."

A crack in the dam that held all of this back and kept the pain over her mother's choices from spilling out grew even wider. "My mother started her serial wealthy-man dating life somewhere, Elle. At first she probably thought she was dating to find the right one. Then she started to like flipping through them, got pregnant with me at twenty and the path was set."

Moving from man to man, uprooting her only daughter and living as a mistress or girlfriend until the man's money or welcome wore out, then hunting again. Her mother made a career out of using and being used by men. Up until recently she lived in Santa Fe as the "special friend" of some slick-talking gem salesman. That ended when she asked for money one time too many and she hit the road with a friend. Now her mom was working her way through the men of the Bahamas.

But it wouldn't end there. There was always a new man. Always that hitch in her mother's voice as she grew excited and described a new living arrangement, commenting on how this guy was "the one" and she knew it. Always a crash when something went wrong. And with seven marriages and eleven broken engagements, something always went wrong.

After a lifetime of watching the sick dance and more than once visiting her mother in the hospital when a benefactor's wife found out about the sex-for-lifestyle arrangement, Jordan gave up. She'd spent years trying to get her mother into other jobs, into another world. And even longer trying not to become her mother.

"Your mom relies on men to survive. She expects to go from one to another, taking then moving on." Elle shook her head. "She chose the life. You run from it, and that makes all the difference when it comes to men."

"Then, why do I keep thinking about Forest." Jordan put words to her feelings and didn't try to downplay them at all. Not with Elle. "It's this weird magnetic pull. I vow to stay away, but I don't want to."

Elle smiled over the rim of the glass. "You should see your face when you talk about him."

"I'm guessing it's the look of wide-eyed idiocy."

"Not at all, but I would point out how you describe him doesn't really match the little we've heard and collected on him."

Jordan leaned her forehead against the glass, letting the coolness of the surface seep into her warm skin. The churning in her stomach that settled in whenever she thought about her mother refused to cease. "Oh, he's as hot as we were told he'd be. Trust me."

"I mean, the whole flirting with you, getting you to his office part, doesn't sound like an aloof guy who insists on a confidentiality agreement before he gets a woman into bed."

There was the weirdness again. Amazing how that sort of talk made Jordan both more and less interested in seeing Forest naked. "I keep hoping you'll admit you're messing with me and making that agreement stuff up. I mean, he does know there's a difference between buying a house and having sex, right?"

No way would she ever believe he confused the two. The guy struck her as way too sure of himself to be accustomed to failure in the bedroom.

Elle wiggled her eyebrows. "I guess you can ask him next time he *challenges* you."

Yeah, about that. "I should leave this assignment before it explodes in my face."

"I'm going to skip the crude joke." Elle leaned over and refilled her glass. She held up the bottle.

Jordan shook her head. No refill necessary here. Somehow in all the Forest and mother talk she'd failed to drink even a sip. "Please do."

"But you're not going to leave him alone." Elle curled up on the corner of the couch again. "You're too intrigued. He's a puzzle and he's got you wanting to move the pieces around and put it together."

Jordan hid her wince. “That doesn’t sound very sexy.”

“Exactly how many hours did it take you to get ready this morning?” Elle waved a hand up and down in the air, looking over Jordan as she went. “That outfit? Hot. I’m guessing you spent more than your usual twenty minutes throwing it together and getting out the door.”

Jordan fought off the urge to smooth down her shirt where it stuck to her from the walking part of her commute. “I thought about wearing my flannel pajamas, but it’s still eighty outside.”

Elle pointed in and around her mouth. “And is that freshly applied lipstick?”

And shaved legs…and mascara. Yeah, the whole female arsenal was on display. “You don’t know everything, you know.”

“I know you and I know interest when I see it. You have it in him. Big-time.” Elle smacked her lips together. “And, again, that’s completely normal.”

“He’s like a science experiment.” Admittedly, it wasn’t the best comparison out there, but Jordan was stuck with it as soon as it popped out. “I’m going to poke around, gather some intel on the male executive staff at Redder Investments. I can make this work for the website.”

“So, you’re refusing to let this be personal for you?”

“No touching, no kissing, no naked stuff.” Even though every one of those things tempted her to the point her muscles shook.

Elle sighed and generally threw out most of the girlfriend-you’ve-got-to-be-kidding signs. “I’ll remind you of this moment when you sleep with him and I get to say 'I told you so.'"

Nothing in Elle's sentence was as upsetting as it should have been. Jordan wasn't sure what to make of that.

CHAPTER SEVEN

Subject Request for Kevin Alford: He seems more interested in his best friend Tom than me. I'm trying not to be paranoid. —Member 99

Response from Member 306: I walked in on Kevin and Tom once...you're not paranoid.

FOREST MANAGED TO get through the entire day without seeing Jordan. He wanted to credit his strong sense of control, but truth was meetings about the southwest waterfront project kept him out of the office all day. Damn Ryan Peterson and his complete incompetence. His failures meant more work for Forest, which made Forest hate the guy even more. Who knew that was even possible?

Even through the dragging exhaustion, Forest heard the hum of vacuums from the cleaning crew down the hall. He glanced over at the chair where Jordan sat during the day. The small lamp over her desk burned, shining a light in a circle around her computer. The rest of the reception area stayed shadowed in darkness.

Not seeing her there gnawed at him. Not that she should be around at this time of night. Hell, he shouldn't be there.

He shook his head and opened the door to his office. The soft click of heels against the hardwood floor of the lounge area kept him from slipping inside and out of sight. He looked up in time to see Jordan exit the bathroom at the end of the hall and head toward the reception area. As usual, she was staring at her cell.

Keys jangled and her humming carried over the muffled sounds of whatever cleaning was happening inside one of the conference rooms. When she glanced up, her off-key tune died on her lips. Then came the blinking.

She opened her mouth twice before any words came out. “Forest?”

He motioned to the phone in her hand. “Your mom?”

“It would appear she’s very happy with John.”

“I thought the guy’s name was Felix.”

Jordan’s shot him a smile that managed to look sad. “You’re a few days behind.”

“Well, it’s nice she’s dating.” He had no idea if that was true. He’d collected some information on her family, because that’s what a guy did when he planned to take a woman to bed, but the family history was a bit hazy. No father, raised by a single mom, and no siblings.

Jordan leaned against the wall as she slipped her cell in the waistband of her skirt. “You say that because you think she’s sitting in a chair looking all grandmotherly and knitting.”

His mother was more the charity-auction type, but the image seemed reasonable. “No?”

“She only admits to being forty, but she’s forty-five.”

He did the math in his head. “Young.”

“You know how you think of your parents and are

absolutely clear they only had sex the number of times it took to create you and your brother and sister?"

"I try never to think of my parents having sex."

This time amusement flooded Jordan's face and met her eyes. "I don't have the luxury of being able to do that. She tells me. She's always told me who she's sleeping with and how good it is."

Forest's brain went blank. "I'm not even sure what to say to that."

"Now you know how I've felt my entire life."

His hand fell from the doorknob as he straddled the inside/outside threshold to his office. "Why are you still here?"

"I wanted to catch up."

Of all the odd things she'd said to him during their short time together, that was one of the oddest. "On what?"

"Work."

He conducted a quick visual search and didn't see a folder or any other sign of business. She shifted her weight around and her gaze did a quick dart to her desk. The whole fidgeting thing struck Forest as out of character. If anything, the Jordan he'd seen pulsed with a coolness vibe. That simmering heat was one of the many things he found so attractive about her. But something had her bouncing around now.

"Jordan, I hand out the assignments. If Wen is piling on enough to keep you here at—" Forest checked his watch as a new wave of exhaustion from his ninth consecutive sixteen-hour workday crashed over him. "It's almost ten."

"By that logic, you should be home, too."

"It's not really the same thing. I own the place."

She waved her hand. "Either way, I'll let you go."

"Or we could finish our conversation." He had no idea why he said it. Well, some idea, but the timing was pretty screwed up.

She stopped in midturn. Didn't look at him, but didn't run, either. "I'm not sure that's a good idea." She made the comment to her feet.

"Because?"

She faced him then. "You mentioned kissing."

He took in her wide eyes and the way she clenched her hands together in front of her. Whatever internal battle waged in there had her cheeks a rosy pink. He decided to take that as a good sign of something. "I'd rather do it than talk about it."

"I doubt your HR department would approve." Yet she took a step toward him.

The urge to reach out rammed into him with the force of a house. But he'd made his move. There couldn't be any doubt that he wanted more than dictation from her. She had to initiate here. Give him some sign. Any damn sign—hell, he'd settle for that blinking thing—and he'd pick it up from there and run with it.

"Again, I own the place." A fact that kept slipping by people for some reason.

"So, the rules don't apply to you?"

She seemed a bit confused about the rules. Maybe a bit obsessed, as well.

Damn, everything about this woman turned him on. Even the usually annoying shit. Maybe it was the combination of the quick mind and mouth with those slim skirts and mile-long legs. The combination built the anticipation inside him until the pressure behind his zipper threatened to explode.

He focused on the least sexy document on the planet instead—the employee manual. "I don't have a prohibition against interoffice dating."

Those sexy lips twisted in a frown. "Do you want to be sued?"

"The people who work here are grown-ups. They attend all sorts of seminars on workplace behavior." Forest had no idea how they got on this subject, but as long as they were… "I've had executives date before and sneak around until their attempts at subterfuge ended up wasting time and frustrating the hell out of me."

"That's very romantic of you."

He leaned against the doorway, ready to slam on the brakes or reach out for her. He just needed her to send up a flare so he knew which way to go. "If they want to sleep with each other, and both agree and know the terms, I'm not getting in the way."

At his words, a definite heat flared in her eyes. "I'd guess that's a very unique business position."

"I'm not sure what that means."

"Just when I think I get you…" Her voice trailed off, but her steps didn't falter. She walked until she stood right in front of him.

A simple lift of his hands and he could touch her. Damn, he wanted to touch her. Kiss her. Lick her. Drag her to the ground. Any combination of those worked fine for him.

Instead, he forced his mind to stay in the moment. "Yes?"

With one last sweeping glance into the office behind him, she balanced her hand on the wall closest to his shoulder. "Fine."

"Excuse me?"

"Let's stop dodging. Kiss me."

Sweet Jesus. The woman constantly zigged when he thought she'd zag. "Here? You're sure?"

"I'm a big girl, Forest. I know what I want. At this second, you kissing me is at the very top of the list." Her other hand went to his tie, traveled from his neck in a sure line to his stomach. "But it's just one kiss."

She had to be kidding. No way would that ever be enough.

Every inch she touched caught fire beneath the surface. His muscles tightened and strained under her warm palm, begging for flesh-to-flesh contact. "That's a start."

"You have my permission for a kiss."

Somewhere in the back of his head a warning bell rang. He barely knew this woman and she could say anything once his lips touched hers. Wanting her was one thing. Wrestling her clothes off in the middle of his office was another. The latter being the type that could cost him everything.

But his mind and his hands moved on different schedules. One went to the small of her back and pulled her in close. The other slipped through her soft hair. With her head cradled in his palm, his mouth found hers. He skipped over the gentle hello kiss and dove right into an I-want-your-clothes-off scorcher.

Lips pressed. Tongues touched. He couldn't pull back or slow down and when her fingernails pinched his skin through his blazer, the heat between them exploded.

He dragged her into his office and kicked the door closed behind them. Heavy breathing and the soft rustle of clothing shut out the late-night office noises. He pressed her back against the wall and crowded in closer. One pluck and he had her cell and dropped it on the floor, kicking it to the side with his shoe.

The tug on his collar had him raising his head. Air rushed through him, pounding the walls of his lungs, as he waited for her to call an end. Instead, she grabbed the lapels of the jacket and pushed the material off his shoulders with the heels of her hands.

"I want this gone."

Her demand sent heat roaring over his skin like a wildfire. Her hands never stopped moving as she undressed him, dropping his suit jacket to the floor. His tie came next. The silk slid and her hands followed the edge down and over his chest to the top of his pants.

It was the sexiest striptease ever.

Strike that, the one he planned to perform on her would be even better.

Every caress, every touch, had his body shaking harder with the need to be inside her. He thought about the desk and his chair. He wanted to suggest his house, but they'd never make it past the elevator to the garage. Hell, he doubted his legs would carry him down the hall at this point.

Then his mouth was back on hers. The kiss deepened as their lips traveled over each other. With each pass, every tiny groan from the back of her throat, his control slipped further until it seeped out of him.

He had to have her.

His fingers skimmed up the outside of her bare thighs, bringing her tight skirt with him. Bunching the material in his fist, he dragged and pulled until she shifted her hips to help him shimmy the confining material to her waist.

The warmth of her bare skin burned through his palm as his fingertips brushed over the edge of her soft underwear. When his finger slipped under the elastic, he felt a slick wetness. Her scent pulsed around him as his heart hammered hard enough to knock him down.

One hand squeezed her ass cheek. “Damn, woman.”

“Yes.” She lifted her leg and wrapped it around the back of his knee, digging the heel into the top of his calf.

The move opened her to his touch. He didn’t hesitate. His finger slipped inside her as her breath hiccupped against his throat. She was tight and wet and two seconds away from having those panties ripped right off her.

His mouth found the sexy spot right under her ear and his finger continued to pump and prime her body for him. “Tell me you want this.”

“Yes.” As if the word weren’t enough, she rotated her hips, rubbing her lower body over his pounding erection.

He would have sworn or begged for mercy, but he couldn’t find the breath to make a sound other than a moan. He settled for taking her hand and pressing the back against the wall next to her head. She kept it there as he trailed a finger down her throat to her breast. One hand cupped and squeezed. The other continued the insistent pumping inside of her.

For this he wanted total surrender, her body open and ready. His fingertip danced around her opening, then dipped inside again. He plunged and retreated, enjoying the buck of her hips as she pressed deeper against him as if seeking his hand.

"Forest, do it now." She unbuttoned the top few buttons of his shirt and kissed the skin she unveiled there.

The passion he sensed inside her exploded. Her tongue licked his skin. Hot breath blew over his chest. Hands and mouth and her body sliding against his.

He needed to taste her. With his knees bent, he hit the floor, ready to suck and taste her until her body went wild. He dipped his head, inhaling the warm heat and licking her wetness off his fingers. But he wanted more.

The roar of the vacuum cleaner screeched through the room.

Jordan froze. So did he. The sound and the reality of what was happening barely hit him before she started pushing at his shoulder and squirming against the wall.

"Forest, stop." Her whisper sounded frantic and out of control as she clenched her legs together and tugged on the edge of her skirt, trying to bring it down despite his head being right there. Never mind she trapped his finger inside her.

He tried to sit back on his heels, but her shifting almost knocked him over. "Whoa, Jordan. Wait a second."

She clearly wasn't in the mood for patience. She shoved her skirt down the rest of the way and pushed his hand away from her body. Before he'd fully regained his senses, she stepped away and placed a good five feet between them. Her body shook as she stood there and the pink on her cheeks was now a bright red.

He hadn't moved from his position kneeling on the floor. He reached out and snagged her cell before stumbling to his feet again.

"Did you know they were out there?" She held a hand over her mouth and spoke in a voice so low it almost didn't register.

When he'd realized how ready she was for him, he'd forgotten everything, including most of his common sense. But he never meant to embarrass her. "Of course not."

Standing there with the top of his shirt open and his belt undone—something he didn't even remember happening—he feared the worst. Tears. He struggled for the right words and realized he wasn't even sure what the wrong ones were so he could avoid them.

They were adults, for fuck's sake. Adults had sex. It was completely normal. The stopping wasn't. His balls would ache the rest of the night from the sudden halt.

Winding up his anger, he'd just decided to fire anyone still in the building when he glanced at Jordan. She stood still with her hand hiding most of her face.

Son of a bitch. Looked like he had to apologize. For what, he wasn't quite sure. But when a woman blushed from head to foot and froze in horror, a guy had to say something calming. Anything. Probably after he rezipped his pants. Shame his bulge made that a nearly impossible task.

He'd just decided to give her a speech about being grown-ups with needs. Reassure her all would be well despite this little scene happening in the middle of his office, when her shoulders shook. Then she doubled over.

"Jordan?"

Laughter bubbled up a second later.

Not the usual reaction to getting half naked with a woman, but at least she hadn't screamed or blamed. "Uh, you okay over there?"

She stood back up and stuttered out a word. "Hysterical."

The vacuum stopped and whispered voices sounded right outside his office door. He couldn't do anything about either of those things. He was too busy staring at the woman who a second ago he'd planned to get to know with his tongue. It was quite possible she'd lost her mind.

Or he had.

Another few seconds passed before she regained control and swallowed the last of her laughter. But amusement lit her face from her bright eyes to the mischief playing around her mouth.

She snorted. "You have to laugh at this."

He wasn't sure what the proper reaction was to a fit of giggling in this circumstance. "I do?"

Stepping in front of him, she lifted her hands and rebuttoned his shirt. Her knuckles brushed against his skin and when she reached for his belt, he clenched his stomach muscles on a sharp intake of breath.

"Care to fill me in?" He was impressed his voice sounded strong. Words spun through his brain, but he couldn't catch them long enough to form a coherent sentence. He'd never been redressed before and the movements mixed with subtle caresses to make it oddly erotic.

She skimmed her hands over his shoulders. "You are the boss, after all."

"Believe it or not, I don't feel like I'm in charge." He handed the cell back to her.

"You poor thing. Derailed by the cleaning staff." She clearly thought it was funny, because she chuckled again. "But you sure can kiss."

That sounded like a good thing. "Does that mean you're going home with me?"

"No."

The woman had him spinning. "Jordan—"

"You said *no* meant *no*."

"That will always be the case." When she threw him a blinding smile, he let out a sigh of defeat. "Fine, then how about dinner tomorrow?"

After a second or two of hesitation, she nodded. "At some point tomorrow you can give me the name of the restaurant and the time, and I'll meet you there."

"What kind of date is that?"

"A woman can't be too careful."

He'd just seen that phrase somewhere. "Dinner it is."

She patted his chest and placed a chaste kiss on his chin. "Good night, Forest."

"I'll drive you home."

"Not happening." She was gone before he could figure out why she thought the night had to end for them.

THE FRONT DOOR to Jordan's apartment opened and Elle rushed in. She had her hair in a ponytail and her hands wrapped around a steaming mug of something. She scrambled over to the couch and sat next to Jordan. "What's going on? What's with the late-night SOS?"

Jordan managed to get changed and scrub the makeup off her face. Now she sat in oversize boxers and a tank top with the remote in her hand. At some point she'd be able to concentrate to turn the television on.

Elle snapped her fingers in front of Jordan's face. "Hey, there."

"I screwed up tonight."

Elle slumped back against the sofa cushions. "Oh my God, you had sex with him."

"So close." Part of Jordan hated how close they came. The other part hated that they only got close and didn't do the deed.

Forest had her spinning and stumbling and generally acting as if she didn't have two brain cells to rub together. When he kissed her, she got smacked with a shot of dizziness. His finger slid inside her and she had to fight the urge to climb all over him. And that mouth…that deserved a page on the Need to Know Hall of Fame. The site didn't have one of those, but she now wanted to add one.

"What does 'close' mean in the context of sex? Like, did he miss, not find the hole." Elle held the mug to her mouth. "And I hope that last part is wrong, because Forest looks like he'd know his way around a woman's body. If that's not true, I give up."

Jordan tried very hard not to think about holes. "Hands up skirt. Finger, mouth, but no more."

"Ah, the critical lack of penetration." Elle made a face. "He knew how, right?"

Talk about a blunt conversation. Jordan was used to it. Sharing love-life information didn't make her squirm. Despite her other failures, her mom made it clear there was nothing wrong with sex so long as it was safe and consensual. It was the healthy message that went along with all the men rotating in and out of her life.

"He did, but that's not the point. He's the exact wrong guy for me."

"Nope."

Jordan flipped the remote in her hands. "Elle, I'm serious."

"Hold that thought." Elle put the mug on the coffee table and went to the desk.

"What are you doing?"

"This forty-something guy who lives with his mother in a one-bedroom apartment—yes, I said one-bedroom—is wrong for you." Elle held a file. As she talked, she held up one page after another. "This one who can't hold a job for more than two months at a time is wrong. Then there's the guy who keyed his ex's car and wrote *whore* on it because she had the nerve to leave him."

Man, Jordan was so out of it she hadn't even looked at the work information Elle had compiled and assessed tonight. That never happened. When she had a temp job, Jordan came home, relaxed and then spent some time in front of the television while she put in more hours on the site.

She shook her head. "That crazy gal, whatever was she thinking dumping that prince."

"She's probably thinking she needs a restraining order."

Jordan got the point, but that didn't solve the Forest problem or her strange weakness for him. "There is a choice between that list of horribles and a controlling business guy."

Elle put down one file and grabbed another. The pages started flipping. "Sure, there's the guy who plays the flute in the orchestra. Nice, but really hasn't dated much, or ever, in thirty years. The hardworking and decent scientist who works about twenty hours a day and travels all the time. He'd be a lot of fun to schedule dates with."

As Elle moved on to the next choice, Jordan stepped in before the list put her to sleep. "They sound lovely."

"*Boring* is the word you're looking for."

She'd had a front-row seat to a lifetime of excitement. Her mother met a man and fell in love in a second. Or she tricked her mind into thinking she did to justify moving in on him regardless of his marital status. If he had money, she gave him a shot.

The cycle kept repeating and it wore Jordan down. "Is that so bad? Boring means safe."

Elle frowned, marring that cute face with harsh forehead wrinkles. "Boring means boring."

The truth was so much worse than the level of dullness. Jordan bit her bottom lip as she debated saying the words out loud. She didn't care if Elle knew, but giving voice to her weakness made it more real somehow. "When I get near Forest, the hardwiring in my brain misfires."

"Good."

Leave it to Elle to boil everything down to one simple word. Jordan thought another word was more fitting—*stupid.* "How is that good?"

"You're attracted to him."

Jordan flipped the remote harder that time. It flew out of her hands and nailed her in the knee. She rubbed the unexpected injury. "I've been attracted to men before."

Elle sat back down, but not before reaching over and grabbing the remote out of Jordan's hands. "But he's good for you. He won't take your shit and you can't walk all over him."

"Uh, hello?"

"He's not hiding a wife and he's not a covert abuser."

"Do we know that?" Jordan basically did. She'd spent far too many hours checking him out online and dropping small comments at work to get people talking. The employees found him fair but tough, which was her assessment, as well.

"It's called dating." Elle smacked her remote against the palm of her other hand. "You started the website to help women find good men to date. Sure, you help them ferret out the assholes, but the goal is dating, right?"

"Sure."

"There."

Clearly Elle thought she made a point. "There what?"

"You found a good guy. Controlling but hot and not a weirdo, as far as we know." Elle wiggled her eyebrows. "More importantly, a guy who seems like he knows how to use his hands."

Jordan remembered the combination of his finger and his mouth and heat flushed through her. "He definitely does."

"Then right now, my friend, you are winning the D.C. dating game."

CHAPTER EIGHT

Subject Request for Seth Greenburg: He wants to make a video & insists I'm the first. —Member 4

Response from Member 211: Oh, honey. Many have fallen for that line coming out of that beautiful face. He's a liar.

FOREST BARELY MADE it to seven o'clock the next night without dunking his head in an ice bath. Seeing Jordan sitting there, just a few feet outside his office door, had his body revving on high alert all day long. And watching her walk out at five, those hips swishing after she bent over and grabbed her bag out of the bottom desk drawer amounted to pure female-induced torture.

That would teach him to keep his door open so he could sneak a peek at her face now and then.

The only thing that prevented him from giving in early and changing their dinner to a late lunch was Ryan Peterson. That guy kept buzzing around, begging to be squashed. Now he had it in his head the damn website, Need to Know, had ruined his reputation and caused him to lose the waterfront deal.

Forest knew the argument was a load of crap. Deep inside Ryan had to know it. Still, he kept whining about the dating website ruining his reputation and interfering with his business contracts. He threw around lawsuit threats against the site and even promised he'd drag Forest's company into the mess. Basically, Ryan was doing everything possible to add to Forest's already seemingly insurmountable work pile.

The last place Forest should be at this time of the day in the middle of the week was a restaurant. He should grab a sandwich and hunker down at his desk. Should but wouldn't.

He was reaching across the table for his water, when movement at the end of his row of tables caught his attention. He knew Jordan stood there before he ever looked up, and when he did meet her gaze he almost swallowed his tongue.

Sweet loving damn.

She wore a short-sleeve black dress that hugged her waist, then flared out over her hips before coming to rest a few inches above her knees. And those legs. Long, lean and bare. Just when he recovered from the memory of his fingertips against those thighs, he noticed the spiky red heels.

But the body, that walk, had nothing on her smile. It lit her face and brought a twinge of color to her cheeks.

There was no way in hell he'd be able to choke down an appetizer tonight.

He somehow got to his feet, but God knew he didn't remember standing. A napkin dangled from his fingers. When she stopped across from him, he threw it down and pivoted around her to pull out her chair.

The subtle whiff of orange wrapped around him as

he leaned down to whisper in her ear. "That was quite an entrance."

She glanced up at him for the briefest of seconds. "I decided to be memorable this time."

His comment at the wedding about her dress came rushing back on him. How he ever thought this woman could blend in, even for a second, stunned him. He'd be able to pick her out in a room full of hundreds of women. Something about the way she carried herself and the confidence that swirled around her had him chasing and wanting and generally forgetting his usual rules about women.

With a broken engagement on his scorecard, he preferred to keep his emotional distance. Not that he shunned commitment. He just preferred his life outside work as simple as possible and long-term dating struck him as the exact opposite of simple.

Enjoy women, date when he had time and otherwise focus on building his business. He'd mapped out that three-part plan the day after his father had security escort him out the lobby doors of the family business. He hadn't been back and, despite all his father's yelling and threats, Forest never had to crawl back and beg for forgiveness, either.

"Thank you for not wearing that dress to work." Forest sat again, deliberately pushing all thoughts of his dysfunctional family out of his mind. "I would have violated more than one HR rule to get near you. Me and half the staff. No question about it."

"There's nothing provocative about this dress." She ran her fingertips across her exposed collarbone. "No plunging neckline and only a minimum of skin showing."

"That outfit is all about anticipation. A guy sees it and hopes he'll be treated to more." And seeing her fingers skim over her skin had him tripping over his words. "So that you know, that's sexier than just about anything."

She unfolded her napkin and laid it across her lap. "Aren't you the sweet talker?"

"You should be impressed I can think at all at the moment." Not that the babble running through his brain made any sense. He saw her and forgot about work and his responsibilities and even about that idiot Ryan.

Forest wanted to talk to her, touch her, run his hands all over her. It had been a long time since attraction smacked into him this hard. The energy to fight it abandoned him almost from the beginning.

"I'm thinking a guy like you can have his pick of any woman." The amusement in her husky voice faded. A thread of anger weaved its way in.

Normally he'd skip over the comment, but something about her tone had him stopping and investigating. "What kind of guy am I?"

The waitress interrupted Jordan with what felt like a never-ending recitation of specials. Fish, lamb…fine. He got it.

When the server left and conversations around them blended into a steady hum, Jordan stayed quiet. She studied her menu. As he watched her, Forest heard an occasional laugh rise above the crowd noise and the clink of silverware as the people two tables down dug into their steaks.

"Well?" That's all he said. He knew she ignored the question on purpose. No way was he letting this one slide.

Jordan lowered the menu and stared at him over the top. She didn't pretend confusion. "Rich, powerful. Born wealthy and used to getting what he wants."

All of it fit in a way, but didn't in most others. "Sounds as if you've been checking up on me."

Her head tilted to the side, sending her hair slipping over her shoulder. "Would that offend you?"

"No."

"Oh, come on." She balanced her elbows on the edge of the table and leaned in.

"Are you referring to checking me out on that website, Need to Know?"

Her smile faded as her expression went blank. "Maybe."

"Look, I can understand a woman wanting to know about the man she plans to invite into her bed. Women do need to be careful. I just think a website can't replace getting to know someone in person."

"Agreed. I poked around and got the vitals, like school and family and dating history."

He doubted she knew one sentence more than his PR department put out there. "Did your investigating tell you I'm the black sheep of the family?"

Those sexy eyes narrowed. "You're a successful businessman. Unless you killed someone, I have a hard time seeing why you'd be considered a disappointment to your parents."

He'd been disloyal, which was much worse in his father's eyes. "You'd be surprised."

Jordan smiled as she took a sip of water. "What, you were a bad boy, so you can't attend the annual family yacht race or something?"

The way she said it pushed him to prove her assumptions wrong. "Being born into a family with money doesn't solve everything."

Her hand froze in the middle of putting her glass down. When it finally hit the table it smacked against the wood with a sharp crack. "You never went hungry and always knew you'd have a bed to sleep in that night."

Looked like he wasn't the only one with a messed-up personal history. He'd refrained from picking her life apart, thinking old-fashioned dating and getting to know each other might be an interesting twist, but now he regretted the decision. "Are you saying—"

She waved him off. "Just offering a response to your general comment."

Wen and a few others knew, but Forest rarely shared the details of his life with anyone, certainly not with a woman he just met and was trying to impress. But for some reason he craved honesty with her, so he supplied the barest of information. "It's a well-kept family secret, something no one in the Redder family talks about at parties, but I assure you my younger brother is the heir. Except for some communication with my baby sister, I don't have any contact with my parents or anyone else in the family. They no longer consider me their son."

Noise rattled around them, but a quiet settled around the table. Jordan moved as if stuck in slow motion. "Are you playing me?"

"No."

After a few beats of silence, she reached across the table and covered Forest's hand with hers. "In that case, I'm sorry."

He hated the sympathy he saw in her eyes, but the warmth of her skin mixed with his and he couldn't pull away. "I've learned to accept it."

"Maybe one day you can tell me how to do that."

"What?"

"Accept a rough family dynamic and not let it define you."

The longing in her voice got to him. "If you need me to, I will."

"You always seem to say the right thing." She sat back in her chair, putting as much distance between them as possible in the small space. "I'm wondering if that's practiced or real."

"What does the website say?" When her eyes widened, he continued. "I'm assuming you're a member, since I've heard you use the tagline more than once and, well, from the article I read today about it, it sounds as if every single woman in town is on it."

"Hardly, but yes. I'm a member." Her hands slipped from her lap to the arms of the chair and back again. "And no."

He was so busy watching her fidget, he missed whatever she said. "Excuse me?"

"You're not on it…yet."

The playful teasing came zipping back into her voice. He welcomed the break to the tension snapping at him. "Will I be after tonight?"

She shrugged. "We'll see."

"Then, let's come to an agreement." Since he had no intention of making a general announcement to the crowded restaurant, he leaned in. His finger traced the outline of her silverware against the stark white tablecloth. "After dinner I will drive you home, not because

I think paying for dinner gives me rights with you, but because I'm not a dick and want to make sure you get back to your place without incident. I'm still kicking my ass for not insisting I see you home after our office run-in."

"Run-in?"

"I thought you'd prefer that to me mentioning how close we came to having sex in front of the cleaning crew."

This time she wrapped her long fingers around the armrests. "Very sweet. Okay."

He ignored the "sweet" part because he feared that led them down the wrong path. One that didn't finish in a bed. "And anything that happens after I drive up is your call. A kiss, me coming up with you—whatever—you have all the control. I've made my play and my intentions can't be a mystery."

"You want me to be the aggressor."

"Oh, I'm happy to take the lead." If she sent him the right look, he'd be all over her. "You'll just need to tell me I can."

"I only agreed to dinner."

But she understood. He saw it in every muscle and the glint in her eye. She got his message. She was in charge.

He nodded. "Then, let's order."

JORDAN HAD NO idea how she forced more than two bites down during dinner. Even as they chatted about safe topics, like Ryan Peterson's loser tendencies or the state of Forest's waterfront project, a part of her mind wandered to what would come later.

It sucked for him, really, because he gave her his full attention. He didn't stare at other women. Didn't say or do anything inappropriate. He'd kept his word and at the end of the evening pulled up to the lobby of her building to drop her off...until she invited him up.

Not that the decision hit her in the car. No, she'd excused herself more than a half hour ago and texted Elle to go over and hide all website evidence in the condo. Jordan wanted Elle to shut and lock everything in the small den the real-estate broker had tried to convince Jordan was a guest bedroom. Never mind she'd have to fold the mattress in half to fit a bed in there.

"Let me do that." Forest reached around her and took the keys from Jordan's shaking fingers.

She didn't realize a small tremor ran through her until the jangling of metal echoing in the hallway stopped and her front door opened. "Sure."

Despite her desire to remain calm and in control, she almost bolted inside. The goal was to get to the bedroom and hide the eleven outfits she'd tried on before this dress. Right now they lay scattered all over the floor and draped over the exercise bike she used as a very expensive hanger.

He held the door for her to go in first. She walked down the short hallway past the kitchen on one side and den on the other and into the open family room. The place looked clean. Certainly picked up. That had to be Elle's doing, because Jordan had long ago given up the battle with clutter. Working from home made stacks of papers inevitable. Not that you could tell at this moment.

Jordan peeked into the bedroom to her left and saw a stack of pillows and a clear comforter. No discarded underwear. If Elle hadn't been her best friend before, she'd have won the title tonight.

Forest's hands fell over her shoulders as he whispered against her hair. "I like your condo."

"Me, too." Her breath stuttered in her chest. A few more minutes of that and she'd start wheezing. Not exactly the perfect setup for sexy times.

His mouth found her neck. Hot breath skipped over her skin right before his lips went to work. The gentle suction had her knees buckling and her head falling back against his shoulder. The way her body melted into his should have embarrassed her. After all she'd made some sort of vow…not that she could remember a line of it right now.

"Tell me what you want." His voice vibrated against her skin.

She let her head fall to the side this time, hoping he'd trail the line of kisses to the base of her neck, then lower. Instead, he hesitated. He didn't stop, but his mouth didn't move over her. He continued to kiss her neck as his fingers flexed against her shoulders.

"Please, Forest." She backed up, pressing her butt into his groin to give him permission.

As if he'd been given a flashing green light, his arm wrapped around her waist and held her steady. Heat radiated off him and burned through her. His erection pressed against her as he rocked his body into hers.

"Say it." His mouth lifted, journeying to her jawline and inflaming the nerve endings there.

She decided to spell it out before she threw him on the couch and straddled him, and that was in about-to-happen mode. "I want you inside me."

His hands stilled for a second before roaming again. "Very soon."

With every cell tingling, she wanted to demand he do it now. She might have opened her mouth and suggested they fast-forward this first round, but the rip of her zipper stopped her. One minute her dress held tight against her body. The next, the bodice fell and his hands slipped inside. His fingers traced her nipples through the black lace of her bra.

When she turned her head toward him, he captured her mouth in a searing kiss. Not gentle or quiet. No, this one claimed. Hot, sensual and carrying a promise of the wicked times to come, his lips traveled over hers even as his hands pushed her dress and the thin crinoline underneath to the floor.

One arm lifted over her head and found his hair. When he lifted her other arm up, she felt a tug as the clasp on her bra opened. Then his hands cupped her bare breasts and massaged the nipples to tight sensitive peeks.

Forest Redder did know his way around a woman.

His hips bucked against her, mimicking the rhythm she hoped to experience within the next minute or two. She heard the shuffle of material, then his hands left her for a second. When her eyes popped open and the protest hovered on her lips, he appeared in front of her.

With his focus transfixed on her breasts, he peeled off her bra. Fingers dipped under the edge of her tiny panties next. His thumb rubbed against her as the pressure began to build inside her. Yet he didn't stop kissing her. His mouth met hers and his finger slid inside her slick opening.

If he hadn't been holding her up, she would have

crumpled to the floor. She felt weightless and boneless. Every care slipped away and her whole being focused on getting him into the bedroom and sprawled across that mattress.

She lifted her head. And faced him head-on. Those green eyes had darkened and a tense passion showed in every line of his body.

"Take me to bed." She whispered the words against his lips and saw a tremble shake through his shoulders as she watched.

"Yes." Then his mouth came back to hers full force and his hands fell to her waist.

He walked backward as she stripped off his tie and unbuttoned the little white buttons on his shirt. She would have shredded the expensive material, ripped the buttons right off despite the cost, but the way their bodies kept knocking against each other and their hands explored, she settled for dipping her hand inside and caressing the bare skin of his chest.

She had no idea how he steered them into place, but when the back of her legs hit the edge of the bed, she sat. The move brought her face in a direct line with his erection. She didn't hesitate. Her fingers went to work as his belt buckle clanked and his zipper screeched through the quiet and punctuated their heavy breathing.

Her head dipped forward as she rubbed her palm over him through the opening in his dress pants. She had his erection out and in her hand before he could finish his sharp intake of breath. She pumped and squeezed while his hands slid through her hair.

"Jordan." He clenched his fingers as he whispered her name.

Not good enough. She wanted to drive him right to the edge so she wouldn't be the only one standing there. Her tongue licked up his length as she clenched his butt cheeks in her hands. When his body tensed, she kept going.

Every single part of him felt right to her. From his smell to his body, he fit her.

Now she wanted it all.

With one last lingering suck, she pulled a moan out of him. Then she fell back against the bed with her hands by her head. She would have lifted her legs or issued a new invitation, but her muscles failed her and the need driving through her had her vision blurring.

But he didn't need help with this part. The second her back hit the mattress, he shrugged out of his shirt and bent down to run his hand over the damp front of her lacy underwear. She was wet and ready and when he stripped the tiny scrap of material off her legs, she almost cried in relief.

Then his knee hit the bed and he shifted until his mouth was on her. His tongue up and inside of her. He licked and sucked and kept going when her hips lifted off the bed and her fingers dove through his hair. As he explored every tiny muscle, she heard the soft growl under his groans and felt her breath hiccup inside her chest.

With each pass of his tongue and fingers the nerve endings flared to life. Her sensitive skin burned everywhere he touched. She thrashed and tightened her legs against his shoulders. Anything to ease the winding sensation pumping through her.

Just when she thought she couldn't take one more second, his mouth traveled up her stomach to her breasts. He took one, then the other into his mouth and licked her nipples until the sensitive areas ached. During all the touching and tasting, he'd stripped off his pants, because she felt the brush of hair on his legs against her soft thighs.

When he lay full against her with his upper body balanced on his elbows above her, she almost begged for relief. He stole what little breath she had when he kissed her again. This time, the kiss lingered. Her head spun and her arms wrapped around his shoulders for balance.

Before she could ask about protection, she felt him shift and heard the rip of paper. His body lifted, but only for a second. Then he came back. He pulled her legs up around him as she felt him right at her entrance.

His gaze burned into her. "You're sure?"

She couldn't speak. Couldn't think. But she knew she wanted this. She told him the only way she could right then. She kissed his shoulder then nipped at his skin in small bites.

As she pressed his shoulders in closer, he started to enter her. He didn't skip right to plunging and pumping. He slid in, giving her body time to adjust. Then he slipped back and pushed forward again. The move was steady, robbing her mind of thought and stealing her breath.

The feel of him over her, around her, had her body clenching even as release hovered just outside her grasp. He didn't speed up. He entered her on a steady rhythm, then retreated and began the slow sensual torture again. After a few minutes, her entire body shook with need.

"Faster." She whispered the plea against his throat. "Now, Forest."

Only then did he speed up. The room filled with the

sounds and smells of their lovemaking. Sweat slicked his back and her fingernails dug into his skin. He plunged deeper, speeding up as his finger rubbed her clit.

Sensations battered her, tossing the last of her control aside. The tightening inside her had her meeting his thrusts while she chanted his name. Just as his body shuddered above hers, something broke lose inside her. Waves of pleasure crashed over her. Her hips lifted and her thighs slammed hard against him. She tried to press and clench, anything to release the energy pounding through her.

With a final push, his rhythm changed. His big body shook over her as her head fell back against the pillows. When the orgasm slammed into her, she inhaled on a mix of shock and pleasure. Every part of her trembled as a soft whisper of his name escaped her lips. Then he kissed her again and she couldn't think about anything other than keeping them right where they were until morning.

CHAPTER NINE

Subject Request for Jake Ballman: He says he can't share info because he's a spy. —Member 163

Response from Member 80: He tried that line on me, too. Then I found my Visa in his wallet. He's a scam artist. Run away now.

FOREST WASN'T EXACTLY a master of the morning after. He'd experienced several in his time, but he was usually the one stepping into the shower, hoping his nighttime partner would be gone before he turned off the water and got out again. He wasn't accustomed to being the guest. That made standing in the middle of Jordan's kitchen extra odd this morning.

Not that he was complaining about the night before. Damn, the woman had him ignoring sleep and hanging on the edge of a heart attack for hours. Now if only he could figure out how to work her coffeemaker. It was pretty fancy. His had a timer and a place for the beans and water. That's it. She had some expensive version that had him thinking about her temp salary.

Owning the condo, the impressive wardrobe. The pieces didn't exactly fit with his image of a struggling office temp. The city was not cheap, but she didn't appear to be in financial trouble. He liked the idea of her being secure. But the question of how kept bumping around the inside of his mind. He knew about her law-firm job. Maybe she saved money. Again, logical, but doubt kept nipping at him.

"You need help?" Jordan walked in, wearing a long T-shirt and what appeared to be nothing else.

Any thought of money and coffee vanished. Those legs went on forever and the shirt did little to cover them. She had her hair up and her face scrubbed clean.

The woman clearly was trying to kill him. Make his heartbeat triple until he passed out or something.

"I've got it." He wasn't sure that was true, but he was more concerned about another topic at the moment. He liked to win and this time the victory carried all sorts of benefits.

She slid onto the barstool across the counter from him and put her cell down in front of her. After a quick scan of the kitchen, she reached over to finish off the coffee prep and press the button to start. They sat in comfortable silence as the machine went to work. Every now and then her phone would buzz and she'd look at the screen.

He glanced over. "Your mom?"

Jordan read for a few more seconds, then sighed. "Good news is she seems satisfied with John."

"That's the new guy?" Forest swore the name kept changing. Probably had something to do with all that dating her mother did.

"The newest one." Jordan waved her hand in the air. "But don't feel the need to memorize the name. It's likely to change when she gets back from the Bahamas."

Bahamas? His parents had been married since before paper was invented. It was a screwed-up mess of a marriage, but it kept ticking. He barely understood their situation. He definitely didn't understand whatever was happening with Jordan's mom. "Excuse me?"

"She's a serial dater. Actually, a serial marryer."

Sounded messy and expensive to him. He had a former fiancée and that was more than enough in the "former" department. "That's a thing?"

"She's the expert."

"She sounds like an interesting woman."

"That's the word everyone uses." Jordan fidgeted in her chair. "I've gotten used to the way she lives her life."

"Are you sure?" When she glanced up at him, he stared in the direction of her chair. The squeaking immediately stopped.

"I know your family isn't close—"

"Understatement."

"—but imagine your sister when she was younger. The idea of her having sex probably would have driven you crazy."

Something in the back of his brain exploded. "I prefer to believe she still hasn't had sex."

"How old is she?"

"Twenty-four."

"Wow, okay. I see you've got that overprotective thing down." Jordan rolled her eyes in a way that said he was being a dumbass. "Well, my point is my mom was upset I waited."

"To do what?"

She gave him eye contact, but she kept swiveling her chair and sliding the placemat around on the counter. "Lose my virginity."

Every single thought in Forest's head slammed to a halt. "You're kidding."

"I was nineteen and she was horrified." Jordan held up a hand. "Not that she wanted me sleeping around, because she totally didn't, but I had a boyfriend when I was sixteen and she couldn't believe I didn't do it then."

"That's kind of messed up." He spent a lot of time dwelling on his family situation. He tried to come up with ways to resolve it or at least ease the tension to make it easier on his sister, who was stuck in the middle. This, Jordan's situation, was a whole different type of dysfunction. He wasn't completely clear on which was worse.

"Only kind of?"

After a few minutes the green light on the coffeemaker flicked on and Forest forced his hands to slow down as he grabbed the mugs. What he really wanted to do was pour a cup and down it.

He waited until the coffee hit the cups and she started humming before he shifted off their bizarre conversation to one he could handle better, but only slightly. "For the record, the interest isn't over."

She eyed him over the top of the mug. "What are you talking about?"

"You said I was all about the chase. Well, I felt pretty caught last night and I'm not going anywhere." It was tempting to call in sick for the first time in his adult life.

A soft pink stained her cheeks as she fiddled with the edge of the placemat under her elbows. "What about the agreement?"

He took a sip of coffee, because at six in the morning he was already a half hour behind on his usual daily caffeine intake. "Should I know what that means?"

"The confidentiality agreement."

Between the words and her sudden refusal to give him eye contact, he stilled with the cup halfway to his mouth. "Excuse me?"

"According to the rumors, you make your bed partners sign a piece of paper promising not to talk." She closed one eye and wrinkled her nose. "That's not on the site, by the way. Just whispers around the ladies' locker room."

He was pretty sure she'd lost her mind. "An agreement in exchange for sex?"

"I'm not sure I'd phrase it that way."

He searched his mind for anything that could fit. The only time a woman he had sex with signed an agreement was when it was part of a separate business deal and unrelated to the bedroom activities. He had no idea how that news got around or how it got so tangled up.

Not that he was surprised. This sort of thing happened when rumors ran the day. "Well, call it whatever you want, but it sounds nuts."

Jordan nodded. "I agree."

When she continued to stand there, he decided to be as clear as possible. "And I don't have that requirement."

"Can't lie, that's something of a relief."

"Yet, even with the possibility out there, you slept with me anyway." That was the only part of this discussion he found interesting.

"Like you said yesterday, information is fine, but it's better to find out the truth for yourself."

Huh, not so appealing when she put it that way. He was hoping for something more along the lines of being unable to resist him.

He eased the death grip on the coffee mug and put

it on the counter. No need to smash dishes. That sure wasn't a great way to end an otherwise fantastic night. Still, her comment refused to settle in his mind. "So I was an experiment."

She nodded. "I did use that excuse."

"Okay."

"It was one of the nicer excuses I gave myself."

Maybe he should carry her back to bed. They worked in there. Out here, not so much. "I'm not sure this morning is going well."

"Let's try this." She slid off the stool and came around the counter to stand right in front of him with her hand pressed against his stomach. "Last night was amazing."

"That's much better." And if her fingers ventured even an inch lower, they would be back in bed again. He'd brought four condoms. He had one left and wasn't afraid to use it.

She smiled up at him. "Don't tell me you needed a little reassurance about this. You have to know you're good."

His palm cupped her cheek. "I am human, you know."

"I'm starting to believe that."

She kept throwing out these lines. Each one knocked him further off balance. "Tell me what that means."

She rested her hand against his. "You're not the first powerful guy I've worked for."

"I figured that but, technically, you work for Wen."

"Uh-huh, right." She lifted his palm and placed a firm kiss in the dead center. "Cy Peters, Gus Atcheson. The list of men who think nothing of pushing women around is pretty long. Then add in the Ryan Peterson type."

The same man who spent most of his day ruining Forest's right now. "Dumbass."

"Asswipe, asshat, asshole. They all work."

She looked so serious with that frown that he had to laugh. "Who knew the word *ass* could be so versatile."

Amusement filled her eyes. "Kind of like *jack*—jackass, jacknut, jackwagon."

Man, he loved listening to her. She tested him, made him smile. And what she could do with those legs and that mouth had him wishing he was the work-from-home type. "All very good terms."

"I dated this guy." She fiddled with his shirt. "Smart, powerful, tough...and a liar. Like, *whoa* liar. Forgot to mention the fiancée and ended up making me the other woman in his relationship, the dumb bastard."

That fact caused tension to zip across Forest's shoulders. Every muscle tightened as if preparing for battle. In a way, he was. "Who?"

She reached up and traced his mouth with her fingertip. "Why? Do you want to go beat him up?"

"Kind of, yeah."

"Sexy, but he's not worth it." She rested a hand against his chest. "And he was only one of many losers."

Forest felt anything but sexy at the moment. Rage-filled was more like it. He wasn't the type to resort to banging heads to make a point. He usually preferred to use his brain, but sometimes violence was the right choice. Possibly now.

The idea of someone hurting this woman made him want to punch something. So did the thought of her loving another guy when she'd been rolling around the sheets with him all night.

Forest had a few rules and absolute fidelity was one of them. He'd experienced fallout and pain from the opposite side of that. Watched his father fool around and flaunt it, no matter how much it hurt Forest's mother. Forest refused to play that game and juggle partners.

He didn't want to be used as a way to forget some loser, either. "Are you still stuck on this guy? On any of them?"

Jordan stretched up on tiptoes and kissed his nose. "I wouldn't have slept with you if I were. I'm a monogamy gal."

A heavy exhale escaped him, taking most of his anger with it. She might be holding things back, but she said the one thing that mattered most. "Any chance you plan to sleep with me again tonight?"

"Subtle."

"I didn't become successful by hiding what I want." While he was at it, he gave her the rest of the information she needed to know. "And, chase or not, I still want you. The desire hasn't abated at all."

He lowered his head then and captured her mouth. Her lips danced over his until he deepened the kiss and pulled her in close. Her body cuddled against him, all warm and promising. Calculations ran through his head on whether he could get her back into bed and then him in a shower in time for his seven-thirty breakfast meeting.

Before he could make the decision, she did. She stepped back and swiped his coffee cup off the counter. "If you're off by eight tonight, come over."

"After that?"

"I change into lounging clothes and you don't want to see that."

Boy was she wrong about that last part.

But the whole offer struck him as a challenge. One he'd accept every time. "Oh, I'll be here."

JORDAN WAS ABOUT to kiss him, maybe do a little exploring using her hands across that impressive chest when the rapid knocking started on the front door. She didn't have to guess who the visitor was. Elle had already texted saying she'd knock first instead of using her key, just in case.

Forest's eyebrow lifted. "You get guests at this hour?"

"That's Elle, my best friend."

He froze in place. "Do you want me to hide?"

That fast, tension rolled off him. It smacked into Jordan and she had to blink to get her bearings again. "Are you supposed to be a secret?"

His shoulders relaxed. "Just checking."

No question about it, men were weird.

She turned around and unlocked the door. Elle stood in the hallway practically vibrating with excitement. "Well?"

Jordan sent a silent keep-cool message with her eyes. "Come in and meet Forest Redder."

He met them in the doorway to the kitchen and held out a hand. "Hello, Elle."

Jordan remembered for the first time he was barely dressed. He had his dress pants on and the white tee he wore under his dress shirt. It stretched tight across his shoulders and highlighted his trim stomach. She doubted he liked being on display, but he didn't show any anger or surprise.

To keep Elle from asking any embarrassing questions, Jordan kicked off the conversation. "I was telling Forest about my mom and men."

"Men in general or hers?" Elle asked.

"Well, he knows there's a website that ranks the men of D.C." Jordan walked into the kitchen. She acted like she wanted to find Elle some coffee. Jordan really wanted to stall and see what Forest would say.

Elle followed and took the mug without question. "Not a fan of dating-warning sites?"

"My only point is that sort of thing can't replace actually getting to know someone." When the women looked at each other, his explanation sputtered to a halt. "What?"

Elle closed one eye as if she was pretending to think his point over. "How about the guy I dated who wore pantyhose?"

Forest's eyes bugged out. "What?"

The reaction gave Jordan hope. It meant she wouldn't be finding out that weird little secret about Forest the hard way. "Or the one I went out with who conveniently forgot his wallet on every date."

Forest shook his head. "Asshole."

"Or the congressional aide who wanted to share me with his friends." Elle blew out a breath. "He didn't ask, by the way. Just invited them over."

Forest's mouth dropped open. "What the fuck?"

Elle shrugged. "They thought I'd consent. My screaming convinced them otherwise."

Jordan noticed Elle left off the part where the two of them had told the guys' mothers. Amazing how twenty-something males scattered when they got tattled on via the internet.

"Then you have your basic losers." Jordan couldn't believe how long that list was. "Mean, demanding. You know, the type who call you a whore if you don't put out in the elevator ride out of the office building to start the date."

"Is it really that bad out there for women?" Forest's hand jerked and coffee splashed over his thumb. With a good bit of muttering, he put the mug down on the counter.

"Everyone has those private things they like, but it can be shocking to run into whatever fetish is out there when you don't hold the same interests," Elle said.

Jordan ran the cold water and soaked a towel for Forest. "One of my favorites is the guy who painted his chest."

Instead of holding it to his hand, Forest wiped the brown drops on his tee. "To be fair, it's not my thing but some sports fans are into that."

Jordan snorted. "Oh, it didn't have anything to do with sports. He liked to do it under his business suit."

Forest's hands dropped to his sides and the towel dragged on the floor. "Oh, come on."

Jordan nodded. "And I guarantee you know him."

Elle pointed. "Oh, there's the one who got home and kicked off his shoes and tried to wear yours."

With a shake of his head, Forest leaned back against the doorjamb. "Please stop."

It felt strangely good to rattle off some of the odd dating experiences. Some were hers and some were Elle's. A few came from the site. But reality was they offered only a tiny taste. They skipped the liars and the really violent ones.

But Jordan was smart enough to know men were not

the only ones who liked some off-the-wall stuff. "Women can't always be a joy, either."

"Remarkably tame compared to what I'm hearing." He hesitated as if trying to figure out if he should reveal top-secret information. "You mostly just need to watch for the three C's."

Curiosity gripped Jordan. "What?"

"Clingy, conniving and crazy." He counted them off on his fingers. "They're all bad, by the way."

"We've met the male versions of those, too."

Forest blew out a long breath. "You know I want names, right?"

"No, you don't. You'll never be able to keep a straight face in a meeting again."

He glanced at his watch. "Speaking of which, I have one."

The news sent a cold chill blowing over Jordan. Having him here, relaxed and charming, made her heart do a little dance. The idea of him walking out, even though he wasn't walking away from her, left her feeling empty.

But she'd get over it. "I'll help you get your stuff in the bedroom."

Elle smiled into her mug. "I'll wait here."

CHAPTER TEN

Subject Request for Alec Cleveland: He seems too good to be true... Good job, decent, smart, sexy and no weird exes hanging around. What don't I know? —Member 87

Response from Member 13: Alec is one of the good ones. Don't let him go.

IT TOOK JORDAN another fifteen minutes to get him out. The temptation to drag him back inside hit her the second the bedroom door closed behind him. But having sex with her friend only a few feet away wasn't Jordan's thing. Luckily, it didn't seem to be Forest's, either.

She'd expected him to be great in bed. There was just something about those commanding business types that worked for her on a sexual level, and Forest always struck her as someone with skills. He sure had those. Everything else was the surprise.

He could hold a conversation that was about something other than his self-proclaimed awesomeness. Then there was the whole black-sheep thing. She knew from her spin around the internet when they first met that he'd been engaged but that it ended with her marrying someone else. That little fact had Jordan wondering what went wrong and what guy could hold more appeal than Forest.

Jordan busied her hands by putting the dirty dishes in the dishwasher and rushing around the kitchen. Not that the constant movement did her any good. Elle was right there, watching it all.

Elle finally piped up. “He’s ridiculously hot.”

That didn’t even come close to covering it. “No kidding.”

“Was he good?”

The things he could do with those hands and that mouth. Nothing selfish about his performance. “Well, I can say this. He doesn’t require an agreement before sex.”

“Well, well, well. Now, that’s more like it.”

“He also knows all about the website. Not my ownership, of course. Its existence.”

Elle’s smile vanished as quickly as it came. “About that—”

“Good job on getting the site in the paper, by the way.” Jordan had read the article online. A membership surge came right after. There were stacks of emails waiting in the business box. At this rate, they’d hit her membership target well before the year expired.

The success filled her with a silent thrill. She wanted to share it, shout it from the rooftops or maybe clue Forest in and see what he had to say. The guy was a business tycoon, after all. Sure, she didn’t know the exact definition of *tycoon*, but she’d bet Forest would have some business ideas she could consider.

It was a shame she couldn’t talk it all through, but there was no way she’d put the business in peril. Not over a man she’d known for less than a month. She wasn’t her mother.

Elle lifted the lid on a container of stale cookies.

One sniff and she snapped the lid back on. "Unfortunately, Ryan is doing an even better job at advertising than I am."

The battling thoughts about Forest and her business slammed to a halt in Jordan's brain. "Peterson? What the hell does that moron want?"

"To blame Need to Know for the demise of his company. He's saying we defamed him and interfered with his business."

That guy was a total crap weasel. But he could ruin her with nonsense paperwork and she didn't want that to happen. "That's insane. We passed on the member reports about his personal life, all of which matched each other, by the way."

"Agreed."

"I really want to punch that guy."

"Ryan implicates Forest in the whole thing. Says Redder Investments colluded with the site owners—us, basically—and made up the information to give Forest some sort of unfair bargaining position on the waterfront project. Ryan paints himself as the martyred hero who refused to give in to Forest's blackmail demands and walked away instead."

Now Jordan wanted to throw Ryan under a bus. Coming after her was one thing. Blaming Forest was another. "That's not what happened. I was in the room. Forest dumped Ryan, not vice versa."

"Looks like your boyfriend and your ex-boss are fighting."

"Ryan was never my boss." The thought of that made last night's dinner churn in Jordan's stomach.

Gone were the days of her stomping into someone

else's office to do someone else's work. Yeah, she did the temp stuff, but that was part of a bigger cause. She didn't see herself as an employee on someone else's payroll. Not really. She could walk out at any time. Once she was financially independent and pulling in enough money from the site to meet her needs, she never had to take another temp position for extra cash. She longed for that day.

Elle made a humming noise. "Interesting how you ignored what I said about Forest."

More like practical. "I don't know what we are or how to define it."

Jordan didn't let her mind go there. She had no idea what she shared with the man other than a mutual case of lust. That sort of thing fizzled fast. She kept waiting for the implosion to happen with Forest. It was inevitable with the sort of electricity that burned between them. Had to be.

"Sleep with him a few more times. That will probably help you figure it out."

She thought about their deal this morning. "Now you sound like Forest."

Elle nodded with a slow wisdom well beyond her years. "Always knew he was a smart one."

LUNCH WAS TWO hours away and Forest already had fifteen files sitting on his desk. What started as an interesting side project, a way to fill a few hours in the evening, had become a necessity. Ryan tied Redder Investments up with this Need to Know website. That made the website Forest's business. This was no longer only a matter of curiosity.

Wen didn't knock before barging into the office. He carried a stack of files and wore a frown. Forest couldn't really blame him. Digging through files and conducting online searches wasn't really in Wen's pay grade, but Forest didn't want the whole company to know he was looking at this dating website. That meant no assistance from the tech crew or the administrative staff.

Wen dumped the contents of his arms on the last open space on the edge of Forest's desk. He removed a yellow legal pad from inside one and put it on top with a smack. "For you. The top includes a list of businessmen complaining about having negative personal information listed on the site."

"Is this everything?" Forest scanned the landscape in front of him. The files amounted to hours of work. Normally, he didn't mind, but he had someone to occupy his extra hours right now, and it wasn't Ryan Peterson.

"All I can find." Wen laid a hand on the top of the tallest stack. "The Need to Know website isn't exactly open about its corporate structure."

"Ryan is on the warpath." Forest had hung up from his third angry call of the day a few minutes ago.

Ryan was going down and taking his family's thirty-year-old company with him, so his desperation leaked into every word and action. There was nothing good about this situation, but his lies involved Forest and Forest couldn't tolerate that.

"It's all bullshit," Wen said.

"Defending bullshit still costs money." And Forest hated wasting money. He sat back and blew out a long breath. He definitely should have climbed back into bed with Jordan this morning instead of coming in to the landslide of media request for quotes. Denial wasn't his thing, but it sounded good right about now.

"Imagine how big a deal that is to a place like the website." Wen absently paged through the few files at the top. "Of course, it might be better if the site goes under."

After all he'd heard from Jordan and Elle about the D.C. dating world, the thought of shutting down the site pissed Forest off. If it was true the women out there were wading through that level of bullshit, he wondered why there wasn't a site before now. Whoever came up with it sat on a potential gold mine. Almost made Forest want a piece of it.

"Why do you care?" Yeah, the place dug too deep and went too personal for his taste, but he understood the need for the service. Hell, he wouldn't mind having one for fellow businessmen on their work practices so he didn't have to rely on his instincts all the time.

"I'm just saying some people are upset."

To Forest's way of thinking, someone was always upset about something. Welcome to reality. "And I'm thinking they shouldn't act like dicks if they don't want to be on the site."

Wen smiled. "You think it's that simple?"

"Nothing about this situation is simple, which is why I plan to poke around until I find someone affiliated with this website who will talk with me."

"And if you don't?"

Not an option as far as Forest was concerned. "I don't lose, so I'll find them."

CHAPTER ELEVEN

Subject Request for Cameron Dillard: I know he has a bad-boy reputation, but I thought maybe it was overblown? —Member 401

Need to Know Response: The site almost crashed from the number of members trying to sign on and warn you off.

JORDAN'S HEAD FELL back. Her legs straddled Forest's thighs and her hands clenched his shoulder and the pillows stacked behind him. She brought her body down one last time and pushed him deep inside.

Naked except for her spiky heels, everything felt right. The comforter bunched around her knees and the soft creak of the headboard still echoed in the room when she collapsed on top of him.

After riding him, guiding her body up and down on him until his breath came out in pants and his hands locked into fists on the sheets next to her, her breathing hammered in her chest. Her bones melted as she slid against him now in the aftermath. All she could feel was the soft caress of his hands up and down her back as his heartbeat thundered under her ear.

He'd walked in the door tonight and they'd made it

this far. No food. No talk. He'd grabbed her hand and walked her to the bedroom, stripping of their clothes as they went. After a day filled with closed-door meetings and never-ending phone calls, here they found silence.

"That made every shitty hour today worth it." His rough words vibrated under her cheek.

She lifted her head and stared into those deep green eyes. "Ryan?"

"You're going to need to find some more *ass* words to describe him."

"I'm on it."

Forest brushed her hair off her face and over her shoulders. His fingers trailed down her throat to cup her breast. "But right now I like you right where you are."

Now that the fire had cooled, she noticed everything. The rough scrape of material against her legs being the most obvious. She glanced behind her before facing him again. "You didn't even get your pants off, stud."

"I was eager." He didn't sound the least contrite. The kiss he placed on her nipple and sweep of his tongue suggested he was ready to find a new topic.

So was she. The idea was dangerous and scary, but the truth always was. "I sat in the room during part of that meeting. I can be a witness—"

"No." Forest delivered the decision between kisses.

Much more of that and she'd never get this out. She lifted his head and pressed her palms against his cheeks. "That was a quick answer."

He looked at her then. "I don't want you involved. Don't want him coming after you or threatening your ability to get work."

To think she'd once viewed this man as shallow and

disconnected. Now she saw the real person behind the title and knew the conclusions she'd jumped to about him were dead wrong. Guilt smacked her, but she pushed it away. She'd been taught hard lessons and she applied them to Forest. Unfair but human, and she refused to apologize for that. She'd given him a chance, opened herself up. Now she saw him for what he really was—tough but decent.

Ryan was dragging them all through the mud, but Forest insisted she stay clean. It was hot and sexy and tempted her to spill the secret she'd vowed never to share with anyone but Elle. Her insides shook and a wave of insecurity washed over her. She recognized the sensation for what it was—vulnerability. She'd learned the hard way not to trust. A lesson that got hammered into her over and over. But with him she wanted to dive in and risk it all.

A buzz filled the room as her cell went off. Before she could stretch across him and grab it, Forest had it in his hand and gave it to her.

"Mom, I'm assuming?" He didn't sound angry or annoyed. More like resigned to the fact sleeping with her included regular check-ins from her mom.

Jordan read the texts, all three of them. "Apparently John continues to be a winner. With her sex life in order, she's asking how I am."

Forest's hands fell to her waist. "How are you?"

"Pretty damn satisfied."

He nodded. "Tell her that."

Why not? She typed in the message and hit Send. The response came almost on top of hers. "She wants to know if I'm having sex."

The woman knew. She always knew.

"What?" He spun the phone around to look at it. "Damn, she did ask."

"Told you."

"Do you hide it from her?"

"Why would I?" A strange question for other people, maybe, but for Jordan it felt natural to tell her mom.

"Okay then." He started typing.

It was her turn to move and shift and try to get a good look at what he was doing. Looked like typing a message was the answer. "What are you saying?"

"I'm giving her my name and telling her we're in bed. Asking if you can get back to her later."

The conversation made her smile. The idea of proper Forest Redder talking sex with her mom was almost too weird for Jordan to wrap her mind around it. He should be repelled. Instead, he took it in stride. Just like he did with everything.

She snagged the phone and saw his message. He hadn't hit Send. She eyed him up. "Are you sure you want to do this?"

"I plan to be around for a while, so I'm good if you are."

Wasn't that the sexiest thing ever? "Done."

With the message sent and the phone down, she snuggled against his chest and used her finger to trace a pattern over the bare skin of his chest. "Why are you the black sheep of your family?"

The question popped into her mind and hit her mouth a second later. She didn't intend to ask. The answer pulled at her, but she understood privacy and was all set to honor that. Then she opened her mouth.

For a long minute he held her while his hand rubbed up and down her back. He didn't stiffen, but he didn't start talking, either. The coolness of the air-conditioned room settled around them and the lamp burned bright on the nightstand. She'd just decided to sit up and make a flip comment about food to bring the lighter mood back, when she heard him sigh.

"It's not a pretty story." He slipped the fingers of his free hand through hers. "My dad was one of the guys you talked about, like the men on that site. Terrible to women and happy to show off a string of mistresses in public, regardless of what it did to my mom."

Jordan closed her eyes on the wave of pain she heard in his deep voice. She bit back words of reassurance because she knew he didn't want them. He was a strong man, full of pride, and it sounded as if every word had been ripped straight from his gut.

"When I got old enough and had a position in the family business—textiles, by the way—I tried to stage a takeover. It wasn't about me or a power grab. I wanted to knock him off stride and use the time and opportunity to give my mother a chance to get away from him and all his strict, unbending rules about how a Redder should live."

She knew the type. A nasty hypocrite. "The same rules he didn't follow."

"Exactly." Forest hugged her a little tighter. "He was pious and judgmental and thought the rules just didn't apply to him."

"What happened?" Her voice came out scratchy and raw when she felt Forest kiss the top of her head.

"People in the company feared him and I was young.

They wanted a sure thing and he got a warning in time to build a defense." Forest cleared his throat. "My mom sided with him."

Jordan sat up then and faced him. "What?"

"They've been married for more than thirty-five years now. She is the dutiful wife. He is the philandering husband."

Forest held her gaze with an intensity that ripped away the last of her defenses. "And you got left behind in the fallout."

"Something like that."

"You did the right thing." She kissed him then, quick and chaste. Not to rekindle the excitement, but to give some sort of comfort. It was her way of stopping the words that raced up her throat. The ones about being sorry. They sounded like pity and he didn't need them.

She didn't feel that, anyway. She mourned his loss of family, but what overwhelmed her was his personal strength. His sense of right and wrong.

"We all have family issues." He said the words, let them hang out there.

She knew he was asking without asking. "I didn't know my father. He was one in a long line of men my mother used to support her. See, that's her career. She uses sex and whatever other skills she has to hold men who should be home with their wives or anywhere without her."

His hand slipped to the back of her neck and his fingers started a gentle massage. "You're nothing like her."

Jordan wasn't sure they knew each other long enough for him to make that leap, but she accepted the compliment because it meant everything. "Most men in your position would run after being told something like that."

"Men can be idiots."

"No 'like mother, like daughter' concerns?" The question hovered there until she regretted asking it in a moment of insecure weakness.

"Do you think I'm my father?"

She didn't hesitate. "No."

On some level she knew that was the truth. A man torn apart by his father's antics wouldn't run headlong into the same trap. And with his firm question, he answered hers. There was a strange comfort that came from having it all out there and meeting on a certain level of understanding.

Well, not everything was out. A huge secret stood between them and the internal battle over telling him or keeping it quiet had her head pounding.

"My fiancée left because I lost my position in the family firm."

Looked like there was more than one item still outstanding. This was her last question for him. The one Jordan wanted to ask, but couldn't put into words because with the information she held back she didn't think she deserved to know the answer to this one.

But now she had it. "Men aren't the only ones who can be idiots."

"Very true." His finger danced over the tip of her chin. "We have something else we need to talk about."

She tensed, waiting for him to launch into a series of questions. If anyone could figure out her secret, it would be Forest. But that didn't mean she had an answer prepared and ready to go. "Go ahead."

"If we're going to keep seeing each other, and I hope to hell that's the case, we need to think about your temp position."

Relief shot through her. This was about appearances and propriety. "I'll tell my office Thursday is my last day."

He frowned at her. "I don't want to cost you work. It's just that—"

"I get it." Decent until the end. "I'd rather see you outside work than in."

The wrinkled brow didn't ease. "Are you sure?"

She let her hand wander down his chest and keep going. "Very."

FOREST SAT IN his office three days later in the middle of a Saturday afternoon and stared at the information piled in front of him. He'd coaxed some of it out of the assistant in his office who he knew was a Need to Know member. Then there were the bits and pieces he collected from fellow businessmen and some stray comments on websites.

He'd taken it apart and put it back together three times. It was all circumstantial, but it fit. The timing of when Jordan started her temp jobs, the locations, the men she worked for and how that coincided with the information confirmed by the Need to Know staff.

Jordan might not run the site, but he'd bet the contents of his money market she was involved in some way.

Since that first night together, he'd stayed there every night. Between quick runs home for clothes, he visited her. They ate, talked, had incredible sex. He'd shared things with her about his family and his ex that he never told anyone. From the second he met her, he'd been falling for her—something unexpected that he didn't try to fight.

And the whole time she'd been hiding a huge piece of

information from him. He understood her motivation at the beginning, but she knew he had Ryan on his ass and spewing out lies. She did nothing to step up and help.

He let his head drop back against the chair. No, that wasn't true. She offered to assist him by telling what happened in that meeting. She just failed to tell him all the information he needed to know about everything else.

And how fucking ironic was that?

"Forest, you okay?"

Her voice cut through the quiet room. He opened his eyes and slowly lifted his head. "Hey."

She smiled at him from across the room. Between that face and the trim dark jeans his mind sputtered. He wanted to be furious, but in some ways he was more numb than anything. He needed her to say it, to open up and confide in him.

She walked over and stood across from him. Only a desk separated them. "You still want to have lunch or are you too busy?"

"I'm working on the Need to Know website."

Her smile faltered. "What?"

"I want to talk to the owner."

"How would that help?"

All his suspicions gelled. Her pale face and the way she balled her hands into fists told him something clicked through her brain and she wasn't sharing. After all those hours in bed, whispering in the dark, she held back.

The reality of her deception nailed him like a kick to the stomach. "I'm thinking a united front against Ryan is the answer."

She clenched and unclenched her hands. "He doesn't have any power. You told me that yourself."

"He's the squeaky wheel and with other people wanting to dig behind the scenes at the website, men who feel like they've been burned, this is hanging around longer than it should." Forest said anything to get her to admit the truth. He did want to talk with the owner and soon had to put the Ryan mess behind him, but mostly Forest wanted her to trust him enough to tell him.

He wanted their time together to mean something to her.

But he buried all of that under business talk. "I need to move the project forward, but I keep having to deal with this crap instead."

"What can I do?" For the first time since he met her, her voice sounded small and weak.

Hell, she was right there. So close. "Is there anything you need to tell me?"

"What?"

"I'm asking. Not judging, not demanding. I only want to understand."

"I don't…" Her voice trailed off and silence descended.

He laid a hand on top of the legal pad in front of him. Her gaze zoomed in on the writing beneath. "Say anything, Jordan."

She shook her head. "It's not that easy."

They'd at least moved to the same page. "It is."

"You don't understand what it's like—"

"To build something?" He was up and out of his chair and standing right next to her. He grabbed her upper arms, forcing his hold to remain loose so he didn't hurt her. "I sure as hell do. You know the story. I got kicked out of the family business and had to start over."

All the blood drained from her face. She rubbed a hand over her forehead as her body started to sway. "I needed somewhere to belong."

He'd lived that. He got it. He just needed her to say the words. "Tell me the truth."

She swallowed a few times. Words came out and sentences started. Then she stepped back, breaking the connection between them. "This isn't just about me."

"I get that."

That determined chin lifted. "Frankly, Forest, this is my thing. It's not about you. It's not your business."

Her words hit him like a body slam and his hands fell to his sides. "You're right, Jordan. It's about us. Or I thought it was."

"What are you talking about?"

A mix of anger and confusion pounded off her. He could see the conflicting emotions battling. She wanted to tell and was desperate to keep the information to herself.

He decided to make it easier on her by backing away. It would be hell on him, but if she needed to stay in control this badly, because of her own dating history or her mom, fine. "I'm not sure there is an 'us' here."

Jordan's eyes narrowed as her anger took the lead. "What are you saying?"

It took every bit of strength in his body to walk away from her and head back to his side of the desk. He dropped onto his chair and picked up the telephone. He didn't have anyone to call, but he needed something to hold on to.

"I have work to do." He dismissed her without looking up.

"Don't do this."

He refused to look at her and see whatever emotions played on her face. He would not give in this time. "When you're ready to talk, let me know. In the meantime, I'm going to handle this Ryan nonsense once and for all."

"How?"

This time he did look up. Saw her face ravaged with pain and wide eyes stark with fear. He fought back the wave of caring and the side of him that wanted to fix this for her and focused on her refusal to let him in. "I'm thinking you don't need to know."

CHAPTER TWELVE

Subject Request for Allan Heard: Went to his house and looked in an extra bedroom. There was this swing. Thoughts?

Response from Member 2: Honey, he is a genius with that swing. Go for it!

FIVE DAYS LATER Jordan hovered over her laptop, waiting for the link to pop up. The news teased an interview with Forest about the Need to Know website. She should be panicked about exposure, but all she could think about was losing him. Not having him in bed beside her.

She'd dragged around, cursing every hour since that scene in Forest's office. He stood there, practically begging her to open up and she couldn't find the words. She'd been tempted and on the verge, but then a lifetime of desperate visions flashed through her head. Her mother depending on this man and that one. The promises they made to her and how she got stuck as each one moved on to someone else.

Forest wasn't like any of them, but he wasn't the problem. She was. Fears swamped her and old insecurities rushed over her. The idea of letting him in had the air rattling in her chest and her stomach dropping to the floor.

After all her examples of what not to do and a string of Mr. Wrongs, she hesitated at that final step. Forest offered her opportunity after opportunity. Even now, giving her a daily call that started and ended with one simple question—is there anything you want to tell me? She begged him to come over, but his response was always the same. That damn question.

And Elle wasn't any better. She was a one-woman cheerleader for Forest's cause. Even now she paced the small space in front of the window.

She stopped and threw up her hands. "What are we doing here?"

"Work."

"You're sitting there, waiting to read whatever Forest says in his interview. Call and ask him."

She'd tried that several times, but he wouldn't budge off that question. The more he asked, the more entrenched she became. "He has the power to unmask me."

"Something you should have done."

A part of Jordan knew that was true. She'd traveled down this weird, lonely road for so long that she didn't know how to step off.

She got up and headed for the kitchen. "We're not having this argument again."

"You've been kicking around here, sad and depressed for days. Since I love you, I will say what you should already know, what with you being a smart girl and all."

Jordan held up a hand. Not that a gesture would ever stop Elle. "Don't."

"You have feelings for him. Serious feelings. Like, falling-for-him feelings."

The words sliced through Jordan. The truth cut right to the bone.

It took her until this morning to realize that's what all of this was about. She'd been hurt and unsure coming out of her last train wreck of a relationship. She'd been so sure about the kind of man she needed next. Not someone like Forest. The exact opposite was the answer. But her heart flipped when she saw him, and the sound of his voice had the power to make her weak.

Her vulnerability, her attraction to him, scared the hell out of her. It shouldn't be like this. "I've only known him a short time."

Elle snorted. "Because that's the test."

Jordan walked to the kitchen and back to her chair. It was mindless, aimless movement. "I made a promise not to tell."

"It is your secret. You can tell whomever you want, and he gave you the opening to tell him." Elle sat on the arm of the couch and stared at Jordan as if willing her to believe.

"He practically demanded it."

"I know trust is hard for you."

"I don't want to talk about this anymore." Every word hammered a crack in Jordan's defenses. She had so little shield left.

The days without seeing Forest broke her. In such a short amount of time she switched from not knowing him to not wanting to be without him. And how sick was that? Maybe she was more like her mother than she pretended to be. So easily caught up in a man that she forgot her promises and moved his needs to the top of her list.

Her computer dinged. "Here it is."

Elle came around to Jordan's side of the computer. "The article?"

"It's a video clip." The little start arrow was right there, taunting her.

Elle reached across the keyboard. "Hit Play."

"Yeah, I know how this works." Jordan got to it first. Her finger hovered, but she didn't push.

Elle sighed. "You're stalling."

With a deep inhale, Jordan clicked the link. Forest's face filled the screen. He stood there in his sharp suit, looking in command and a little tired. She wanted to touch the screen, but knew that bordered on pathetic. After a few introductory remarks, they got to the good stuff. Forest's deep voice broke through her small condo.

"Despite all the accusations, I ended the deal with Ryan Peterson and his company due to performance evaluations. I am trying to be respectful here, but this had to do with management flaws and financial concerns. This was a business decision unrelated to his personal life."

Elle lifted a fist in the air. "Score one for the hottie."

Jordan wasn't quite ready to celebrate. Every word he spoke was the truth, but he still held the power to mess up her world. And when he opened his mouth again, she feared the end was coming.

"But I would like to say that I find nothing wrong with the Need to Know site. Dating isn't easy and women do need to protect themselves, because not every man is worth trusting. But some of us are."

He looked straight into the camera as he delivered that last part. She expected a rush of relief, but it never came. The flipping sensation in her stomach didn't ease.

He supported her and she walked away. The reality of that disparity made her dizzy.

The final question had to do with his dating status. She held her breath, waiting for him to declare he was single.

"I'm in a relationship, but that's all the comment you're getting on that."

Jordan had to grab on to the edge of the desk to keep from falling over. A relationship. The scared and insecure part of her shouted that he meant someone else, but deep down she knew that wasn't true. He was talking directly to her.

Elle slapped her hand against the desk. "Well, there you go."

Too stunned to say anything coherent and still reeling, Jordan went with the obvious. "He didn't out me."

"That man just made a huge gesture. He kept your secret and gave you that flirty smile through the camera."

Jordan saw it all the same way. "I don't—"

"Don't think. Don't try to reason it all out. Feel." Elle slipped to her knees beside Jordan. "You deserve this. You get to be happy, too, and I'm thinking this guy could be it."

The denials died in her throat. "He's everything that's always scared the crap out of me."

"And he's proven over and over that he's worth the risk. If I were you, I'd go to his office and drag him back to bed. Or finally try that desk chair." Elle shrugged. "Your choice."

"I'm just supposed to walk in there and spill it?" Jordan knew that would be the scariest walk of her life.

"The man made his big play. Now it's your turn."

"You know I'm terrified." He could turn her away. He could be a jerk. Anything could happen. The interview went well, but Jordan knew how quickly the wind could change.

"The only worthwhile risks are the big ones." Elle hugged Jordan. "But you know that."

Jordan held on. "Really?"

"You are a woman who created a business and is building something on your own. You get risks."

Her friend always knew the right thing to say. "I love you, you know."

"Then listen to me and go after your man."

THREE HOURS LATER Forest sat in his office and tried to ignore Wen. The man wasn't making that task easy, since he kept hovering and even now leaned in the doorway with one leg crossed over the other.

"That interview was impressive," he said.

Not exactly what Forest was going for, but he appreciated the support. "Yeah, you're not the one I was trying to win over."

"I'm hoping I was." Jordan's voice cut through the room.

Forest's head popped up and he jumped from his chair, nearly knocking it over behind him. "Jordan?"

Wen smiled down at her as she brushed past him wearing one of those dresses that held together with a tie in the front. He looked her up and down, then winked. "About time you showed up."

She stopped long enough to place a hand on Wen's crossed arms. "I'm slow, but I make up for that with staying power."

As far as Forest was concerned there was one too many people in the room. "Wen, disappear."

"Yes, sir." Wen didn't even try to hide his grin as he shuffled out and closed the door behind him.

Forest wanted to rush to her, but he forced his body to stay still. She needed to make all the moves this time. He'd laid it all out there, gave as much of a public plea for her as he could without causing more trouble for her business. "You heard the interview."

"Yes, but I didn't need to, to know I owed you an apology."

Shit. "That's not what I want from you."

"You're getting it anyway." She pointed to his chair. "Sit."

Now, this was the Jordan who haunted his dreams all week. Feisty and in charge, knowing what she wanted and how to get it.

So, he obeyed. Hell, right now he'd do just about anything to get them back on track. "Fair enough."

"As you've probably guessed, I've spent my life trying not to be my mom."

"You are not her." He had no idea how she could think that. The differences were so obvious. He didn't have to spend even a second to come up with the list. "You might have her charm, but your drive and will are your own."

"I love her and would fight to protect her, but growing up with her affected me." Jordan came around to his side of the desk and leaned against it, right at the side of his leg. "I saw what was happening and let it taint how I dealt with relationships. I rushed to do the opposite of what she did, to not look to men for security."

"You pushed me away."

"I did and I'm sorry." She stood there. "I was just so sure the answer was to limit the uses in my life for men."

"We do have some skills." He was working on listening and accepting. "Sometimes, if you let us, we can be a partner."

"Definitely." She slid in closer.

He held her face in his hands. "And, for the record, you are independent and fierce. You are not someone who wants other people to pay for her."

She smiled. "You get me."

"I have been proud of you, impressed by you, since day one of meeting you." Forest hated to walk into a bad topic, but the words needed to be said. "And if Ryan somehow still outs you, you'll handle it because that is who you are."

"You'll stand by me."

"Always."

He thought she'd wiggle her way to stand between his legs, but she did something even better. She pushed him back into his chair and dropped into his lap. One hand went to the back of his neck and the other pressed against his chest.

He shifted to get more comfortable. "I like this position."

"Shh." She put a finger over his lips. "My turn for admitting things isn't over yet."

He nodded, afraid to say the wrong thing and scare her away. He went for draping his arm across her legs and pulling her in tighter instead.

"When you came along, I got it in my head that wanting you so much, so fast, meant I was turning into her. I was ready to put aside all my personal vows about keeping the website quiet and mine and private. I wanted to share with you."

The last bit of tension twisted in his gut broke free. A feeling he could describe only as hope spiraled through him. "Why didn't you?"

"Because I wanted it to stay mine."

"And now?" He'd pull every word out of her if he had to. With her history, he knew this level of intimacy was hard for her. Having lost so much of his family, he craved it. Being burned by family, she revolted.

"I wanted to keep you at a distance." She spread her fingers against his shirt and the coolness of her skin seeped into him. "But not anymore."

"Sweet hell, I hope not." His free hand traveled up her back, soothing even as he dragged her closer.

"I own the website. It's all mine." She smiled as she said the words. The pride bubbled up and out of her and flowed all over both of them. "It's not part of some revenge scheme as people are saying. It's about filling a need. Building something."

A concept he understood well. "I know."

"Yeah, you do, don't you?" She leaned in and kissed him, but pulled back before he could stop her.

"Can I talk now?" He trapped her hand against his chest. "Because if I can, I want to say you're quite the entrepreneur. It's pretty amazing what you've accomplished. You have most of D.C. watching."

"I could use some advice about expanding and when to reveal my identity, if at all."

This is what he wanted. The give and take. "Ask anything. We'll talk it through. Just the two of us."

"And Elle."

He chuckled. "I figured she was in on this."

"I do need you to know I trust you."

Tension eased out of him. "I know that from the way you're talking now. From the fact you came to the office."

She brought their joined hands to her mouth and kissed the back of his. "It scares me to need you and I'll probably mess up and get plowed under by all my insecurities, but with you I want to try. All I'm asking for is time and understanding."

"The fact you're sitting here, telling me all of this, proves you trust me." He couldn't hold back another second. He leaned in and kissed her. Not deep, but firm to let her know he wanted more but could wait. "That's all I wanted."

"All?"

"Well, there's some naked stuff and the part where I am dying to pull the end of this knot, but for now I'm good with trust." He toyed with the material belt around her waist, wondering the whole time if she wore anything underneath. He sure as hell hoped not. "You see, we need that if we're going to go forward, and I am desperate to move forward with you. We've built businesses. Now I want something deeper, just for us."

Her smile almost sparkled now. "You're comparing my site to your multimillion dollar business?"

One more insecurity he needed to help her conquer. "We all start somewhere. I'm betting you work as hard, if not harder, than I do."

"I want you to know I believe, deep to my soul, you're different."

He didn't know how desperate he was for the words until he heard them. Something deep and dark inside him burst open. All those years of looking in and missing what he'd lost, no matter how dysfunctional it was. With the comfort of family gone, he leaned on Wen. Now he wanted to lean on her.

"Any chance that's a sign you're falling for me?" It actually hurt to force the words out. They were new and his feelings grew and shifted as the days went by, but he knew the truth. She was the one. It would take time and some healing, but she was it.

She wrapped her arms around his neck. "I'm definitely falling."

The last of his worries washed away. He could handle scandal and Ryan and anything else their relationship brought down on them. "Good, because I didn't want to jump alone."

Her hand brushed over his hair. "So, we're dating."

"Only each other."

"Then I have one more thing to give you." She dipped her hand into her bra.

"Does it have something to do with the tie to the dress, because I'm having a hard time concentrating on anything else at the moment." She shifted her position and his erection fit into the space between her thighs. "Oh, that works."

"Here." She held something between her fingers.

He tried to focus, but the combination of her body and her smell had his brain misfiring. He blinked a few times. "A key?"

"To my condo. My life is there—business and

personal—and I want you to have it. No locked doors. No restrictions on what you can see or where you go."

The gesture was about so much more than easy entrance to her place. It was a vow of sorts. "I'll have one made for my place for you tomorrow."

She laughed. "I haven't even seen your house yet."

"We'll go there. Later." He glanced at the closed door. "First, I want to show you what I can do in this chair."

She reached for his hand and put it on the end of the belt tie. She gave it a gentle tug. "You're the boss."

Subject Request for Forest Redder: Heard rumor he's seriously dating. Please say it's not true!
—Member 8
Need to Know staff: Confirmed. He definitely is not available.

* * * * *

SPECIAL EXCERPT FROM

Presents®

Harlequin® Presents® welcomes you to the world of ***The Chatsfield****, synonymous with style, spectacle… and scandal!*

Read on for an exclusive extract from Maisey Yates's story of passion in the desert…
SHEIKH'S DESERT DUTY

* * *

"I'm a lot stronger than I look."

And that was all she said before he dipped his head, pressing his mouth against hers. Their lips were slick with rainwater, and he angled his head, sliding his tongue across her upper lip and her lower lip, sipping the water from her skin. She shook, the decadent contact washing through her like a raging river devastating everything in its path, reshaping the landscape, uprooting the anchors that had always held her fast.

He kissed the corner of her mouth, then the center, moving to the other corner before going back again. "Kiss me," he said, his lips moving against hers.

She realized then that she was frozen, simply letting herself be washed away on this tide of pleasure, on this wave of need. And while it was a wonderful feeling, she was not the kind of woman to allow herself to drift out to sea.

HPEXP1214-1

She would swim against the current.

She wrapped her arms around his neck and pressed herself more firmly against him, parting her lips and allowing him deeper access into her mouth, his tongue sliding against hers. It was like the darkest, richest, smoothest chocolate dessert. Imbued with the kind of richness that made you feel as though you couldn't possibly take another bite, while at the same time making you feel as though you could go on tasting it forever.

That was what kissing Zayn was like. Like too much and not enough, all at once. Like something she needed more of, while needing badly to break away, and taking gulps of air.

But she continued to indulge, because he was holding her tight. Because he was so firm and sure. A pillar for her to cling to in the storm.

He was stability and desire. Strength and heat. And she wanted nothing more than to cling to him until it all subsided. Though now, she could not tell if the greater storm raged above them, or inside of them. Between them.

She squeezed her eyes shut tight and kissed him with all of the ferocity in her body. Because she wanted to, and because she wanted him to know that he was okay.

* * *

HPEXP1214-1